Anger

OF THE

KING

J.B. Shepherd

Cover illustration by Jessica Ellen Lindsey
www.jessicaellen.com

Map and interior illustrations by Sandy Mehus

ISBN-13: 978-1-945976-34-6

Published by EA Books Publishing, a division of Living Parables of Central Florida, Inc. a 501c3
EABooksPublishing.com

Dedicated to my own dear children—
I pray that you will "run to Teacher" early
to become faithful servants of the King.

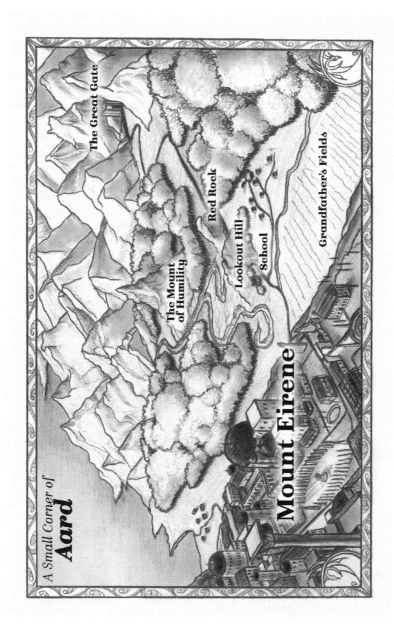

A Small Corner of *Aard*

The Great Gate

The Mount
of Humility

Red Rock

Lookout Hill

School

Grandfather's Fields

Mount Eirene

And the LORD said ... this people ... will forsake me, and break my covenant which I have made with them. Then my anger shall be kindled against them in that day, and I will forsake them, and I will hide my face from them, and they shall be devoured, and many evils and troubles shall befall them; so that they will say in that day, "Are not these evils come upon us, because our God is not among us?"
Deuteronomy 31:16-17

ADAM SONNEMAN II

Prologue

Adam rubbed his fingers across the folded, palm-sized piece of papla leaf. *Crude writing material for such a potent message.* He doubled it over a second time and creased it before setting it on the wooden floor where he crouched.

Sunlight from the window fell on his hand. He jerked it back, putting the knuckle of his middle finger into his mouth. The taste of salt, dirt, and dried blood coated his tongue, but the dark-red stain remained.

So did the memory.

Images of Vaace's body in the ropes, the pounding hammer, the white-faced executioners, and the extended fingers flashed before his eyes afresh. Adam pressed his hands over his face and let them slide through his sweaty hair. He needed to keep moving.

He stuffed a cloak and a large knife into his sack. What else? He scanned the stone walls and wooden shelves of his one-room house for any items he had overlooked. Dried goat

1

meat? He had enough for the journey. A bundle of green funja stems? Edible, but since Susan, his wife, wasn't here yet he could avoid them. Extra water? He needed to conserve it, but maybe he should bring a little more for planting the seed.

The seed.

Adam felt the lump in his pocket. Could it really grow a tree of life? By then, the famine would have finished them. But maybe the very act of obedience to the king's command would appease his anger. Maybe that was the greater need anyway. There wasn't much hope otherwise, not after … he glanced at the papla leaf.

He stood to grab a rope off the nail by the door when the sound of crunching dirt brought him up short. Heavy crunching. *Those can't be Susan's footsteps.* Turning back, he dropped to his knees and scooped up the papla leaf just as the door thudded open.

"Adam, are you out of your mind?" Tari's voice filled the room.

Adam kept his back to his brother and pushed an extra cloak into his sack for his wife.

Tari stepped over the pile of clothes littering the floor. Though younger by two years, he stood almost a head taller than Adam and never seemed to let him forget it.

Tari squeezed Adam's shoulder. "Please tell me Father was lying."

Adam slid the piece of papla into his pocket before turning to meet his brother's gaze. Their faces mirrored each other. Thick black hair crowned high foreheads and dark-blue eyes.

"He's not lying." Adam stood, lifting the sack to his shoulder. "I've put this off long enough."

Tari rose with him. "But why? What good will it do? You're only throwing your life away."

Adam gestured out the open doorway. The last rays of the setting sun fell across miles of brown, baked fields. "What good will it do? I remember when this land was green, when the funja plants produced purple fruits as big as a man's hand instead of mouthfuls of stringy leaves and stems. I remember when people smiled at each other ... before the king left. And now look."

A group of men in the distance struggled to carry a limp figure in their arms—another victim of hunger and labor. Adam took a deep breath. "That makes at least three in one afternoon. How long do you think this can go on?"

Tari stepped in front of him and slammed the door. "I can see for myself, but"—he scanned the room—"you can't save those men by planting a seed on a mountaintop!"

Adam gritted his teeth. In his pocket he squeezed the small, hard seed right next to the folded papla. "King Eliab promised—"

Tari cut him off with a wave of the hand. "That trees of life would grow from those special seeds if we planted them in the Mount of Humility. I know. But where are they then? Where are these trees of life? The king's been gone for over thirty years. Mother planted her seed at least three times way back at the beginning, and"—he lowered his voice—"you know what happened to *her*."

"What do you know about that?" The words erupted before Adam could stop. His cheeks burned, and he turned his face toward the window. Tari hadn't been old enough to remember when Father banished Mother.

But Adam remembered. The light in Mother's eyes and the firmness in her step had dogged his memory until now. Always, he had longed for the courage to follow her.

Tari sighed. "I'm sorry, Adam. I'm not trying to be hurtful. But I don't want to lose you. Whether Father's right or wrong, he's still the governor, and he might banish you as well. Won't you reconsider?"

"Not this time. My mind's made up."

"Then wait until morning. The Keeda roam the woods at night. You're no match for a pack of forest warriors."

Adam studied the blood stains on his hands.

"Some say a dragon lives on that mountain. Adam, have you no fear?"

"Yes!" Adam whirled to face his brother. "I fear the king. Our city has betrayed him, broken his laws, and murdered his messengers." He uncurled his reddened fingers. "I don't believe this famine is mere coincidence."

"Surely you don't think—"

"Stop. He has the power of the Ruuwh. Even now, he may be listening."

Tari snorted. "You actually believe he can see everywhere? Even if that legend were true, whatever the Ruuwh is supposed to be, you can't expect him to control the weather."

"The Ruuwh is greater than you imagine. I don't understand it all, but from what I've learned from his messengers, the king's spiritual force controls all Aard."

Adam pointed out the window to the distant mountains.

"At night I dream of royal soldiers pouring into our city with swords and torches. It could happen any day. Already the prophesied famine ravages our city, just as the Stones predicted. And now—"

Adam broke off and drew the papla leaf from his pocket.

Tari furrowed his brow. "What is it?"

"I spoke with Vaace this morning after distribution. I needed answers. Father must have noticed, or someone told him. This afternoon the Keeda took Vaace to Red Rock. I tried to stop them, but Father had given the official sentence."

Tari pushed against the floorboards with his boot. "They hung the king's messenger in the bleeder?"

Adam shuddered. Images of the black rope and bleeding form flooded his mind afresh. "The Keeda have been executing King Eliab's messengers one after another. I cut him down, but it was too late to save him. I"—he swallowed—"I pulled the spike out of his wrists with my own hands."

He hesitated, trying to find the right words. When none came, he thrust the papla leaf at his brother.

Tari unfolded it and read the words aloud.

When next the bleeder o'er this rock doth swing,
That Day shall fall the anger of the king.

He looked up. "Vaace gave you this?"

Adam nodded. "Just before he died. It's his final prophecy."

"But what does it mean? Isn't the king angry *every* time his messengers are killed?" Tari handed the leaf back.

5

Adam returned it to his pocket. "Did you notice the capital 'D' in 'Day'? This is talking about final destruction for our city. All it takes is one more execution and—" He shook his head.

Tari drummed his fingers on his leg. "It wouldn't hurt for me to mention it to Father. There's a condition involved. The bleeder has to swing above Red Rock to fulfill the prophecy. Maybe he could find a different place for executions."

Adam yanked open the door and grabbed the rope off the nail. "You're wrong. As long as we rebel against the king, we deserve his judgment." The sky had grown dark.

He took a step out the door and turned back to face Tari. "Why don't you come with us? Plant your seed with ours. We can leave as soon as Susan returns."

Tari slumped into a chair. "I've got a wife and two sons to care for. Lichten and Liptor need me. What if I didn't come back?"

He leaned forward and fixed a worried look on Adam. "What about Little Adam? Don't forget you're playing with more lives than just your own."

Adam trailed his fingers along the edges of the rope and stared at the small straw bed nestled against the wall. *Tari knows too well where my tender spot lies.* He shut his eyes and forced his mouth to speak. "My mind is made up. I'm going to honor the king."

Susan's footsteps crunched the dirt outside. Adam swung the rope over his shoulder and opened his eyes. "We're leaving Little Adam for the night at Father's. It isn't as bad as you think. I have a promise from Immanuel."

Tari sighed. "The schoolteacher? Don't tell me he gave

you an assurance of safety."

Adam stepped out into the young night and shut the door before Tari could make any further arguments.

Susan took his arm and smiled up at him. Her gray-blue eyes twinkled in the fresh moonlight. A faded ribbon tied her long brown hair behind her, and she wore walking boots beneath her dress.

"I'm ready," she whispered.

Adam nodded and returned her smile. But his chest tightened. Was he right to bring his wife into such peril? What if the trees of life never grew? And how could one act of submission appease the king? Still, Immanuel had promised.

Glancing back at the door, he murmured, "No. It wasn't safety he promised."

Squeezing Susan's hand, he turned with her to face the path.

ADAM III

Chapter 1

Ten Years Later

"These things have I spoken unto you in proverbs."
John 16:25

The quill pen shook as Adam Sonneman the Third set it to the corner of the parchment and signed his name. He shot a glance at Liptor, his cousin, seated at a desk near the front of the polished, hardwood schoolhouse. The older boy was already scratching away at his test. The other students were also writing.

Adam turned his eyes back to his own test. This wouldn't be easy.

Immanuel, or "Teacher" as they all called him, wanted them to write as much as they remembered from the last month of studying plants. Adam scribbled out a few sentences about desert flowers. Those were some of his favorites. He'd once even seen a few on the edge of Grandfather's fields.

Halfway through a new sentence about nectarines, Adam got stuck. He rested the quill and stared out the window, running his fingers through the hair on the back of his head. Outside, a yellow fog of dust hovered in the air, hiding the distant forest from view. In between lay miles of cracked, dry fields and a handful of stone houses.

Fruit was such a foreign concept! Why Teacher wanted them to study flowers and fruit trees was more than Adam could guess. Especially when the only significant plant common on this part of the island was funja, the staple crop. And no flowers or fruit had appeared on the tall, dry funja plants for decades, at least not anything significant.

Adam's eyes traced the road in front of the school as it wound its way up to Mount Eirene, the city where he lived with Grandfather, the governor. Mount Eirene was the capital of the Twelve Cities, the place where Adam would someday be governor, sole ruler of the Eirenian people.

At least in his dreams.

He shared the same name as Grandfather, Adam Sonneman. Since the night Adam's parents disappeared, he had lived in the governor's mansion. Uncle Tari showed no real interest in becoming the governor, and neither did Lichten, his oldest cousin.

I would have a chance of inheriting the title, Adam thought, *if it weren't for Liptor.*

Adam frowned at his cousin's back. Liptor always came out on top. He made no pretensions about his lust for leadership. If Liptor had his way, Adam was sure he'd try to rule not only Mount Eirene but also all of Aard, the vast lands that covered the island south of the mountains.

Ink had pooled on his test where he rested the quill. Adam wiped if off with his thumb and smeared the ink into the palm of his opposite hand. Back to nectarines. He found a way to finish the sentence and moved on.

At the front of the classroom, Teacher scraped the chair back from his large walnut desk and rose to his feet. He wore a simple pair of breeches and a long, loose shirt called a thrick, tied with a belt—the standard garb worn by Eirenian men. His thin face and small goatee appeared young, but his deep brown eyes and strong voice gave him an air of authority beyond his years.

He walked across the front of the room and peered out a window.

Adam heard a faint sound of shouting in the distance and raised his head. He couldn't make out the words, but the calls were getting louder every second.

Other students began shuffling. Two boys stood up.

"Stay seated." Teacher's voice filled the room.

"Alarm! Alarm! Doene's been taken! Alarm!" A gray horse pounded into the schoolyard, and a lone rider leaped from the saddle. He swung open the solid oak door and thrust in a head of sweat-matted hair. His fist still gripped the door handle.

"They've taken Doene. I'm headed up to the city to spread the word. Be on the alert."

Teacher frowned. "Who took it? Do you mean another raid?"

Adam gripped the sides of his desk. Doene was the farthest east of the Twelve Cities. For a month, raiding parties from nearby Ar Sabia had been attacking its perimeters at night time, setting fire to fields and plundering the outlying villages.

The messenger shook his head. "Not this time. Troops of those cursed Arsabians marched in through tunnels during the night and overthrew Doene itself. They're holding the survivors captive in the stronghold. I'm riding to notify the governor."

The door slammed, and hoofbeats thudded out of the yard. A buzz of student voices filled the room.

Christy Carpenter, the girl on Adam's left, shot up her hand. Her brown braids flopped against the back of her long, checkered dress. "Teacher, what does it mean? What should we do?"

Jackson, a big-boned boy near the front, pounded on his desk. "If the dirty Goiim want fire and death, let's give it to them."

A roar of assent went up from the other boys. Adam pounded his own desk with enthusiasm. Though few in number, the Eirenians had pride in their heritage and looked down on all other nations. They lumped the Arsabians together with all other non-Eirenians in a single derogatory term—*Goiim*.

Christy stood and rested her fists on her desk. "Our swords aren't the only answer, boys. Don't forget we have a king to take care of us."

Adam pursed his lips. Officially, King Eliab ruled over the Twelve Cities and the rest of Aard. He was their creator. But he lived beyond the mountains and never interfered with the Eirenians as far as Adam knew, except for sending them monthly provisions.

Jackson glared at Christy. Several boys started to protest,

but Teacher raised his hands. "Finish your tests. We're not under siege in Mount Eirene. In the meantime, I'm going to get something. Keep on working. Don't forget the Ruuwh will still be here."

Adam looked at his test and then out the window at the settling dust. He could never figure out exactly what the "Ruuwh" was. Teacher had explained it on different occasions, and Adam kept trying to unravel it in his brain. The king had used the Ruuwh to create the land of Aard and the Aardians. It also involved the king's supernatural ability to watch everything, and yet it was more.

In this case, Teacher was warning them not to cheat.

When he reached the doorway, he turned back. "Remember, this is a test." He spoke with a twinkle in his eye, the kind that made Adam think he had something deeper in mind. Teacher often spoke like that. It was too much to figure out at present. Adam needed all his attention for the test if he was going to get higher marks than Liptor.

For years he had been secretly competing with his cousin. Adam wanted Grandfather to recognize his accomplishments and be proud of him. But the attention always went to Liptor.

For one thing, Liptor had all the Sonneman features: height, thick black hair, a high forehead, and bright-blue eyes. Adam was only average height with brown hair and gray-blue eyes. People said he took after his mother. Adam sighed inwardly. *I wish I could remember her.*

Liptor was smart too. If it weren't for him, Adam would be first in the school for high marks. On every test, though, Liptor came out a few points ahead.

And Grandfather noticed.

Adam flipped over the parchment to the back side and dipped his quill in the inkwell. He was making good progress. He shot a glance across the aisle at Hancock, or "Hank" for short. His friend's bright-red hair reflected the afternoon sunlight. At the moment he was chewing on the back of his quill, deep in thought. He looked up wistfully at Teacher's desk, then caught Adam's eyes and gave him a grin.

Adam refocused on the test. Maybe this time he would have a chance to score higher than Liptor. He finished within a few minutes and scooted the parchment to the edge of his desk. Everyone else was still writing. Now he could daydream of his ambitious future.

One by one, the others finished. The whole room was soon filled with hushed conversations about Doene. Still, Teacher did not return. It wasn't like him to be gone for so long.

Camdin, one of the younger boys in the back, folded his test in the shape of a bird and launched it toward the front. Unfortunately for him, his "bird" clipped Jackson on the ear before dropping to the stone floor. Jackson picked it up and crumpled it into a ball. He stomped to the open window and tossed the wad into the yard. "Get your test, boy."

All eyes turned toward Camdin. He stood, his freckled face glowing red but still sporting a mischievous grin. When Jackson sat down, Camdin crossed to the window and peered out in both directions. Then he bolted through the door. Student voices buzzed once more, but they were cut off by a shout from outside.

Camdin charged back into the room, his eyes wide.

"Horses are coming from the city!" He dove for his seat and worked furiously to spread out his wrinkled test.

Hoofbeats thundered to a stop in the yard. A gruff voice called, "Adam! Get out here."

Adam's pulse quickened. He tried to avoid eye contact with all the stares that followed him as he jumped to his feet and headed out, but a small smile toyed with the corners of his mouth.

Grandfather was waiting for him astride his black stallion. His muscular, leathery arms stuck out of his sleeveless thrick. Sweat ran down in rivulets from his bald head and trickled through the gray whiskers that speckled his jaw. Despite his age, he commanded respect by the strength with which he carried himself.

Behind him the chief servant, Roberts, balanced on a brown, bony mare with white patches. The man reminded Adam of a bungling bear, extremely tall and very awkward. Like most villagers, Roberts' face was hollow with hunger. In contrast, his stomach jutted out from his waist like he had a small kettle hidden beneath his thrick. A shaggy gray beard flopped against his chest.

Grandfather dismounted and handed Adam the reins. "Tie the horses and then get back inside. This is a time for action."

"Yes, sir." Adam's heart raced. He admired Grandfather's ability to take control of a situation.

As Grandfather shoved through the door into the schoolhouse, Adam seized the reins of both horses and dashed for the fence. He didn't want to miss anything. Roberts remained seated on his mare, scratching his bony fingers across his belly.

The mare started slightly at Adam's pull. She jumped forward to keep up, causing the old man to flail his arms. "By my beard and my belly!" he shrieked. "What are you trying to do to me? I tell you the world will end in a bad way, and all for young people always being in a hurry."

Adam suppressed a grin as he looped the reins around a fence pole. "You're welcome to join me on solid ground."

The chief servant snorted. "I've got to keep an eye out for 'Caiah. He's coming on foot." He peered down at Adam. "You do know my brother Micaiah's the best scout in all the Twelve Cities, don't you, boy? He knows the forests so well he'd notice if an anthill was relocated."

Adam rolled his eyes. "What's he coming for?"

Roberts motioned him closer. The reek of greasy fish fouled the air around him. "Keep your mouth shut about it, you hear?"

Adam nodded and held his breath, partly with anticipation and partly to keep from smelling fish.

"We got a report that some of them Goiim have been sighted in this area. Now that Doene's fallen, we're not wasting any time sniffing them out. Me and 'Caiah are going with your grandfather down to Red Rock to see what we can find."

Adam had never seen Red Rock, but he knew it wasn't far from home. Arsabians in far off Doene aroused his spirit of adventure, but enemies nearby gave him the shivers. "I better get inside."

Grandfather had never visited the school before. This was a meeting Adam didn't want to miss.

ADAM III

Chapter 2

*"Whosoever committeth sin transgresseth also the law, for
sin is the transgression of the law." 1 John 3:4*

Grandfather towered over the class from the front of the
room. He propped a boot against Teacher's chair.

Adam slipped into his seat just as Grandfather began to
speak.

"Drastic times call for drastic measures. I'm not here to
banter words. You've heard that Doene has fallen. What you
don't know is that Arsabian armies have been mustering
along all our borders, near Garda, Sheera, and Zeulban."

A murmur ran around the room. Adam glanced out the
window toward the distant forest. Were Goiim roaming the
woods near Mount Eirene even now?

Grandfather scratched his whiskers. "I understand that
what I'm about to suggest goes against the law as it stands in
the King's Stones. But this is no time for sticking to rigid
codes. We can be glad your teacher isn't here. How many of

you boys are sixteen or older?"

A dozen hands lifted. Adam wished he were sixteen. But he'd have to wait four more years. Thankfully, Liptor fell short too or he'd get another advantage over Adam.

Grandfather clasped the hilt of a sword that dangled by his side and ripped the blade out of the scabbard. "I'm giving you the choice. If you want to keep your nose in a pile of parchments, that's up to you. But those who raised their hands are free to come with me. I'm freeing you from the king's school. It's time to grow our army."

He sheathed his sword and strode out of the classroom.

Jackson leaped to his feet, along with eleven others, and headed for the door.

Just as quickly, Christy blocked the aisle. "You can't walk out on the king and all we've been taught. Quitting school is breaking the law."

The boys paused. Hank gasped then put a hand to his mouth. Adam could barely hear his friend mutter, "This is a test."

Jackson shoved Christy back into her seat. "Get out of our way. How would you understand war? You're just a schoolgirl."

He marched out into the yard. The others trailed close behind. From the window, Adam watched the boys follow Grandfather back toward the city.

Within minutes the door opened, and Teacher stepped in. His gaze swept the room, clearly taking in the empty seats. He frowned. Then he looked up as if he could see through the polished rafters to the sky, breathed deeply, and walked to the front. He carried a small branch, frayed at the end where it had been recently torn. A few green leaves tinged with brown clung to it.

Teacher looked into his students' eyes for a long minute before he spoke. "I brought this from my garden so you could see my dilemma. For weeks I've been trying to rescue this branch. It keeps growing down into the shade, where it can't get the light it needs. I tied it with rope to redirect it upward, but it resisted and cut into the rope so it could keep pointing downward. Perhaps it thinks it can get to the nutrients in the soil that way."

Adam frowned. *Is this part of the test?* They'd studied plants for a month, but what Teacher was saying now didn't make any sense. Branches didn't have wills of their own. Why didn't he say something about the missing boys?

Teacher lifted the branch for the whole class to see. "So, what can we do with it now? Will it work to stick the branch in the ground outside and let it have all the soil it wants? I could even put it in a sunny place."

Adam's hand shot up. This must be an extension of the test, strange as it seemed. He wasn't going to let Liptor be the first to answer. "No, sir. The branch needs the tree in order to live. If it's dead, the dirt and the sunlight won't do it any good."

Teacher looked deeply into Adam's eyes, as if he were searching his soul. He smiled, but in a sorrowful way. "Yes. The branch needs the light and the nutrients in the soil, but it must be attached to the tree."

He walked to the window and gazed toward the city. Then he rested the branch on the sill and turned back to the class. "If you understood what I'm saying, then don't forget it. Hand in your tests. Class is dismissed."

Adam made his way to the front with the others. Teacher took his test and gestured at his desk. "Can you wait for me? I have something to give you."

What could it be? Adam walked to the walnut desk and leaned against it. Hank was there too, picking at an ink spot on his sleeve. He furrowed his brow. "Did you understand what he meant?" He nodded at the branch on the window sill.

Hank might enjoy digging into weighty matters, but Adam wasn't sure he wanted to know what Teacher meant. He shook his head. "It must have been something extra for the test."

Christy walked up with Mayleen just then. Jacob followed, along with a few others. They were all about Adam's age, twelve.

Teacher came and stood with them in a small circle. "Today's a big day for you all. I was going to wait until the new year, but under the circumstances, I've decided to make this presentation now. The older students have already received theirs. Now it's your turn."

"Received what?" Adam cocked his head.

Teacher reached into his pocket and pulled out a fistful of small, dark balls. He placed one in Adam's palm. "Your first seed. This is a gift from the king. From now on, you'll receive one each month on Supplies Day."

Christy beamed. "I've been waiting for this day!"

Hank nodded. He slid his seed into his pocket.

Adam let out a long, frustrated breath. Did everyone else already know about these seeds? "What are they for?"

Teacher dusted off his hands. "They're seeds of life. The king is offering you a chance to make a difference by planting them on the Mount of Humility. This is both a privilege and a command. I'll go over the details this evening. I want all of you to meet at my house in an hour." His look turned somber. "On the king's authority."

Adam swallowed hard. Disobeying the king's appointed schoolteacher was breaking the law, but if he put them under the king's authority, the order carried extra weight. The penalty of breaking such a command—according to official law—was death.

Would the king really execute us for missing? Adam wondered.

"We'll be there." Christy hugged Teacher.

The students moved toward the door, with Adam bringing up the rear. His mind bounded back and forth like a rabbit between Doene's fall, Grandfather's army, the lurking Goiim, seeds of life, and tonight's meeting.

He was halfway through the door when Teacher's voice brought him up short.

"Adam." Teacher stood by the window, fingering the brown-tinted leaves of the branch. "Don't forget."

Don't forget what? He couldn't forget the meeting in one hour. "Yes, sir." Adam waved and stepped into the yard.

A hot wind swept over him, blowing dirt into the sweat on his skin. Roberts still perched on his spotted mare. Micaiah, his brother, stood beside him looking like a long, knotted walking stick.

To Adam's surprise, Grandfather had returned to the schoolyard. He leaned forward in his saddle, speaking and laughing with Liptor.

A knot tightened in Adam's stomach. The sight of any boy enjoying a father-figure always moved him. He couldn't put a name on the feeling. Longing? Jealousy? Regret? He halted, wondering if he could speak with Grandfather once Liptor moved on.

Hank looked back from where he stood by the road. "Hurry, Adam."

"Go on ahead. Join me in an hour for the meeting."

A harsh laugh followed his call. Liptor pointed his thumb at Adam and called to the other students, "Yeah. Hurry back for Little Governor's meeting. Don't be late."

Grandfather sat back in his saddle and laughed too.

Adam's face burned. He had told Liptor about his aspirations a couple years ago in a moment of weakness. Ever since then, Liptor taunted him mercilessly. It always hurt, but this time it was worse—right in front of Grandfather!

The two resumed their conversation. Every now and then, one of them glanced Adam's way. Hoping to avoid any more attention, he joined Roberts and Micaiah.

Micaiah winked. "Don't let Liptor get you down, boy. What's he got against you? You want to be governor like your grandfather or something?"

Adam stared at the dirt. Yes, he did want to be governor, but not because he craved power, like Liptor. He wanted to make someone proud of him. Father, maybe? But Father and Mother were gone, presumably dead. They had disappeared when he was a child, leaving him alone and feeling unwanted. If he could rise to power like Grandfather, perhaps someone would finally notice him and love him.

Roberts harrumphed. "By my warts and my whiskers, the world will end in a bad way, and all for young people taunting each other."

Micaiah patted Adam on the shoulder. "Maybe you *will* be the governor someday." He turned to Roberts. "But I wonder who will be left to govern. These attacks have been foretold since the beginning. It's our inevitable fate for rebelling."

Adam wanted to ask what Micaiah meant. Before he had a chance, though, Grandfather trotted his stallion toward them and gestured up the King's Road, away from the city. "Let's ride."

Micaiah laughed. "I'll walk. That'll keep old Kettle Belly from being pushed too fast. He might fall off." He nudged his brother in the leg.

Roberts glowered.

Adam watched them follow the dusty road into the distance. They passed Teacher's house on the left then wound their way up Lookout Hill, the boundary of Mount Eirene's surrounding territory. When they had crested it and disappeared on the opposite side, Adam turned back toward the city.

Liptor stood waiting for him, feet spread and arms crossed over his chest. He smirked. "I let Grandfather know I got the best score on the test."

The hair on the back of Adam's neck rose. "You don't know that! I'm sure I did as good or better than you."

"Little Governor, I always score higher. Grandfather believes me."

Adam's jaw dropped. The knot in his stomach grew

tighter. "He didn't take you with him to be part of his army."

Liptor's face darkened. "He said maybe he will. You'll see. Give me a little time."

Adam trembled. He had to do better than Liptor. He *had* to! "Did he? Well, he invited *me* to come along on a dangerous scouting mission. The only reason I'm staying is for the meeting I'm required to attend with Teacher."

"Ha! You expect me to believe that? If he invited you, then you'd be with him. You wouldn't miss an opportunity like that for any old meeting."

"You weren't there when I went out to tie the horses."

Liptor scowled. His blue eyes searched Adam from top to bottom. "Prove it. Go ahead and join him. I'm watching."

Adam looked behind him at Lookout Hill. Fear gripped him. He'd never crossed the hill in his life. What if there really were Goiim out there? Liptor had called his bluff. He always got the upper hand. Always.

But he wouldn't win this time. "All right. I'm going. You'll have to eat your words."

Adam turned and ran for the hill. His heart thumped as fast as his footfalls. *What was I thinking?* Before he could find an answer, he reached the hill's peak. He leaned forward on his knees and panted. The sun burned his neck and hands.

A vast forest stretched out before Adam, the largest part of Aard he'd ever seen. Like Grandfather's dry fields of funja stalks, a dull gray color dominated the scenery. Patches of dried-up hardwoods mixed with ubiquitous tangles of giant rhododendrons. Their gnarled, skeleton-like branches held crackly brown leaves aloft, covering the forest floor in shadow.

Adam could see over the treetops to the place where the road reappeared in the distance. It stopped at the base of the mountains before the Great Gate. Beyond that point lived King Eliab and the native islanders, the ones who had been here before he created the land of Aard.

King Eliab.

By the power of the Ruuwh he could possibly see Adam at this very moment. Teacher had bound him by the king's authority to attend the meeting. If Adam went forward, he would most likely return too late.

His pulse pounded in his ears. He'd never consciously broken the law before. Then again, drastic times called for drastic measures.

In the distance, he saw the stallion and spotted mare tied to a branch near a boulder. If Adam ran, he could overtake Grandfather while he was on foot. But what would Teacher say? What would happen to Adam? He tugged the hair on the back of his head, his habitual posture for deep thinking. He had to go to the meeting.

He turned back—and spotted his cousin.

Liptor had followed him! The older boy stood watching Adam from the bottom of the hill, with his arms crossed in front of his chest.

Adam's face flushed with heat. *How dare you mock me all the time!* Well, Liptor would be disappointed.

Adam spun back toward the forest and started running down the hill. Law or no law, he wasn't going to turn back now.

ADAM III

Cнapтer 3

*"I sware unto thee, and entered into a covenant with
thee, saith the Lord GOD, and thou becamest mine."*
Ezekiel 16:8b

The boulder where the horses were tied rose higher than
Adam had guessed from above. When he reached it, the
rock stood at least three or four times his height. Large, red
stains crowned the top and spilled over the sides in dark
streaks.

Was this Red Rock? Thorn bushes surrounded the
boulder, and Adam thought he saw a small path cutting back
under the rhododendrons.

He squeezed his body against the rock's surface and
eased past the thorns. Sure enough, a small path opened
before him like a tunnel, winding its way into the forest.

He paused and drew a deep breath. What if Goiim were
in there?

Adam forced himself to take a step forward. A tuft of

gray hair dangled from a branch swaying in front of him. It didn't take a scout to see that old Roberts had come this way. Fighting back his doubts, Adam walked deeper into the shadows.

Branches like giant hands clutched at him from both sides of the narrow path. More than once he was forced to crouch and twist through ropes of thorns. He could barely see his way. The dense foliage surrounded him, blocking the sunlight.

Adam hesitated. His heart raced with uncertainty. What if he lost his way? Perhaps he should retrace his steps. He could make it back in time for the meeting.

Yet, he had come so far. Grandfather might be close by. *If I hurry,* he thought, *I can catch up. Then I'll be safe.*

Adam raced forward, charging with his arms extended as a shield. His breathing came in gasps. Branches scratched his arms and face.

Then he lost his balance and fell sideways into a bramble bush. He tried to get up, but the branches clung to his thrick and breeches. He could hardly see in the dark confusion of the moment. Images of murderous Arsabian warriors flooded his imagination. Gasping, he tore himself free, ripping his clothes.

Muscular arms suddenly wrapped Adam in an iron grip. A large, sweaty palm covered his mouth, stifling his cries. He swung his arms wildly. He thrashed and tried to kick, but he struck only air.

"It's a little one," growled a voice in a harsh whisper. "Let's get him in the light where we can see."

A wave of dizziness passed over Adam as his captor

hoisted him into the air and swung him around. A patch of light shone in his face, blinding him for a moment.

A tall man leaned into his vision. "By my ribs, my wrinkles, and a bad rash! It's only Adam." Roberts' voice had a tremor in it.

The grip on Adam's chest relaxed. The strong arms spun him around, and hot, red-pepper breath flooded his nostrils. Grandfather held him close to his face. "What are you doing here?"

Adam tried to stop trembling, but he couldn't. "I-I wanted to come with you."

"Don't you know you could have gotten yourself killed?" Grandfather signaled at Roberts and Micaiah, who returned large knives into the sheaths strapped across their chests.

Micaiah looked in each direction. "Do you want me to take the boy back to the road?"

"We don't have time. If he gets hurt out here it's his own fault." Grandfather tightened his grip on Adam's shoulder. "But mark me, boy. You better be quiet and not interfere with our work."

Adam nodded. This wasn't the reception he had hoped for. Still, the thought of being on a mission with Grandfather stirred his spirit. Micaiah started forward, and Adam eagerly took his place behind Grandfather. He worked hard to keep his feet from snapping twigs as he walked.

A little farther on they came to a halt. Micaiah knelt and studied the ground. He groped along the trail on all fours while the others waited. Roberts' stomach rumbled.

Adam crouched. He couldn't believe he on a dangerous mission only hours after studying about flowers.

This was so much more fulfilling. And exciting!

Micaiah tugged at a large bramble bush. "There's something unnatural about this spot. Someone's been here."

Grandfather took Roberts' arm. "When we get back, dispatch a message to Father Dementiras that we need more weapons."

Micaiah lifted his head. "This war can't be won with metal weapons. We've been handed over to our enemies because of the king's anger."

Adam wrinkled his brow. Micaiah had said something similar earlier. "What do you mean?"

"I told you to keep quiet." Grandfather glared at him.

Micaiah stood. "Let him ask. The boy has a right to know. His father believed what I'm saying. He—"

A rock hurtled through the air and smashed into Micaiah's temple. He sank to the ground in a heap. Roberts flopped prostrate in the dirt beside him. Grandfather dropped, rolled, and kicked Adam's feet out from under him.

Adam crashed onto the path. *What's happening?* Another rock sailed over his head, taking out a branch right where he'd been standing.

Grandfather crawled past Roberts to where Micaiah lay and flipped over the body. "He's gone."

Roberts groaned.

Adam's stomach turned over. He thought he should cry, but he felt only a numb awareness of what had happened. He pushed himself along the ground to get closer to the men.

"The Keeda tribe." Grandfather handed Roberts the rock that had struck his brother. The stone was round and smooth, with strange red markings. Roberts let it drop to the ground.

Several more rocks crashed into the trees behind them. Then shouts broke out.

Grandfather grabbed Adam and pushed him and Roberts along the trail. "It's too dangerous to go back. Run. Head up the river. Wait for me at the old lookout point. Can you still find it?"

Roberts acknowledged Grandfather's instructions with a nod then scooted back to his brother. The old man dug into Micaiah's pockets, seized an object, and then jumped to his feet and started running.

Grandfather scooped up the rock with one hand and drew his sword with the other. "Go, Adam!" he ordered. Then he ducked into the trees.

Adam fled behind Roberts. The path was difficult to see, but he kept his eyes on the chief servant's back and stayed close on his heels. He dared not lose Roberts in the heart of this perilous wood. The old man could move surprisingly fast for his age and size.

Branches whipped at Adam's clothes. A spiderweb struck his face, and he shut his eyes. When he blinked them open again, Roberts had stopped. Adam reached out for branches to halt his charge, but his momentum was too strong.

Oof! Roberts buckled when Adam crashed into him, and the two landed in a heap on the trail. Something bounced out of Roberts' thrick and rolled into the bushes.

"Are you all right? I'm so sorry!" Adam pushed himself to his knees and grasped Roberts by the arm. Trembling, he waited for the tirade that would surely follow.

Roberts pushed Adam away. A thin line of blood cut across his forehead. Brambles and leaves were matted into his gray beard. He didn't appear to be hurt.

Adam crawled after the object under the bushes. This must be what Roberts had retrieved from Micaiah. He lifted it to a patch of light.

A pear.

The fruit was crusty, yellow and dry. But it was fruit. Adam's mouth began to salivate. Food in Mount Eirene was strictly rationed. The primary staple was silfun soup, a stringy porridge made from the stocks of the funja plants. Fruit of any kind came only from the king's wagons once a month on Supplies Day.

"Here." Adam brushed off the dirt and handed the pear to Roberts. He felt a strong reluctance to let it go. Hunger gnawed at his insides. *Maybe Roberts will share a bite.*

Roberts snatched the pear, engulfing it in his long fingers. "Help me up."

He took Adam's hand and raised himself out of the dirt. Staggering forward, he rounded a sharp bend in the trail. Adam hurried after him. The bushes ceased as a small clearing opened. Adam found himself blinking against the setting sun.

"Watch where you're going this time." Roberts' voice sounded heavy. Perhaps the old man had been hurt worse than he appeared. His quietness bothered Adam more than the expected tongue-lashing.

The path descended before them into a dry riverbed. Adam shook his head in amazement as he eased his way down the steep side. He knew from studying in school that rivers once flowed here, but he never would have guessed they had been so large. When full, a fishing boat might have sailed comfortably here.

His steps crunched on the hard-packed dirt as they reached the bottom, which was bare except for rocks, deadwood, and occasional cracks. Roberts glanced back at the trail above them, then turned north and began running up the riverbed. Adam had to sprint to keep pace with Roberts' long strides.

A minute passed. Then several more. Adam's side cramped from running. He couldn't catch his breath and slowed to a walk.

Roberts paid no attention and continued running.

"Wait!"

His words came out hoarse and weak. Roberts either didn't hear or didn't care if Adam fell behind. Terrified of being left alone, Adam raced after him. On and on they ran, winding between the walls of earth. Adam's feet and legs ached.

Finally, when Adam felt he could go no farther, Roberts stopped. The old man held his stomach and gasped for air. Sweat ran through his beard and drenched his thrick. He scanned the path and began walking, slowly enough to let Adam keep step beside him.

They went at this pace until their breathing became less forced. Adam kept looking back but saw no indications of pursuit, or of Grandfather. The shadows slowly lengthened.

Roberts gazed up at the dry river bank above them.

Can enemies follow us from above? Adam wasn't sure. But the rhododendrons and brambles were so thick, he doubted anyone could keep up with them there. He relaxed.

Now that Adam had a moment to think, Micaiah's sudden

death weighed heavily on his mind. How could he have gone so quickly? What danger were he, Roberts, and Grandfather in now?

"Who are the Keeda?" Adam's question broke the steady rhythm of their crunching footfalls. "Are they the ones who attacked us?"

When Roberts answered, his voice sounded distant. "They're nomads. One of the tribes of Ar Sabia. Most of them live underground and don't come out unless it's dark."

"Why would they attack us?"

Roberts waited a long time before answering. "The war, I guess. They used to have a truce with your grandfather. He hired them to carry out executions at Red Rock. A nasty lot, the Keeda. Their skin is white and sickly-looking from their time spent underground."

Adam glanced behind him and quickened his pace. "It's hard to imagine I was studying flowers this morning. The war makes all that seem so unimportant. No one's ever seen flowers in Mount Eirene except in Teacher's garden. Too bad we didn't study sword fighting."

Wind blew across the top of the riverbed, tossing down broken twigs and briars. Adam rubbed his sleeve across his face. When he looked at Roberts, he saw tears making brown paths across the man's cheeks and disappearing into his beard. Perhaps he had been hurt in the tumble, after all.

"Are you all right?"

Roberts glanced up at the bank. "We used to." His voice came out muffled.

"Used to what?" He followed Roberts' gaze but saw nothing but skeleton-like branches reaching over the edge.

"See flowers."

Adam looked back at the path, unsure of what to make of this sudden statement. "When?"

"In the beginning." Roberts snorted back and heaved a deep sigh. "The king loved flowers. There was a garden in the city full of roses, orchids, daffo-dandies, and ..."

He shrugged. "Well, I don't remember names very well. Bushes were full of every color you can imagine. The trees were full of blossoms too. And the fruit? It was like a feast every day. We had the sweetest mangoes you ever tasted, pineapple, and bananas too, all sorts of them."

Adam smiled. He wasn't surprised food had come into the conversation. But the humor didn't cover the sense of loss he felt, thinking of a time he had never known. He was surprised to hear about it now. Roberts had never spoken of such things before.

"What was it like here in the forest?"

Roberts stopped and looked down at the dry riverbed. "It was underwater."

"I didn't mean right here."

"It was too beautiful for me to describe. The rivers were clean. Pure."

Roberts gestured at the bank and started walking. "There used to be a footpath with white stones, and I would come here to walk. There were no thorns then, and it was easy. I remember the birds—hundreds of them. I used to know their names. My favorites were the bright blue and gold ones. They came and sat on my hand if I held out a finger. All the animals were that way then."

"Were there flowers here too?"

"Oh, yes. In the grass, the bushes, the trees, and even on vines. There were berries too." He sighed and rubbed his belly. "The king told me the ground contained gold, but I never got to see."

"You talked with the king?" Adam stared at him with bulging eyes. It was hard enough to imagine grass, flowers, and a river. But to talk to the king? Incredible!

"Many times. He used to come here, and I loved to walk with him." A sob shook Roberts, and he put the back of his hand to his nose.

"But how?" Adam asked. "I don't understand. No one sees the king."

"We did at that time. He used to talk with me and tell me about his plans for Mount Eirene. He listened too. I always felt like he—never mind. You wouldn't understand."

"What?"

Roberts shook his head.

"Please. You have to tell me."

Roberts sighed. "I always felt like he loved us, the way a father would."

The hair on the back of Adam's neck stood on end. *What do you know about a father's love?* A wave of longing washed over Adam afresh, choking him.

"Not long after Aard was created, King Eliab gathered us all together. He told us that he loved us and had prepared a special place for us to live. That was when he first took us to our city and named it Mount Eirene. He planned to make it his capital in the future and—well, I guess it doesn't matter now."

"No, what is it?"

"He said he would build the palace there someday. Mount Eirene would become the greatest mountain in the island. But of course, I don't see how."

Adam's thoughts swam. He had always wondered why their city's hill was named "Mount Eirene," when the mountains on the horizon rose so much higher. Sometimes he called it "Eirene Bump."

"We loved our city," Roberts went on. "It was simple enough, mind you, but it was beautiful. All the fountains and gardens and food. You just don't understand what it's like to live in a green world instead of this gray one we live in now."

Adam tried to imagine, but it was indeed difficult. Even the water from the creek was brown most of the year.

"He made a covenant with us. We agreed, of course. We were excited about all his promises. Your grandfather signed the pledge for all of us, and everyone shouted for joy. The king set up a special stone with the two parts of the covenant in writing—our part and his part."

"What is our part?"

"I don't remember. Probably to keep the laws of the land or something. His part was to take care of us, and maybe rule us."

Adam glanced at Roberts. His casual answer seemed out of place. He thought of the City Center, with the towering King's Stones surrounding it.

"Was the covenant stone one of the King's Stones?"

"No. The king set up the King's Stones afterward. I used to read them a long time ago."

Roberts licked his lips. "We had a great feast with goats

roasted in the pit—fat ones, mind you—and every kind of fish and fruit. And the juices! I laughed too, but not like normal, empty laughing. It was laughter from the heart. It was very nice. It was peace."

Roberts toyed with the pear. "I wish it could have lasted forever. The king said we should gather to celebrate every year and read the Stones for the entire nation."

"Why don't we read the Stones?"

Roberts scowled and didn't answer. He bit off half of the pear in one bite.

Adam's mouth watered, but he fought back the desire to interfere with Roberts and his food. Besides, an even greater hunger was gnawing at him, a hunger he couldn't put his finger on.

"Why doesn't the king come to see us anymore? Why is everything so bad?"

Roberts wiped his sticky fingers on his beard and swallowed. "He's angry."

"Why?"

"Ask the governor," Roberts snapped.

"But why? I don't understand. Do you mean we've offended him?"

"Never mind. I don't want to talk about it."

They continued walking in silence, mingled with the old man's heavy breathing. Adam shivered as an evening breeze swept by him. Branches glowed with the disappearing light of sunset. Shadows covered everything else. He hadn't noticed the change to dusk, but now he felt it and hung his head.

What if King Eliab does love us? Could he be the father-

figure I've always longed for? Surely not. But I wish I hadn't broken the law. I wish I could go back to Teacher's house.

It was too late now.

He touched Roberts' arm. "Is there any way for a person to make things right with the king after he breaks the law?"

Heavy breathing was Adam's only answer. He tried to make out Roberts' face, but the shadows had grown too deep.

He tried again. "Do you think our city could make things right with the king? Would that make things the way they were before? Could he rescue us from the Arsabians?"

More silence.

Adam waited for a long time, hoping Roberts would finally answer.

But the silence only continued, and the darkness grew.

ADAM III

Chapter 4

"We will not have this man to reign over us." Luke 19:14

Just as the darkness reached its height, Adam and Roberts came to a place where an enormous oak rose out of the bank on their left. Massive roots sprawled across the riverbed floor. Far above them, its branches covered the sky. Roberts checked over his shoulder and then raced to the tree.

To Adam's surprise, the old man began ascending the trunk. Fascinated, he followed and discovered a set of barely visible steps carved into the wood. He shinnied up after Roberts and mounted a platform of carved boards, large enough for several men to sit on.

Roberts felt around the platform with his hands. "Help me look for a torch. There should be at least a few, if they haven't rotted away by this time."

Adam joined the search and discovered a small pile of wood. He reached one out toward Roberts, prodding his elbow with it.

Roberts jerked his arm and squeaked before he caught himself. "By my beard and my belly!" Grumbling, he took the wood and lit the prepared end using a set of flint rocks from his pocket. A flower of red flame illumined the surface of the platform and their faces. Roberts set the torch into a notch cut for the purpose in one of the branches.

The scuffle of footsteps sounded beneath them, approaching the tree at a brisk trot. Roberts drew his knife out of its sheath and held his breath. Adam squeezed against the bark and looked down. A figure just beyond the circle of light reached out a hand to the trunk.

Adam's heart leaped. "Grandfather?"

"Of course it's me, you fools. Put out that light." Grandfather climbed the steps and hoisted himself onto the platform, his face red and perspiring. Before Roberts or Adam could react, he plucked the torch from its socket and stuffed out the flame, beating the wood against the tree trunk.

Adam lost sight completely for a minute, but he could hear Grandfather panting and then squatting between him and Roberts. The familiar smell of red-pepper breath felt somewhat reassuring.

"They were Keeda," Grandfather said. "Two young warriors this time, hardly men at all. I finished them off, but I suspect there's a larger group behind them. We better wait here for a while. I could have been followed."

The warm night air did nothing to stop Adam from shivering. But in spite of the horror he felt, a sense of admiration flooded his veins. Grandfather had outsmarted and overpowered the Keeda warriors, even in the dark, which usually gave them the advantage. He wished he could say or do something that would earn him the respect of such a great man.

Minutes dragged on in silence. Adam's eyes adjusted to the dark, and he scanned the riverbed. Thoughts of his conversation with Roberts continued to burn in his mind.

"Grandfather?"

"Keep your voice down. What is it?"

"Why doesn't the king come to Mount Eirene? Does he have anything to do with the war?"

Grandfather grunted. "Who's been filling your head with that bunch of nonsense?"

Adam couldn't make out Roberts' face, but the old man hacked a couple times and changed his position on the platform. "I was just wondering."

Grandfather let out a slow breath and drummed his fingers against the wooden boards. "I guess it's about time we had this discussion."

Adam waited in silence.

"Perhaps you're aware that the king was more involved in our lives when Aard was first created. He said he had made us free. But he stayed here constantly, watching our every move. To make sure he had us under his control, he forced us to sign a covenant."

"Forced?"

Grandfather was close enough that Adam could see him squint. "Yes, *forced*. The covenant bound us to do everything the king desired. Every rule. To make sure we never forgot them, he erected stones—covered from top to bottom with laws—right in the middle of our city. All this we are compelled to do by this covenant, this binding agreement."

His voice dropped to a hoarse, angry whisper. "Do you know what the penalty is for breaking the king's covenant?"

Adam said nothing.

"The penalty for breaking the covenant is death for every offender. For the entire city. Death."

Adam's voice shook. "But why?"

Roberts cut in before Grandfather could reply. "Did your teacher tell you *nothing* about kings, covenants, and consequences? How do you expect him to keep peace for his people without the power to enforce what he says?"

"But death?"

Grandfather frowned at Roberts' exclamation, but he held his gaze riveted to his grandson's. "Never mind what he says, Adam. Listen to me. Think about what I tell you. Death—for you, for the city."

Adam shifted on the platform. He looked up into the branches of the tree as if they might be full of spies ready to report him.

Grandfather went on. "The king gathered everyone together. With all eyes watching, he placed a large brown seed in my hand. 'Adam,' he said to me, 'this seed, and many more to come, are the keys that will bring glory to this city.' He also said we would reign with him. He said these seeds would produce trees of life."

Adam sucked in his breath and then immediately hoped Grandfather hadn't noticed. He slid his hand in his pocket and clutched the hard, dark seed Teacher had given him.

Grandfather didn't give any indication of noticing. "I was eager to find out more, but it wasn't what I had thought at first. The king told us he would send seeds with every supplies wagon, seeds for every family, for every individual. Our job would be to plant the seeds. Not just anywhere, though. He wanted us to plant them all on the Mount of Humility."

"I've never heard of it," Adam said. "Where is this mountain? What kind of a place is it?"

"Look out across the riverbed."

Adam strained his eyes in the direction Grandfather indicated. As he looked, the form of a tall, rocky mountain began to emerge through the darkness. The top was far away, and from there, the mountain appeared to slope down by degrees until it touched the riverbed on the opposite side from their tree.

"I see it now."

At that moment, a cloud slid away from the moon, bathing the landscape in silver light. Adam gasped. What he had mistaken for a gradual slope of solid rock he now saw to be a series of tall, thin ridges. They rose at jagged intervals to the peak.

The whole face of the Mount of Humility was a maze of valleys, clefts, and deep holes.

"How could anything grow in such a terrible place?"

Grandfather nodded. "That was my thought exactly. It was unreasonable. But we went out and looked just the same. I tell you, boy, there's hardly an inch of soil or a drop of water on the entire mountain. Even the pine trees that used to stand there have fallen. We were baffled for a while. We almost went to the king to ask what we should do. But we got tipped off beforehand."

"What do you mean?"

Grandfather's voice dropped to a low growl. "One of the old islanders gave away the king's true intentions. His majesty was afraid of us getting too much power."

"I don't understand."

"Think about it."

Adam gazed at the Mount of Humility. He tried to imagine people carrying seeds through the valleys and ridges. *How could the king expect us to do something like that?*

He felt betrayed. Surely no one who loved him would require a thing like that. "Do you mean the king did this just to waste our time?"

"Aha!" Grandfather sat back. "You see, Roberts? He has Sonneman blood in him." He squinted one eye at Adam. "Yes, boy, to waste our time. To keep us too busy to think for ourselves or to make anything out of ourselves. If nothing else, I credit him with foresight."

Grandfather shook his fist toward the mountain. "He should know that with enough time, a Sonneman will rise to power!"

Adam smiled. *A Sonneman will rise to power.* But another thought crowded in upon the first. "What did you do with the seeds?"

"I did what any man of ambition would do. I threw them by the backyard wall to rot."

Adam put a hand over his pocket, covering the seed inside. "Did everyone else follow you?"

"Not at first. Many protested and went off to plant their seeds. It was during that time of instability that B'laadin led a revolt, and the Arsabians separated themselves from us, curse them. Soon, others followed and formed their own nations, until we were left small in number. Over time, we've built the Twelve Cities. But the other nations of Aard have grown much larger than we have."

Adam's mind whirled in circles like a dust storm. Although he felt exhilarated by discovery and ambitious for his city's glory, he was more overwhelmed than anything else. The thought of leadership began to strike him as a fearful burden.

"What did the king do? You said that breaking the covenant would lead to death."

"He left us. Alone."

Adam remembered his fear earlier that afternoon, when he was by himself in the forest. *Alone.* Now he sat beside two strong men, and yet the same emotions rushed over him.

"At least we didn't die. Right?"

"Not yet," Roberts broke in. He frowned. "But I'll tell you one thing. We lost *this*." His knobby fingers clutched the core of his old pear. He shook it at Adam.

Grandfather stood. "I'll tell you one thing. I, for one, will be no man's slave." He beat a fist against his chest. "*This* Adam will be free."

Adam began to rise, but Grandfather dropped to his knees and pulled him down. "Hush."

They huddled against the boards, listening. Murmuring voices in the darkness moved toward them from the riverbed. Adam strained his ears but could not hear what the men were saying.

He felt Grandfather's large hand on his back and

welcomed it. It wasn't exactly affectionate, but perhaps one day it would be. He often imagined his father placing a hand on his shoulder and saying, "I love you, Son. You have pleased me well."

If only Father was still alive.

Four or five men glided beneath them. Adam could barely see their features, but he marveled at the brightness of their white skin reflected in the moonlight. One man lingered, running a hand against the bark of the tree. Grandfather reached for his sword. But the man grunted and moved on without appearing to notice them.

They sat in silence for several minutes. Then Grandfather grabbed two unlit torches. He thrust one into his belt and handed one to Roberts. He swung by a branch to the steps and from there dropped to the ground.

"Go." Roberts prodded Adam in the back. They followed Grandfather down the steps.

Grandfather led them at a light run back the way they had come. Adam's heart thumped wildly in his chest. Would the Keeda warriors return and pursue them? How many remained in the forest?

Sooner than Adam anticipated, they arrived at the place where the path in the woods above them intersected the riverbed. Grandfather ascended the bank first and searched for a minute before waving Adam and Roberts to join him.

Roberts' voice trembled when he spoke. "Can we risk a light? I want … to bring him back with us."

Grandfather hesitated. "Hurry," he said at last. He drew his sword and waited while Roberts lit his torch. Then he charged forward.

Adam hurried to keep up. The crunching of his feet echoed through the woods, and he felt vulnerable with the light on his back.

Then Grandfather stopped and motioned at Roberts. At the side of the trail lay Micaiah's body, face down in the dirt. Someone had stripped his thrick off, leaving his back exposed. Adam moved in front as the two men extinguished the light and lifted the body between them.

A wave of nausea passed over Adam. He forced his feet to move and tried to push back the branches and thorns to help the two behind him. Slowly, they struggled toward the King's Road. The rustling leaves made Adam's skin crawl. He longed to see the open sky above him once more.

Finally, they emerged beside Red Rock. Its stains ran black in the moonlight. Grandfather took the full weight of Micaiah's body from Roberts and slung it across the spotted mare, which had remained tied to a branch.

He handed the reins to Roberts. "Go ahead of us. Adam and I have one more thing to discuss."

Roberts set a hand on Micaiah's bare shoulder and swallowed hard before giving a slight nod. He tried several times to lift himself onto the saddle and eventually succeeded. With a parting glance in Grandfather's direction, he headed toward the city.

A knot formed in Adam's stomach. What did Grandfather want to discuss? Adam tried so hard to impress him, but nothing ever went the way he intended.

Grandfather lit his torch and handed it to Adam. Untying his stallion, he led them both by foot away from Red Rock. They walked in silence for a while.

"Little Governor, huh?"

Adam's hand trembled as he held the torch. Was this what Grandfather wanted to talk about? Anger flared toward Liptor. He kept his mouth shut tight and cringed.

"So, you have aspirations to rule like your grandfather?"

"No, sir. I mean yes, sir, but I ..." He didn't know what to say.

Grandfather scratched his whiskers. "Don't be afraid to say it. And mean it. Your name is Adam Sonneman, isn't it?"

They had reached the peak of Lookout Hill. The woods behind them and the fields before them lay still beneath the moon. Grandfather reached into the pocket of his thrick. "I have something to show you."

He drew out a large copper coin and held it in the torchlight so that it shone. Adam had rarely seen a coin before, let alone thought of possessing one. His eyes fixed on the coin with rapt attention.

Grandfather pointed at the crown that covered the coin's face. "This will be the symbol of your authority. This coin can be yours. It's your choice. Are you willing to follow me?"

"Of course."

"Then you can join me tomorrow morning."

Adrenaline surged through Adam's veins. He could be part of Grandfather's army! Then doubts crowded into his thoughts. "What about school?"

"Is that any concern to you still?"

Adam considered. He had already broken the law. Perhaps, though, he would have a chance to make amends.

At the bottom of the hill he could see Teacher's house. A light glowed in the windows. What had Teacher said to him earlier that afternoon?

He looked at Grandfather. "What about Teacher?"

Grandfather released the horse's reins and gripped Adam's right shoulder. His words came out fierce. "What about him?"

Adam wrapped his sweaty palm around the seed in his pocket and took a step back.

"Your teacher won't take you back now, boy. Didn't you tell your friends you had a meeting with him this afternoon? Now, you've gone against him."

Adam hung his head.

"Immanuel is far too loyal to the king. But his ideals will never rescue us from the Arsabians. There's something you don't know. He isn't one of us. We don't know where he came from, but I do know one thing. He's not on our side."

Grandfather stood to his full height and held out the coin. "You have a choice. Be a slave to a distant king or follow me and freedom."

Adam squeezed the seed in his pocket and stared at the coin. For the second time in one day he had to make a decision. In spite of all he had been through, he didn't want to keep breaking the law. Roberts' words about the king had made him see things differently.

Adam felt torn. For once, Grandfather was giving him the attention he craved. At this moment Adam, not Liptor, was being offered position, perhaps even the promise of being the future governor. *What should I do?*

Adam looked at the coin in Grandfather's hand.

Torchlight danced on its shiny surface.

He took a deep breath and released the seed. Then he took the coin and curled it into his fist. "Yes." Mustering as much strength as his shaky voice could command, Adam beat his fist against his chest. "*This* Adam will be free."

Grandfather grinned. "Spoken like a man. Keep that coin safe. Whenever you have any doubts about your decision, look at it and remember."

Adam nodded. There was no need to encourage him to look at it. All the way home he peered at it in the moonlight. He turned it in his hand under the table during his hasty dinner. When he flopped exhausted into bed, he clutched the coin in his hand.

"This Adam," he whispered to himself, "will be free."

ADAM III

Chapter 5

"To whom ye yield yourselves servants to obey, his servants ye are." Romans 6:16

Crash! The door to Adam's bedroom slammed open. Adam bolted upright in his bed. Camdin stood in the doorway, grinning. A lick of hair shot out the left side of his head. He must have just come up from his bed in the kitchen quarters, where his mother, Rhenda, served as Grandfather's cook.

"Roberts sent me to find you," Camdin burst out. "You'd better hurry. He's awfully upset!"

Adam threw off the blanket and scrambled for his clothes. He chafed at being ordered by the younger boy, but he knew better than to argue with Roberts. He jerked on his breeches. "Why? It's still dark outside. What's going on?"

Camdin disappeared with only another door slam for an answer, leaving Adam to fumble around by himself.

Something poked his leg, and he yanked the large seed

out of his pocket.

The events of the previous day came rushing back. Sorrow choked him as he thought of Micaiah's death. Then he thought of Doene and the mustering army.

Something good had happened, though. He dove for the bed, fished the coin out from under the covers, and held it in front of his face.

"I'm a free man today."

Adam dropped the coin and the seed into his pocket and made the bed. He raced down the stairs two at a time, following the scent of silfun porridge, and came to a stop just outside the kitchen.

The large room had clearly been beautiful in years past. Carved oak paneling covered the walls, rich with details. Stone flowers unfolded around the fireplace. Much of the splendor had been lost over time, but a faint sense of richness remained.

No one noticed Adam standing in the doorway. His gaze found Roberts sitting at one of the tables, as he had expected. He scraped at an empty bowl like a starving man and then lifted it to the light for a closer inspection. Rhenda, the cook, stirred her pot by the fire. The other servants devoured silfun porridge at different tables around the room.

Adam coughed. "You sent for me, sir?"

The chief servant dropped his spoon with a loud clatter and clutched his bowl. "For goodness sake! Why must you always scare people out of their wits and their wisdom?" He paused for breath. "What have you been doing all morning?"

Adam hesitated, unsure what to say. After all, the sun had barely risen.

A servant shot him a pitying glance. Rhenda set a small bowl of porridge on the table by Roberts. She wiped her long, thin fingers on her apron and nodded at Adam. "Not much time. You'd better start shoveling."

"Why?"

Roberts looked ready to say something feisty but checked himself.

Grandfather appeared in the doorway just then. He stood close enough to lay a hand on Adam's shoulder if he wanted to. Several servants darted out past him with bobbing heads.

"Good morning, Grandfather."

"And to you. Are you ready to begin your first day of work?"

"I'm sorry. I haven't eaten yet. But it won't take long."

Grandfather scowled. "Do you think you're a schoolboy still, to begin with the rising sun? If you've missed breakfast, it's your own fault. Let that be a lesson to you. We have work to do. Come on." He turned and left.

A grin twitched across Roberts' face. He replaced his own bowl with Adam's and gestured with his spoon at the door. "Better get going. Let that be a lesson to you."

Adam hurried after Grandfather, his stomach protesting. From now on he would have less sleep or less food. Neither option appealed to him. Somehow, this aspect of his new freedom had escaped his attention the night before.

He followed Grandfather out to the great courtyard in front of their house. He moved closer and reached out to touch his arm. "Will I get to stay with you today?"

Grandfather appeared not to hear. He knit his brows and glanced first at the outbuildings and then at the stone planters, long bereft of any life but spiders. He reached up to rub his forehead, letting Adam's hand flop away.

Adam sighed and followed out the gate in silence.

A path lined with dead rose bushes led them to the main road, the King's Road. They turned right and went north, away from the center of town. The road led downhill and out into the funja fields. From there it passed through a scattering of houses, curved past the school, and eventually arrived at Lookout Hill.

They stopped at the funja fields, where most of the men from Mount Eirene eked out their living, working for the governor. Miles of crusty earth rolled off into the distance, striped with lines of knee-high funja shoots. Adam recognized a good number of the workers. They glanced at him through glassy eyes.

In a rocky patch of ground closer to the city, he saw Uncle Tari training the older boys how to fight. Jackson and the others were drilling with sharpened sticks. A group of men were engaged in similar drills a little farther away. Adam noted their maneuvers carefully, so he would be able to catch up.

On a small rise in the middle of the field stood a short man staring at him. He looked away when Adam noticed but resumed no task. His feet were spread wide, and he fingered a whip.

Adam shuddered. The man's face struck him as unnatural and roundish, not at all like the sunken cheeks of other villagers. His bald head didn't match his young face. Tight muscles covered every inch of his frame.

"Who is that man over there?" Adam asked.

"Ah," said Grandfather. "There he is."

He began marching across the field straight toward the man. Adam hesitated and then trailed behind. The man made no move as Grandfather and Adam approached.

"Here, Schala." He motioned at Adam. "I brought you the help I promised. I hope you'll be content with that."

Schala grinned, and the corners of his eyes tightened. "Good. Any more?"

"That's all for now, and you'd better be thankful. Sometimes I wonder if you think you're the master and I'm the slave, instead of the other way around." Grandfather shook his head and started back toward the road. He glanced at Adam in passing. "Listen to Schala, boy. He'll tell you what to do."

"But I thought—"

"We need the men to defend the city," Grandfather said, "but someone has to take care of the fields."

Adam's heart sank. He wanted to run. Instead, he stood motionless, watching Grandfather walk away. *Would Father have treated me like this?* Adam thought. *Perhaps he would have squeezed my shoulder. He might have said, "Do well, Son."*

An image of Teacher's kind smile crossed Adam's mind. He shook his head to clear the cobwebs and squeezed the coin in his pocket. *These are no thoughts for a free man.*

Schala's eyes stayed fixed on the governor's back. A smirk played about the corners of his mouth.

"Well?" Adam finally ventured.

Schala jerked his gaze from the road. "Come with me."

The two picked their way across the rough soil, swatting

at dust clouds. Schala ducked inside a small cluster of trees and emerged with two wooden buckets.

Adam wrinkled his nose at their moldy smell and stepped back.

Schala eyeballed him. His smirk reappeared. "These are for you." He set the buckets on the ground and started walking across the field. "Follow me."

Adam lifted the buckets. He cringed at their unexpected weight and jogged after Schala.

"Down there." Schala pointed his whip at the brown stream that ran below the fields.

"You want me to fill the buckets from the creek?"

Schala tilted his head.

I guess that means yes. Adam sighed and headed for the water. He'd gone to the creek many times before. It was the primary source of fresh water in Mount Eirene.

Conscious of the eyes behind him, Adam hurried down the slope. He reached out his right foot to a small stone in the stream and bent over, extending the first bucket. The water was shallow, barely sloshing over the lip. He stretched for what he hoped would be a deeper spot. His back cramped with the effort, but the bucket filled more quickly. He held on until he thought it was full.

When Adam tried to stand, the full bucket was heavier than he anticipated. His foot slipped, and the bucket fell toward him, thudding on its bottom before rolling sideways.

He refilled the bucket and set it upright. By now, he'd soaked his shoes.

A quick glance over his shoulder increased Adam's discomfort. Schala stared at him with the same sinister smirk that was becoming too familiar.

Schala's smirk followed Adam everywhere he went that first hour. It mocked his vain attempts to keep the water from escaping through cracks in the buckets. The smirk dogged Adam's steps as he trudged between the creek and the fields, watering the small shoots of the funja. It laughed every time he winced with pain. And there it was again, to hurt him most whenever he hoped for approval.

After an hour, Schala left him on his own. Adam let out a sigh of relief and exhaustion. His arms ached from the unfamiliar exertion. His ankle throbbed from a gash, where he'd slipped in the creek.

Worst of all, his hands burned like fire. Nasty blisters bubbled up all over his palms because of the rough rope handles. He padded them with mud from the creek, but the pain didn't go away.

Adam trudged back and forth all morning. He distracted himself by thinking about the coin. About the time the sun reached its full height, he made an encouraging discovery. A little way downstream, around a bend behind a hill, the opposite bank rose steep. As a result, the creek narrowed and deepened.

At last! Adam could submerge and fill his buckets to the top. He filled them both and sat down to rest. The cool water flowed over his hands and through his fingers.

After a little hesitation, he pulled off his shoes, tossed them aside, and lowered his sore feet into the water. *Ahh!* The water felt so good it almost hurt. He rested, shading his eyes to block out the bright light from the sun. How he ached!

Several times Adam decided to get up, but each time he thought a little more water would feel good. A shadow fell across his face. *Oh, no!* He jumped to his feet and glanced around. What would Schala say if he caught Adam resting?

He looked up. A cloud had flitted in front of the sun. His heart slowed down, but it was time to get back to work. He pulled on his shoes, seized the rope handles, and charged up the bank and around the bend.

Except for a few scattered tools, the field was empty. The men had probably gone to lunch. The thought of missing a second meal threw Adam into a panic. He dropped the buckets and sprinted. Sweat poured down his forehead.

A loud whistle brought Adam up short.

Schala stood by the clump of trees where he'd given Adam the buckets. He motioned for Adam to join him.

Adam considered ignoring the summons and running. But he thought better of it and jogged toward Schala, hoping to get back on course as soon as possible.

He cringed as he drew near the man, anticipating a rebuke. To his surprise, Schala smiled. "You have worked hard. You should be proud."

The words stoked immediate pride in Adam. Schala signaled for him to follow and ducked into the trees. "I have something for you."

Adam frowned, running his hand through his hair. His heart beat out a warning, but he pushed the feeling aside and entered. Surely, he deserved something for all his efforts this morning. Schala sat on a rock in a small clearing within the trees and stretched out his legs.

At his signal, Adam sat on another rock, waiting.

Schala pulled a cloth bag from his vest, took out a few large berries, and tossed them into his mouth. From its shape, the bag appeared to hold a large number of berries, and Adam's mouth began to water. When Schala held out the bag, Adam cupped his hand. Schala dumped several berries into it.

"Thank you." Adam tasted the first berry. A rich sweetness surprised and thrilled his taste buds. He tipped back his head to toss in a couple more. His eyes widened. "I've never tasted anything so good in my life. What are these?"

Schala snorted with apparent disgust. "You're not *that* naïve, are you?"

"Why? What are they?" Adam held up the remaining berries for a closer look. They were bright-red and soft but firm. He saw nothing special. He wracked his brain, trying to remember anything important he had learned from school.

A terrible thought crossed his mind. "Surely these aren't wedding berries!"

Schala snorted again. His voice oozed with sarcasm. "You mean you've never before enjoyed the sweet fruits of love?"

Adam frowned. Teacher had spoken to the class several times about wedding berries. They grew on sacred bushes, cultivated by King Eliab himself. For every wedding in Mount Eirene, he would send one of his bushes as a gift for the new couple. It was a token of his love for the people and of his blessing on marriage. The couple could plant the bush at their new home and enjoy its fruits for the rest of their married lives.

Because of the bushes' sacred nature, the king forbade anyone except the married couple to partake of its fruits. Stealing wedding berries was a capital offense, according to the King's Stones, although Adam didn't think Grandfather ever enforced the punishment. Once though, when Darbey, the wife of Adam's older cousin Lichten, had shared some of her berries with a servant, Grandfather had raged with fury.

"Many mighty have been destroyed for a handful of berries," Teacher had repeated over and over again. He urged his class to wait for the king's good gift.

Adam trembled at the memory. Perhaps he should go to Teacher for help. Grandfather said Teacher was trying to enslave them, but even Grandfather thought it was wrong to steal wedding berries.

He rose, but the berries left in his hand caught his eye. His gaze locked on the fruit. His mouth longed for another taste. *Just one more!* He sat down and nudged one of the berries with his fingernail.

Adam didn't like being called "naïve." And after all that had happened yesterday, why worry about breaking the king's laws? Somehow, that didn't sound right, but only a few berries remained.

Three more won't make any difference.

He ate the remaining berries. Then he wanted more. He looked at Schala, who was staring at him intently. He proffered the bag.

Adam opened his palm. "Just a few more."

Schala turned the bag upside down. The entire contents poured into Adam's hand until it overflowed.

Adam's heart thudded. His tongue remembered the

sweetness. He raised his hand and ate two more. "What would happen to us if King Eliab found out about this?"

Schala's eyes flashed. "Don't mention that name to me again!" His forehead turned bright red, and his nostrils expanded with his rapid breathing. "Never!" He spat near Adam's feet.

Too frightened to respond, Adam lifted the rest of the berries to his mouth and gulped them down.

Schala's chest heaved, clearly trying to regain his composure. "Listen to me, boy. If you run your life by those concerns, you'll never be happy. *He'll* never let you enjoy anything good! Do you hear me?" He spat again.

Adam nodded dumbly. Berry juice seeped out from between his lips.

Schala pointed the whip toward the fields. "Good. Now get back to work!"

Adam was only too glad to obey, running in search of his buckets. The men had returned from lunch and were resuming their duties among the funja. Adam dumped out the water where he stood, wincing at the knot of hunger in his stomach.

The berries were sweet, but they did not fill him up or sustain him.

The rest of the day passed in a blur, a haze of blistering ropes, sore feet, and aching muscles. Adam went straight to bed after dinner that night. He didn't even bother to undress. The last thing he remembered before falling into a troubled sleep was clutching the coin.

"Freedom," he whispered in the darkness.

But the word sounded hollow.

ADAM III

Chapter 6

"Faithful are the wounds of a friend." Proverbs 27:6

A dam Sonneman the Third! Where in the island have you been?"

Adam almost dropped the bucket he was lifting out of the creek. Above him, a few paces away on the opposite bank stood Christy, her eyebrows raised and her hands planted on her hips. Her brown braids lay back against her checkered dress.

Adam cocked his head and shaded his eyes against the sun. "What are *you* doing here?"

"This is the path to my house. But that isn't fair. I asked you first. What are *you* doing here? And where have you been the last few days?"

Adam stood as tall as he could. "For your information, I happen to be working for Grandfather."

Christy knit her brows together. "That doesn't explain why you've missed school. Are you coming back tomorrow?"

Adam lifted the bucket in answer. "I'm not going back at all. As long as the war is upon us, I think surviving is a little more important. Besides, this is my great opportunity to make something of myself. You'll see."

Christy stomped her foot. "Missing school is against the law, and you know it!"

"So?" Adam tried to sound indifferent.

"So? What do you mean *so*?"

"Just what I said. So what if I break the law? What difference does it make? Nothing bad has happened to me. Besides, I kind of like not being in school."

Christy gaped at him. "It makes all the difference in the island! You can't go around doing whatever you want, not when the king has told us what is right and wrong. Are you going to ignore the king? There are penalties for breaking the law, you know. We all have to give an account of ourselves one day, and King Eliab will either reward or punish us. That affects everything."

Heat rose in Adam's cheeks. "As far as I can see, the king has left us to ourselves. If I'm not in school, he isn't here to do anything about it." He scowled at her.

"That still doesn't make it right," Christy said, clearly astonished. "Just because the king doesn't judge you right now doesn't mean he won't judge you later. What are you going to say when he asks you why you broke his law?"

Adam felt like he was being backed into a corner. "I'll ask him why he's caused all these problems for us. Look how hungry we are. Where are all the gardens and the birds and the music and everything else that used to be here? Where has he been all this time?"

Christy's lip trembled, and tears glistened in her brown eyes.

This conversation is getting worse and worse, Adam thought.

But then, Christy had started it.

He struggled to keep his voice level. "If it weren't for the king, this land wouldn't need so much water, and then I *could* go to school."

"Adam Sonneman!" Christy doubled up her fists, tears brimming over. "If it weren't for the king, we would have nothing at all. No supplies wagon every month, no houses to live in, no land to take care of, no school to go to. If it weren't for the king, you wouldn't even be here!"

Adam looked away. It hurt to see Christy cry. She had never acted so passionate before. He didn't have an answer for her, either. "Humph. You're just saying that because you're on the king's side."

Christy's expression turned to one of perplexity. "Of course I am. We're the king's subjects. This is the king's land. Whose side are *you* on, Adam?"

"Yeah, Adam. Whose side are you on?" a sarcastic voice cut in from behind Christy.

Liptor, with Hank right behind him, stepped forward and smirked at Adam.

Adam glared at Liptor. "I'm on my own side."

"Hah!" Liptor laughed. "Adam against the island. Who do you think you are, Little Governor? Don't expect to have anyone join *your* side, whatever that's supposed to mean."

"Laugh now, but someday you'll be sorry, when I really am the governor of all Mount Eirene." Adam reached into his pocket and held up his coin with a flourish. "Behold the symbol of my authority!"

The light reflected the crown even better than Adam could have hoped.

Hank's mouth dropped open, and his eyes bulged.

Liptor looked scornful, but Adam could see that his coin had made an effect. He was enjoying his moment of glory.

But it was short-lived.

Christy burst into a peal of laughter. "Oh, Adam! You don't know how funny you look. *Your* authority? Don't you know whose crown it is you're holding up? It's the king's crown. It's stamped on every coin in the village. My father gets a coin like that with every supplies wagon."

Silence.

Then without a word of explanation, Christy burst into tears and ran away up the path.

The boys stared blankly at one another.

Adam's cheeks burned. Not knowing what else to do, he faked a shrug and reached for his second water bucket. "If you'll excuse me, I have important work to do for the governor."

He turned and marched toward the fields. When he chanced a quick look behind his shoulder, Liptor and Hank were running back the way they had come.

Adam clenched his teeth. What was Liptor up to now?

ASTERIK

Chapter 7

"Through the wrath of the LORD of hosts is the land
darkened, and the people shall be as the fuel of the fire."
Isaiah 9:19a

The wind rushed around Asterik's body as he rode,
stinging every inch of the sunburned flesh that lay
exposed outside his armor. Sweat flew across his scalp and
through his short, black hair. He leaned low in the saddle,
shielding his face against the mane of his faithful bay.

The horse's hooves thundered along the road in perfect
unison with the hooves of ninety-nine other steeds. They had
all been hand-picked by the king for the critical campaign
they had just won, fighting a horde of Dragonian warriors in
the far East. To Asterik, the perfect rhythm of the hoofbeats
sounded too much like the drumming before an execution.

In this case, it would be.

Asterik's companion Malakan rode beside him on a white
stallion. He stood in the saddle and let the wind blow his

blond curls behind him. Enthusiasm sparkled in his emerald-green eyes. With a great bow over his shoulder and hardened muscles adept at firing such a weapon, he looked every part the valiant warrior of the king.

Charging into conflict is like a picnic for such a man, Asterik thought.

Ahead of Asterik and Malakan rode the rest of their division, perfectly balanced in two columns. Asterik admired the expert soldiers before him. Sunlight glistened off their royal blue and gold armor and the metal of their weapons. They were all Pre-Aardian islanders from beyond the mountains, faithful servants of the king since before Aard's creation. The passing of time had done nothing to age them like it had the Aardians. Life was different in the king's country.

Asterik leaned closer to his horse as the road ascended sharply. They left the forest and mounted a high ridge. The eastern part of the Twelve Cities spread out behind them, and beyond that Ar Sabia.

Asterik shot a glance back at the forest—a collage of various patches of green and brown, like a vast quilt that spread for miles beneath their feet. Pillars of smoke rose from distant villages, a reminder of the war carnage they had seen over the last two days of riding.

His stomach churned. He was no warrior. Gardening was Asterik's calling, as well as medicine because of his skill with plants. If he could, he would turn and ride back into the Twelve Cities to bring them healing. Certainly, the Eirenians had found a special place in his king's heart.

But today his skill in plants was required for other

purposes, and in a foreign city beyond the Eirenians' borders: Morgos. They would reach it momentarily. He fingered the leather bag that swung from his belt. It bounced lazily against the single blue arrow he kept strapped to his right leg. He hoped he wouldn't need either the bag or the arrow.

A succession of trumpet blasts cut through the sound of pounding hooves. Horses reared at the front of the line. Men shouted. Asterik pulled hard on the reins of his bay, halting his charge just in time to avoid crashing into the steed ahead of him.

The ridge had widened near the front of the line. The road ran between large rocks on the one side and the start of a forest on the other. Arrows whizzed from both directions. Riders with black-striped shields charged into the line.

Dragonians.

"Ambush!" Malakan's shout sounded almost glad. He lifted his sword high and called encouragement to the soldiers at the front. "Fight for the king! Fight for the king!"

The troop rallied, driving back the first assault. They circled the horses at the front with shields raised. A band with lowered lances charged into the trees.

Asterik pulled out his dagger, but he had trouble holding it and managing the reins at the same time. *I'd rather be holding my pruning shears.*

Frustrated, he shoved the dagger back into his belt, steadied his mount, and grabbed a sack of medicinal herbs tied in front of his saddle. A survey of the battle revealed none wounded so far, except the enemy. A red horse with a lance in its neck lay dead on top of its Dragonian rider.

Another Dragonian sprawled on the rocks. Several arrows stuck out of his armor.

Asterik grimaced at the sight. Dragonians too were Pre-Aardian islanders, but they no longer served King Eliab. Instead, they had betrayed him. As a result, they had been banished from the king's country. They now made it their primary business to destroy Aard and to fight against the king's faithful servants.

Two rounds of high-pitched notes blasted from the trumpeter. Malakan and his horse leaped forward with a shout. He waved his bow at Asterik. "That's our signal. Follow me!"

The back of the two columns parted to make way for Malakan and Asterik. They pounded toward the front of the warriors. The battle moved into the trees as the king's soldiers pursued their enemies.

Malakan and Asterik reined their horses beside their commander, Michael. He waited for them at the place of initial combat. His golden hair reflected the light from his armor, and he extended his heavy sword in greeting.

Behind Michael, three other soldiers straddled their mounts. The first was the trumpeter on a dappled stallion. Beside him on a sleek, gray steed rode Bandier, the Master of Pronouncement. Sweat shimmered like diamonds on the dark skin of his forehead. He was the strongest man in the troop but carried no weapon. Instead, he gripped a heavy flagpole twice his height, which held a bright-red banner tied close to the wood with a rope.

A short man with a bulky beard rode behind Bandier as his guard. He more than made up for Bandier's lack of weaponry. Blades poked out in every direction from his armor and from his saddle. On his back, he carried a double-bladed battle axe.

Michael nodded to Malakan and Asterik. "I expected opposition from the enemy. However, with the presence of the Ruuwh we can overcome them. You two ride ahead and enter the city as planned. Bandier will follow. If the time comes for you to raise the signal, the rest of us will be in position."

"For the king." Malakan saluted and charged forward.

Asterik hurried to catch up. The sound of hoofbeats from Bandier's and his guard's horses following mixed with the distant noise of clashing steel. The scent of pine trees reminded Asterik of the peaceful days when he had planted these very trees with King Eliab before the war.

The road rose higher into the mountains and then peaked before dropping almost straight before them into a green valley. The four riders halted their horses along the edge of the cliff. Beneath them spread the great city of Morgos. Stone towers rose into the sky. The buzz of city life echoed through the valley.

"Here we part ways." Bandier turned his steed to the side and began working his way north around the rim of the cliff with his guard. He would wait here for the rest of the soldiers to join him.

Asterik fingered the string of his leather bag. Now came the hard part. He eased closer to Malakan. "Do you think we might be able to avoid raising the signal?"

"Are you expecting to find anything good left in a city that has sided with traitors?"

Asterik's heart sank. He longed to spare the Aardians. Yet he knew as well as any the depths of corruption that had permeated them since the rebellion. "Don't forget the king loves them," he whispered. "These are not Dragonians."

Malakan grunted. "We won't do anything until we have enough evidence." He shrugged. "I doubt that will take very long." He kicked his heels into his steed and edged his way down the cliff.

Asterik sighed and trotted his horse behind his companion. They picked their way along the winding road into the valley. As soon as they reached level ground they galloped toward the gate.

The gate of Morgos loomed high as they approached. At its peak a disfigured crown remained barely visible beneath a crude image of a dragon's head nailed together on top of it.

Asterik's blood pressure rose as they rode under the gateway and into the city.

Malakan shot a glance back at Asterik. "Evidence number one."

Stone dragons stood on each side of the entrance. Malakan pushed his horse forward through the crowd standing in their way. Angry shouts filled the air as the citizens scattered. With a swift kick, Malakan sent the statue on the left crashing to the ground, where it split into pieces.

"Make way!" he called. "Make way for the servants of the king! Today your city is held accountable."

The two warriors wound their way through the filthy streets toward the center of the city, while Malakan proclaimed the coming judgment. Serpentine icons in red dye had been etched above the doorways. Women spit at their passing horses. Richly dressed merchants shook their fists.

They passed a narrow alley, where a line of mud-smeared boys stood tied together by a rope around their necks. Asterik flushed and turned toward them. The boys began to shout and grab for broken stones or handfuls of mud to throw at him.

Asterik turned back and hastened after Malakan. A knot of teenage girls in ragged dresses parted before him. Their fingernails and eyelids were dyed red with berry juice. Wedding-berry juice. One of the girls raked her fingernails across his horse's flank.

Asterik gritted his teeth.

"We've seen enough. Give me the arrow." Malakan leaned back in the saddle. His face burned red.

"Not yet," Asterik said. "You never know. There's a chance a loyal remnant could be hiding here."

Malakan snapped the reins and leaped forward, crashing through a drink stand that jutted into his path. "Make way! Make way! The judgment of your city has come!"

They reached the plaza and headed straight for the wooden platform in the middle. Black banners with hideous faces encircled it. On the north side stood a metal gong with a mallet dangling on a chain. Beside it on the stone pavement a firepit gaped its wide mouth and heaved out a steady stream of smoke.

Malakan leaped from the saddle and onto the platform. Drawing his sword, he began slashing the black banners to ribbons. Asterik remained in the saddle and held the reins of Malakan's white stallion.

The citizens of Morgos poured into the plaza from between the wooden and stone edifices surrounding them.

Malakan waited for the mob to gather and then paced with his sword still raised. "Hearken to me, all you rebels! You have lived in wickedness and rejected your king, who made you. The blood of the oppressed cries out from your streets. You have cheated, and stolen, and drowned your consciences with strong drink. The dye of evil stains your hands."

He glared fiercely around him. "But now, thus says the king, 'He who formed the ear, does he not hear? He who formed the eye, does he not see?' Your works are ever before his face, and the stench of your crimes has come into his nostrils. This day he will bring your violence upon your own heads, and this city shall be removed from his presence."

Shouts filled the air. People threw dust. A tall man with a bronze ring in his cheek climbed halfway up the stairs. The noise subdued. Asterik guessed by the man's demeanor that he led the city.

"What right do you have to disrupt our peace?" the tall man demanded.

Malakan beat his fist against the golden crown on his chest. "I am a servant of the king. This day we have come to examine your city."

Asterik untied the leather bag from his belt and held it ready. He was content to let his companion wax eloquent. In the meantime, he'd better prepare for what would follow. The two of them were surrounded on all sides. He searched the cliff for any sign of Bandier or the rest of their troop.

A boy in rags climbed the stairs behind the lead man and threw a rock at Malakan. "Curse you and your old king!" He shot out his tongue and began prancing back and forth.

The lead man signaled with his hand. "Ring the gong. Kamosh will tell us what to do with you."

The crowd took up the name and began to chant it. "Kamosh. Kamosh. Kamosh."

Malakan waved at Asterik. "Ready the arrow."

One of the lead man's slaves rang the gong, filling the plaza with a dull, metallic ringing. Asterik untied the blue arrow from his leg and sniffed the metal point. The scent from the chemicals he'd soaked it in still remained strong.

The dirty boy on the steps made faces at Malakan. "You're in trouble now. Just wait till Kamosh gets here."

A giant of a man galloped into the plaza just then. His red horse was streaked with black war paint. From his saddle hung a whip, and in his hand he wielded a mace. A small vest flapped wide, revealing a hideous red dragon tattooed on his muscular bare chest. His shaved head sported a thick, white mohawk.

Kamosh was a Dragonian.

As Kamosh steered his charger toward the platform, the crowd fell on their faces before him and extended their hands on the pavement. He dismounted and climbed the steps. The people rose.

"Why have you summoned me?" He avoided eye contact with Malakan and glared at the man with the bronze ring in his cheek.

Malakan took a bold step toward him. "We are servants of King Eliab. Your power over these people is at an end."

Kamosh spat at Malakan's feet but still refused to make eye contact. He pointed his mace at the king's servants and spoke to the lead man. "These scum must die. How dare you pollute my presence with them! Nail their wrists together and hang them in the bleeder." He grinned at the mass of ropes dangling from a spike on the edge of the plaza.

Asterik shivered and looked to the cliff. He couldn't see anything. Malakan pulled his bow from his back and held it ready, watching for the first sign of anyone approaching.

"And for disturbing me," Kamosh continued, "I demand payment. Give me five children for the fiery branding."

The heat of anger rose into Asterik's face. He searched the crowd for any soul who still remained faithful to the king, but only angry eyes blazed back at him. "Oh, my king," he whispered, "help us now."

The lead man bowed to Kamosh and spoke in a trembling voice. "Yes, my lord. We will give you whatever you require. We can begin with this piece of trash."

He seized the dirty boy on the steps and pinned his arms behind him. The boy's face turned white as a Keeda's, and he began to scream.

The boy's cries tore at Asterik's heart. Passionate hatred of evil flooded his soul. He felt the king's Ruuwh surround him, infusing him with strength. He lunged his horse forward toward the leader and kicked as hard as he could with his boot. The blow connected with the man's shoulder and sent him sprawling on the stairs. The boy jumped to his feet and disappeared into the crowd.

Asterik turned in the saddle and faced the people. "How dare you! Don't you know that the king made you? He loves you. And yet you worship your enemy. Even now in the face of imminent destruction, will you continue to rebel? Now is your last chance to repent. Reject this servant of the Dragon. Turn to your king, and he will show you mercy."

Silence filled the plaza. Wide eyes looked back and forth at each other. The lead man lay on his back, rubbing his shoulder. Malakan lowered his bow.

Then a deep, throaty laugh shattered the silence. Kamosh threw back his head, letting his laughter roll into the sky and fill the plaza. The people began to laugh as well, nervously at first, and then louder and louder. Soon every man, woman, and child was roaring.

The lead man stood to his feet. "Seize them! Take them to the bleeder."

The crowd surged forward, pressing around Asterik's mount. Hands reached for him. His heart pounded, and his palms broke out in slippery sweat. He fought his right boot free from someone's grasp and drove his horse forward. The steed forced his way through, knocking the Aardians back.

He reached the firepit. Extending his blue arrow, he thrust the tip into the smoke. It instantly burst into flame. "Malakan!" Asterik turned his horse and circled the platform, tossing the burning arrow to his companion.

The mob pressed closer. "Kill them! Kill them!"

Malakan caught the arrow and put it to his bowstring.

Now came the critical moment. Asterik balanced the leather bag in his hand, crushing the compound inside. Heat radiated through the fabric. "My king, I trust myself to your Ruuwh."

He sensed no surge of power, yet he knew in that second

that the king was with him. Arching his arm, he threw the bag high in the air, above the heads of the people. All eyes turned to watch its flight.

At the perfect moment, Malakan fired the blue arrow. The metal tip tore through the leather, bursting the bag into a ball of blue flame. Thunder roared through the plaza. Black dust filled the air, settling on the crowd.

The people nearest the platform went blind. They began to scream and fight with one another. The Aardians surrounding Asterik fled. The lead man fell on his face and clutched Kamosh's heel. "My lord, help us."

Kamosh kicked the man in the face with his free boot and leaped into his saddle. He charged into the mayhem, trampling on the people who got in his way.

Asterik looked up. High up on the cliff, gleams of light reflected off the armor of the king's soldiers. Near the center, an immense red banner unfurled and snapped in the wind. Black flames covered its face. Bandier had seen their signal and was proclaiming the king's verdict.

"Hurry!" Asterik broke through the Aardians nearest him and charged for the city streets. He heard Malakan mounting and then pounding behind him. They had little time.

The bay's muscles rippled beneath Asterik. He flew past houses, markets, goats, and people in a blur. All condemned. The horse's hooves pounded out the drumroll of execution.

Guards braced themselves in a group by the gate, extending their spears. Asterik halted his flight, but Malakan raced past him, swinging his sword. The men scattered before he reached them. From the cliff, a volley of arrows filled the sky. Smoke trailed behind them.

"Hiyaa!" Asterik sprang forward with his mount in one last charge. He flew through the gateway just as the rain of fire surged into the city. Another wave of arrows flew over him. Asterik tore up the turf in his flight, following Malakan's charge.

They climbed the twisting road toward the top of the cliff. Several more flaming volleys shot over their heads. When his horse rounded a curve, Asterik looked into the valley below. Far in the distance, a rider on a red horse fled into the mountains. Morgos was a giant ball of flame. Even at this height the heat reached him, stinging his skin. Sweat dripped down his sides beneath his armor.

By the time they reached the top of the cliff, the soldiers were forming into columns once more. Michael saluted Asterik and Malakan. "Well done. You have honored our king." He rode to the front with the trumpeter.

Asterik dismounted and rested while he waited for the troop to pass in front of him. He and Malakan stood side by side looking into the valley. Everything was scorched, including the grass and the trees. One of the tallest stone towers collapsed as they watched.

"May all the king's enemies so perish." Malakan clapped Asterik on the shoulder. "You did splendidly. There's no one I'd rather ride with into such danger. Congratulations."

Asterik smiled weakly, but his heart ached as he stared into the fire. The heat of anger had passed, and sorrow filled him. The echo of Kamosh's laugh rang in his mind.

He answered with quiet words. "I almost feel like this is a victory for the Dragonians."

"Nonsense. Kamosh has played perfectly into the king's

plan to judge these traitors. If they sell themselves to a destroyer and then get destroyed, I call that justice. They've had their chance. At some point it has to be too late."

Asterik sighed. "Yet, the king takes no delight in the death of the wicked."

Malakan frowned. "He delights in his glory. Any of these clumps of dirt who rise up to mock his holiness should be wiped off the island. Even Mount Eirene itself might burn if it continues in its rebellion."

Asterik turned to watch Bandier roll up the red flag and ride after the troop. Malakan mounted and followed. Asterik climbed into his saddle and twisted for one last glance. In the distance, farther north along the cliff, he saw another soldier. A crown of gold gleamed upon the man's brow, and light shone around him.

Asterik's muscles went weak all over his body. From this distance, all he could read was the man's posture. The figure held his head high, looking down on the scene of wrath. It was the picture of perfect justice.

Asterik trembled before the anger of the king, even though he knew it was not directed toward him.

Then he saw the crown bend low. The king's shoulders slumped.

Asterik snapped the reins and hurried to rejoin his troop. In spite of his victory, he felt defeated inside. He had tried so hard to change the people's minds, but they refused even in the face of judgment.

Morgos was gone. But how could Malakan say that Mount Eirene might burn? *The king loves the Eireneians.* Asterik knew he did. He loved all the Aardians. But then again, how could he spare a city of rebels and still preserve his honor?

Asterik shut his eyes and fell into place beside Malakan. He gave his steed its head and rode in silence.

The drumming of horses' hooves pounded on.

ADAM III

Chapter 8

"The carnal mind is enmity against God: for it is not
subject to the law of God, neither indeed can be."
Romans 8:7

Nighttime shadows danced on the ceiling above Adam's head. Cool air floated in through the window, teasing his sweaty hair. If only he could fall asleep!

He rolled over and closed his eyes. Christy appeared in his mind's eye, arguing with him. *"You can't ignore what the king says."*

He began to argue mentally with her afresh, weaving elaborate explanations that sounded good at first but ended in confusion. How long would this go on?

Adam sat up, flipped the pillow to the cold side, and lay back down. As soon as his eyes closed, Christy reappeared. Her blue-checked dress snapped in the wind as she challenged him. *"Whose side are you on, Adam? Whose side are you on?"*

Christy's image faded, only to be replaced by King Eliab himself sitting upon his great throne of judgment. He gazed at Adam with eyes that knew his deepest secrets. *"Why did you break my law, Adam?"*

Adam climbed out of bed and walked to the window. From his room on the second floor he could look out over the town to the distant forest. Poking up out of the middle rose the Mount of Humility. He had noticed it there in the past, but for the first time he recognized it and shuddered.

Beyond the forest he could make out the outline of the great mountains. He imagined he could see the Great Gate at the base—the closest he could ever get to the king. He combed his hand through his hair and drew it back, soaked with sweat.

"I will never break the law again," Adam whispered. "I promise I won't." He stared in the direction of the Great Gate. *Maybe I should say more. But what?*

Teacher often spoke to the king as if he was present. The Ruuwh was real to him. Perhaps even now the king was watching Adam and listening.

He returned to his bed, but another thought occurred to him. "I still have to go to work." What would Grandfather think of him if he didn't? "I promise I'll be the best water carrier ever." He let out a deep breath and lay down.

When Adam closed his eyes this time, he fell asleep.

Any rest and relief were short-lived, however. Adam overslept and found himself running to the fields late, and without breakfast. He rubbed his protesting stomach, clenching his jaw against the painful, empty feeling.

He ached all over from two days of intense labor.

Muscles he hadn't known existed throbbed.

In keeping with his promise from the night before, Adam ignored the aches and hurried to fetch the water. His resolve faded, though, as the morning stretched on. The heat beat down on his unprotected head and shoulders. His progress in the fields diminished, while his times at the creek grew longer. It was hard to keep his mind on his work.

When Schala checked on his progress, he gave Adam a nasty scolding. Discouraged and angry, Adam didn't work harder. Instead, he became more distracted than ever.

Interacting with Schala reminded Adam of wedding berries. He swallowed. A sudden craving for another taste of the forbidden fruit filled his mind. His imagination rolled the berries back and forth, feeling their texture and tasting their sweetness. His stomach groaned with hunger.

"No!" He tightened his grip on the rope handles and walked faster. "I promised to keep the law."

As if mocking his promise, his thoughts raced back to the berries. He mentally savored them all over again.

"I can't," Adam whispered, trying to focus on his work. A sense of loss and strong desire overpowered him. Without intending to, he began to think of ways he could have some berries. His mind stayed in turmoil the rest of the morning.

Adam decided to seek out Schala during lunchtime. It occurred to him that he should show good progress, so with a sudden resolve he began to fly through his work. He ran with the buckets, not only when they were empty but also when they were full. His hands, rubbed raw from the ropes, screamed for relief.

Adam hardened himself and continued to run. He blocked

out everything from his mind but the taste of those wedding berries.

The men began to leave the fields for lunch. The smell of dry funja passed over Adam like a wave of loneliness. He suddenly desired to follow the men—to run away from Schala, from the berries, and from breaking the law. But he clenched his teeth and stayed where he stood.

He faced the trees on the edge of the field. His feet began to move in that direction, slowly at first but then faster and faster. His eyes flicked from side to side, searching for anyone that might see him, as if someone might appear out of the ground. His heart raced. He looked back while his feet continued to run.

Adam's foot snagged the leg of an old man snoozing behind a bush. He threw out his hands to catch his fall. Dirt and rocks tore his blisters open. "Ow!" He cried out in pain and leaped to his feet, rubbing his hands against his breeches.

He recognized Doke, the old man he'd tripped over. His fluffy white hair ran down the sides of his face into bristling sideburns. Of all Grandfather's servants, Doke was one of Adam's favorites. He sometimes told Adam stories about his father. Right now, however, Adam felt ashamed to talk to anyone.

Doke, on the other hand, appeared glad for the interruption. He sat up and smiled at Adam. "That was quite a trip you had there. Are you all right?"

Adam winced and pressed his burning hands against his legs. "I'm fine. Really. I hardly feel a thing."

"You're not fine," Doke said, tugging at his sideburns. "I

can see that well enough. You're shaking like a leaf, and your face is white as chalk. Now tell me, where were you going in such a hurry?"

Adam paused. This was his chance to get some help. But maybe Doke would never think of Adam in the same way. Besides, the taste of wedding berries seemed so close.

"I'm ... I'm heading to lunch."

Doke looked toward Mount Eirene. "Lunch, huh? I might be old, but I'm pretty sure I remember which way the city is, and it isn't the way you're running. Why don't you sit here with me and share my lunch? I've got enough."

Adam shook his head. "I have to go." He took off running, slowing his pace only when he came closer to the trees.

Adam tried to stifle his heavy breathing. He stood outside the copse of trees, doubled over. He clasped and unclasped his sweaty, burning hands, wondering if he dared to enter, after all. He might regret it for a long time.

But the berries drew him closer.

His heart rate stayed elevated. Regret filled him for lying to Doke about lunch. *I promise I'll never lie again.*

A noise from inside the trees startled Adam. *Run away! Leave this place!*

The thought of the berries made him stay. Clenching his fists, he forced himself not to think about anything else, pushed his way through the trees, and stopped short.

Schala was nowhere inside the clearing. Instead, Liptor sat on Schala's rock. Hank sat on another rock. They were eating lunch but stopped and stared at Adam.

Adam stared back, struck speechless in bewilderment.

Heat crept up his neck.

A minute went by before anyone spoke.

"Have you lost something?" Liptor smirked, breaking the awkward silence.

The question snapped Adam back to his senses. "I ... well ... y-yes," he stammered. "I thought I left my lunch here. But maybe not." He glanced around as if searching for it. "I don't see it."

So much for never lying again.

Liptor took a large bite of bread and spoke with his mouth full. "I'm sorry to hear that. I'd share my lunch with you, but I'm going to need all the strength I can get. I have important business to attend to for the governor. Isn't that right, Hank?" He shot a grin at his companion.

Hank stared at the ground and scratched at the ink spots on his breeches.

"How dare you mock me," Adam shouted. "What right do you have to be here?"

"Why, Adam, I never thought you would question your own cousin." Liptor slid his hand into his pocket. He chuckled as if enjoying a tremendous joke. "But allow me to show you my 'right.' Behold, the symbol of my authority!" He held up a large copper coin.

Adam's eyes widened. "You have a coin too? But how–"

"It was easy enough. We went to Grandfather and asked if he needed any more work done. Don't forget he's *my* grandfather too, Adam." He scowled at Hank. "Hank has a coin too, if he'd stop moping long enough to show you."

Hank's cheeks turned as red as his hair. "I need to leave. My parents are going to be so disappointed."

"You didn't tell them you're working for the governor?" Adam asked.

Hank rested his head in his hands and said nothing. The answer was obvious.

Liptor bit off another mouthful of bread. "I don't care what *my* folks think. It's not like they keep the law, except in public. I suppose everyone's parents are like that to some extent, even Hank's."

"That's not so!" Hank jumped to his feet, clenching his fists. "My parents love the king. They do what he says at home, as well as in public. My dad studies the King's Stones and loves to talk about them with our family."

"In that case, I suppose they *would* be disappointed." Liptor narrowed his eyes. "Especially if they knew you'd been eating *you know what*."

Hank buried his face in his hands. His shoulders shook. "Schala made me do it. I couldn't help it. I never wanted to."

Liptor brushed the crumbs from his hands. "You're afraid of Schala? That old fellow doesn't scare me. I'll tell you one thing. Nobody's going to make *me* do anything I don't want to do. Here's another thing. You won't catch me eating wedding berries. It's a shame, Hank, a real shame."

"It's not just a shame." Hank rubbed his sleeve across his eyes. "It's wrong. This whole thing is wrong. We never should have come here. We need to leave right now and go back to school."

Adam's heart filled with his own shame and guilt. By the time Hank was finished, Adam was ready to agree and leave the fields at once.

He opened his mouth in assent. "I think Hank's—"

Crack!

Hank shrieked and fell to the ground, clutching his leg. A large, bleeding welt appeared through a tear in his breeches.

Schala strode into the small clearing, brandishing his whip. "You boys have been talking long enough. Get back to work." He seized Hank by his thrick, dragged him to his feet, and gave him a shove.

"Listen well." He gestured with the whip. "If any of you ever, *ever* double-cross me and go back to school, I'll hunt you down, no matter how far you run on this island. So help me, when I catch you, I'll make you wish you'd never lived."

Adam shook all over, but he raised his chin. "You can't do that. My grandfather is the governor. I'll tell him what you said!" He tried to look defiant, but he felt like a mouse confronting a tiger.

Schala turned to Adam and cuffed him. "That's for your sass." A taunting smile spread over his face. "You'll tell him, eh?" He snorted. "I have no fear of your precious governor. My master has far more power. Besides, what would your grandfather say if I told him you've been eating wedding berries?"

Adam stepped back, rubbing his throbbing cheek. He said nothing.

Neither did the other boys.

Schala cracked his whip. "Now, get back to work!"

Liptor stood and walked out as if Schala's words hadn't scared him. Adam knew better. His cousin's hands were shaking. Hank limped out behind Liptor.

Adam glared at Schala before leaving. "You tricked me.

That's why you offered me wedding berries."

"I never made you reach out your hand the second time. You made your own choice. Now, get back to work!" He raised his whip. "*Or else.*"

Adam stumbled out of the clearing, pushing his way through the trees. His heart sank. The field workers were returning to work. No breakfast this morning for Adam. And now, no lunch.

He watched Doke stand and brush the crumbs off his thrick. *If only I had stayed and told the old man the truth.*

Adam wished for more than that. He wished he'd gone to Teacher two days ago. He wished he'd never opened his hand for more berries. He wished he could somehow please the king, but ... he wanted to keep his coin as well.

"It's too late now, anyway," he mourned. Even when he wanted to obey the law, he couldn't. Maybe if he worked extra hard the king would be pleased, especially if he didn't break the law ever again.

But he didn't think so.

ADAM III

Chapter 9

"The name of the LORD is a strong tower: the righteous runneth into it and is safe." Proverbs 18:10

Cool water splashed against Adam's burning fingers as he headed back to the fields with his newly filled buckets. Shadows of fear from his lunchtime encounter with Schala surrounded him.

"Adam, wait!"

He turned back to the creek. Christy stood elevated on the opposite bank, like yesterday, holding her hands behind her back.

Adam hesitated. *What if Schala catches me talking?* He scanned the fields. There was no sign of him ... for now. "What is it?"

"Come here."

Reluctantly, Adam set down his buckets, glanced around a second time, and approached the stream.

Christy took a deep breath. "I wanted to say I'm sorry for

laughing at you yesterday about the coin. It wasn't kind of me, and I felt badly about it all night. Will you please forgive me?"

Adam's shoulders relaxed. "Of course. You're still my friend. To be honest, I'm sorry too."

"For all the bad things you said about King Eliab?"

He shrugged. "Well ... I'm sorry for making you cry. I didn't mean to make you feel bad. Will you forgive me?"

"I hope you're sorry to him as well. But yes, I forgive you. You're still my friend."

Adam smiled. "Thanks."

Christy pulled her hands from behind her back. "I brought you something." She held out a large green leaf, folded on the corners around something wrapped inside. "It's daidoush."

"What's daidoush?" Adam peered at the leaf. His stomach turned over in hunger.

"Banana fritters. I made them last night and brought them to school today. The little boys tried to eat them all, but I saved a few for you."

"Where in the island did you get bananas?" Adam stepped out to a rock halfway across the creek. He checked again for any sign of Schala.

"It's like my mother says, *'The king always provides.'*" She stretched out the hand that held the daidoush. "Try a piece. Are you hungry?"

"Yes, actually." Adam climbed the opposite bank. Now he could see the path coming from the King's Road and passing by the stream on its way to Christy's house. "*Very* hungry, in fact. Thank you."

Just as he reached for the leaf, Christy shrieked and stepped back. She jerked her hands in the air. The leaf and daidoush plunged to the ground, scattering crumbs everywhere. "Your hands! Oh, Adam! What happened to your hands?"

Adam dropped to his knees and scooped up the pieces of daidoush. He glanced at his palms. They did look terrible, all red and blistered. "I guess it goes with the job," he muttered, keeping his eyes on the ground.

"I'm sorry for dropping the daidoush. But your hands are so red. They must sting terribly. Have they been that way for long? Have you put anything on them?"

"I hope they'll eventually heal. I don't have anything to put on them." Adam shoved a whole piece of daidoush into his mouth and chewed it hungrily. The sweetness permeated his throat.

"They get like that from carrying the buckets, don't they? You should go to Teacher. You know he's a powerful healer. He could heal your hands."

The words *powerful healer* sounded familiar. Adam had heard the phrase in the King's Stones ... or somewhere.

"Are you listening to me?" Christy raised her voice.

Adam jumped up, brushing the crumbs away from his mouth. "I'm thinking, that's all. The daidoush is amazing and"—he hurried on before she could reply—"you'll be proud of me when I tell you what I did last night."

"What did you do?" A hint of excitement filled Christy's voice.

"I was having a hard time sleeping. I guess I kept thinking about all the things you said yesterday. And—" He paused, trying to find the right words.

"And?" Christy's wide eyes fixed on Adam's face. The back of his neck burned under the sun's unbearable heat.

"I promised I would never break the law again." Adam didn't feel as good as he'd hoped he would for telling her. After all, he'd already broken that promise several times this morning. He looked at the ground, afraid to say anything else.

Christy made up for his silence by bursting into a string of excited chatter. "Oh, Adam, I am so glad to hear that! What a relief! I was terribly worried about you. It's a horrible feeling to have your friend be against the king. This morning in school we were all feeling bad about it, and it's so sad. Liptor and Hank have left too."

This was no news to Adam.

Christy kept up her chatter. "We decided to write a letter to the king and ask him to do something so you could come back to school. Everyone agreed, and then Teacher himself signed the letter with his own hand and sent it."

Adam gaped at her. They did *what?*

"And now, look!" Christy twirled around, extending her arms. "You've already changed your mind, and things will be so much better."

Adam's eyes widened with fear. "You sent a letter to the *king?* Now he'll know what I've done, and then what am I supposed to do?"

"Oh, Adam." Christy shook her head. "He already knows everything that takes place. Don't you remember? Teacher told us that many times, and we read it in the King's Stones:

For the eyes of the king run to and fro throughout the whole land to show himself strong on behalf of those whose heart is perfect toward him.

"So, he already knows. We just wanted to ask him to help you."

Adam furrowed his brows. It bothered him to think the king knew everything he did.

"It will be so *nice* to have you back in class tomorrow."

"I ... I wasn't planning to go back to school."

Christy's face changed from happiness to confusion. "But you said you were going to keep the law from now on."

Adam scowled. "I am, but that doesn't mean I'm going back to school. It's not as easy as you think. I've been working hard to carry the water, and I'll get even better later on. I don't see how the king can find fault with me if I work hard enough."

Christy's mouth dropped open. "You mean that instead of doing what the king has plainly said, you're going to do something else? And you expect him to judge you by your own made-up rules?"

"If you were in my position, you'd understand. I can't quit now. It's impossible." Schala's threats hung over Adam like a dark cloud. "I don't know what else to do."

Christy frowned and trailed her shoe through the dirt. "You need to go to Teacher. He can help you."

It was not the advice Adam wanted to hear. "That's your solution for everything. For every problem you say, 'Run to Teacher. Run to Teacher.'" He thought about Grandfather, about Schala, and about the berries. He fingered the coin in his pocket.

No, he couldn't run to Teacher. "It's not as easy as you think."

Christy cocked her head back and closed her eyes. "Yes," she said in a quiet, thoughtful voice. "You're right. That is pretty much the solution to everything."

"What? Did I say something?"

"Run to Teacher!" said Christy, opening her eyes. "That's it. It's the best solution, just like you said. It's the solution for pretty much everything."

"But why *Teacher*? Listen, I wasn't going to tell you this, but maybe I better." He stepped closer and lowered his voice. "Teacher isn't one of us. Grandfather told me."

To Adam's surprise, Christy smiled wider. Her brown eyes sparked. "You've heard it too? I'm so glad. It's been terrible keeping a secret. I heard about it just this week."

"Heard what?"

"Just what you said." Christy put her hands on her hips. "Teacher healed a man, and the man was telling everyone about it, but Teacher told him specifically not to tell. So, I didn't think I should say anything, but apparently you know already. Doesn't that make sense?"

Not in the least, Adam thought. "You mean that he's not one of us?"

"It's not so much who he *isn't*. It's who he *is*. Don't you know? He's—" She broke off and stared at something past Adam's shoulder.

"Well?"

Christy pointed. "Who in the island are *they*?"

Adam spun around. From where he stood, most of the field was hidden. But crouched in the small space that remained open to their view, three men were bent low in conversation. The man on the left was huge and had a fierce-looking white mohawk. The man in the middle had a black cloak with a hood pulled over his head. The third was Schala.

"Never mind." Adam scrambled down the bank and splashed across the stream. "I've got to go. You better go too." He motioned her to run before grabbing his buckets and charging back to his work.

HANK

Chapter 10

"I sought the LORD, and He heard me, and delivered me from all my fears." Psalm 34:4

Hank traced a crevice in the rough wood of the kitchen table with his fingernail. Father stood in front of the table, facing the window. The setting sun glowed in his fiery red hair. He was a fifty-year-old version of his son.

What will Father say?

Hank had just poured out his heart about everything that had happened that day. Acknowledging his crimes was the hardest thing he'd ever done.

Father sat at the table. "Son, I'm glad you had the courage to tell me. What you did was wrong, and it will bring its own consequences. But we can make it right with each other, and ultimately with our king. You'll need to write him a letter. We'll also have to send one of our lambs."

"One of the lambs?" Hank's heart sank into his stomach. "But we have only a few lambs, and you were planning—"

"I know. But following the king is more important. You know he requires a sacrifice. It is the way he has provided for our forgiveness so we need not die when we break the law."

Hank nodded miserably. "You're right. I want to do whatever the king says. It's my own fault for not obeying." He sighed. "But why does the king require a sacrifice? Isn't there enough death already?"

Father turned his face back toward the window. "There are some things I still don't understand. But we know what the king has said: 'Without the shedding of blood there is no remission,' no cleansing from our guilt. In spite of how we might feel, the most appropriate punishment for defying the king is death."

He looked at Hank. "The king has designed our lives to be fulfilled in our relationship with him. He loves us more than we can understand, and his purpose for creating us is to enjoy that love. He intends for us to rule with him over the rest of the island someday. So, what do you think the king most wants from us?"

Hank smiled a little. "To love him back."

"You're right." Father returned his son's smile. "Think what it means when we break his covenant—when we reject his love. We are going against our very purpose for living. As long as our relationship with the king is broken, for all practical purposes we are already dead."

His face contorted. "Here now, where's the inkwell?"

Hank grinned. Dozens of inkwells lay scattered around the kitchen. He waved to one sitting on the window sill.

Father snatched it, as well as a papla leaf, and drew up

next to Hank at the table. After dipping his quill, he scribbled the word "Life" on the leaf. "What is life?" he asked, poising the quill.

Hank's heart leaped. It excited him to see Father's passion for truth. But he couldn't guess what answer he was looking for this time.

Father scratched out the words "breathing," "moving," "thinking," and "choosing" under the word "Life." He looked at Hank. "Is that all there is?" Without waiting for an answer, he wrote another word, "PURPOSE," and circled it.

"Real life is fulfilling our purpose, which is loving our king and serving him." He set down the quill. "When the king requires death as a punishment, it is only the ultimate fulfillment of a person being dead already—dead toward the king and toward his purpose."

Father closed his eyes and wrinkled his forehead, clearly searching for the right words. Then he opened his eyes and continued. "In a nutshell, Hank, the king has given us life so we can love and serve him. If we betray him, he has authority to withdraw that life. Does that make any sense?"

Hank traced his finger through old ink stains on the table. "It makes my brain hurt. But it does sort of make sense. How does the death of a lamb make any difference, though?"

"I've studied the stones while asking that very question, Son. However, it still remains a mystery to me. The lambs can't fully substitute for people. There must be a greater substitute that can atone for our crimes. Yet, I do not see how."

He put his arm around Hank. "For now, I am glad he has made a provision for us so that I lose my lamb and not my son." He squeezed him. "Come along. Let's see to the animals."

They went outside to bed down their livestock. Hank stopped when he saw the lambs. "I still feel sorry."

Father looked at his palms in the moonlight. "I've had to send my own sacrifices. But I'm glad I sent them. There's a traitor to the king in every one of us, and we'll have to fight against it all our lives. But I can tell you one thing. When King Eliab restores our city forever, the fight will have been well worth it. I've read that in the King's Stones. It's a promise. I'll be glad to be on his side when he comes."

Hank nodded. "What do I do tomorrow, though? What about Schala? He'll try to kill me."

"I'll do whatever I can to help you, but there's only one man who can set you free. Go to Teacher. I think you know why."

Hank thought he did. He was glad that he had talked with Father. That night he went to sleep in peace.

By late afternoon the next day, however, all peaceful feelings had dissolved in the blistering sun.

Hank grunted, giving one last tug before a rock tore free from the dirt. He dropped it on the pile beside him and wiped his sweaty face on his sleeve. Standing upright, he squinted to see the road.

It's almost time.

Liptor threw a rock onto his own pile. "How many times are you going to look at the road? My pile is almost twice the size of yours. If you don't get busy, we'll never get this new plot cleared, and the whole city will suffer from hunger.

You'll never be promoted, either. You'll end up digging out rocks for Schala the rest of your life." He forced his spade into the hard dirt and started working at another rock.

"Not if I can help it," whispered Hank. He saw Camdin running up the road toward the city. A number of other children followed the boy.

It was time. "School's out!" he called to Liptor.

"What does that matter? We're working for the governor now. Have you forgotten how that whip felt yesterday?" Liptor threw down another rock and began tightening the bandages around his hands. "I'm just saying it for your own good."

Hank hadn't forgotten Schala's threat. The welt from the whip still burned. But he had made up his mind what to do about it. He set down his spade and started walking toward the creek. "I need water."

Liptor gave his bandage one last yank. "I know why."

Hank stopped dead in his tracks and turned around. "What do you mean?" He fought to keep his voice steady. Surely Liptor hadn't guessed, had he?

"You're scared," Liptor said. "That's why you're so thirsty. Fear dries out your mouth. You've been licking your lips all day."

It was true. Hank's mouth felt like cotton. He licked his lips again before he could catch himself.

Liptor shook his head and pushed in his spade. "Did your parents see that welt on your leg?"

Hank didn't answer. He had already started for the creek, and he wasn't going to turn back now. Besides, Liptor wouldn't understand.

Fear tied a knot in Hank's stomach as he crossed the fields. He knew what he had to do. He had rehearsed his plan a hundred times that morning. He would cross the creek at the edge of the field and run down the path to the King's Road. From there it was a straight run to school. If he didn't arrive too late, Teacher would still be there, preparing for tomorrow.

Hank licked his lips and glanced around. Schala was nowhere in sight. Every fiber in Hank's body urged him to run. To fly across the remaining part of the field. To never stop running until he was safely in the schoolhouse.

He didn't dare run. A thought plagued him that he was being watched, and although the effort made him break into a sweat, he forced his legs to walk at a normal pace.

Hank was close to the creek now. His heart beat faster. He wished he'd gone to Teacher this morning instead of waiting until now. At the time, he'd thought it would be better to wait, but now he realized it was the most foolish thing he could have done.

And yet, there was still one thing he must do. *Adam, please be there!*

Hank rounded the bend by the water. No Adam. He stooped and took a drink from the stream, fighting to keep his knees from trembling. The water felt good against his face. He looked up again and breathed a short sigh of relief. Adam was coming with his buckets.

Hank waved him over. *Hurry!* he ordered his friend silently.

Adam glanced around and then ran to the creek, letting the buckets roll to one side. He crouched beside Hank.

"What is it?"

Hank licked his lips. "I'm leaving. I talked to my father last night." He reached into his pocket and pulled out his coin. "It's not right for me to keep this, so I came back today to give it to you."

He slipped the coin into Adam's hand. "Will you return it to your grandfather for me?"

Adam turned the coin over in his hand. "What if you're caught? I think Schala was deadly serious about what he said yesterday. He'll try to kill you and maybe succeed. Here—" He tried to put the coin back into Hank's hand.

"No. Please." Hank pushed Adam's fingers closed. "I have to leave. It's the right thing to do. If something happens to me, it's my own fault. I never should have broken the law in the first place. But I'm going to Teacher, Adam. I think he will help me."

I should invite Adam to come too. No. What if the attempt failed? What if Adam were killed?

"I hope you make it safely." Adam squeezed Hank's hand. "Be careful."

Hank squeezed back. "I better hurry." He darted across the creek and climbed the bank. Then he hesitated. How could he let his friend remain in bondage? *I have to say something.*

He turned back to urge Adam to come with him, but the words stuck in his throat. A man in the fields was staring at him, eyes squinted in anger. His hand gripped a whip.

Schala!

Terror seized Hank. He spun around, kicking up little rocks with his feet and stumbling to keep his footing. He ran with all his might, forcing his legs to push hard. No matter how hard he worked them, though, he felt as if he were crawling. His breath came in gasps. He put on an extra burst of speed. The King's Road was not far away now.

Hank knew he could not maintain this pace for long. He chanced a quick glance behind him. Schala was scrambling up the creek bank. His face was red, and his eyes burned with anger. Hank's stomach knotted. Schala was gaining on him! He tried once again to increase his speed.

He reached the King's Road and turned right, preparing mentally for the long stretch of road to the school. Off to the side he saw Schala leaving the path and racing at an angle to cut him off. He was gaining by leaps and bounds. It looked like he might reach the road at the same time Hank passed the spot. If not, Schala would be right on Hank's heels.

Panting, Hank changed directions and darted across the road. He had to put as much distance as possible between him and his pursuer!

This side of the road was covered with trees, sparsely at first, and then gradually becoming part of the forest. Hank plunged in without slowing his pace, glad to be moving out of sight. Roots and branches clutched at him from all sides. A string of thorns on a thick vine caught him across the chest and pushed him back.

Oof! Hank sat down, hard.

He scrambled to his feet in panic and shoved all his weight against the vine, hoping it would yield and let him through. The thorns held, pressing deeper into his skin. He spun and pulled away, stumbling backward.

Hank ran this way and that, but the foliage turned dense.

His eyes darted back and forth, searching for an opening. He found a gap in the branches and crawled through.

The ground dipped suddenly, and Hank crashed down a slope, rolling until he reached the bottom. Looking up, he recognized the broad ditch he lay in, the remnants of an old, dry riverbed. He waited, listening and refilling his lungs with air.

All was silent. He glanced up and down the riverbed. He had played here many times with the other school boys. If he ran up the riverbed far enough, he knew of a place that came out close to the school.

Heartened by the thought, Hank stood up. Everything was quiet. Maybe he could avoid Schala completely. Just in case, he picked up two fist-sized stones, one in each hand. *If I'm attacked—*

Well, he would rather not think about that.

He took a cautious step. Hard dirt cracked beneath his foot. He tried to find soft places to walk, but every footfall sounded like an alarm. Giving up the attempt at silence, he broke into a jog, keeping a careful eye on the bank above him.

A noise caught his attention, and he stopped. Only silence. He started walking again, and then on an impulse began to run. Loud footsteps resounded on the ground from above, then—

Hank gasped.

Schala thudded into the ditch no more than twenty paces behind Hank. He yanked a large knife from his vest.

Hank panicked and hurled a stone. The rock sailed wide of Schala and landed in a bush. The man paused only a second before charging.

Hank fled with renewed energy. He could hear Schala's footsteps gaining on him, intermingled with heavy breathing and loud curses.

Hank's thoughts whirled in terror. *What can I do? My family are scholars, not warriors!*

He jumped over a fallen log, ran a few more paces, and then—summoning all his courage—stopped and turned around. He planted his feet and took careful aim. His remaining stone flew from his hand.

Hank hoped to knock his assailant in the head. Schala, however, was just leaping over a log, and the rock hit him full in the chest. He stumbled backward, missed his footing, and fell on his side in front of the log.

Hank used his advantage to gain more distance. He bolted for the dip in the bank that would lead him close to the school. He scrambled up the crumbling bank, pulling himself along by a large, protruding root. His foot slipped, but his fear gave him the strength to push on. At last, he hiked himself up on the woody bank, jumped to his feet, and started running toward the road.

Where's the school?

Hank's stomach turned over. He'd either mistaken the place or forgotten the actual distance. What hope was there now? He reached the King's Road and followed it, but he could hear Schala pounding through the trees behind him.

Almost there. Would Teacher still be at school? He stretched to run faster than he had ever run before. His lungs burned. His breath came in gasps.

A flash of pain burst through Hank's leg. He was on the

ground and rolling across the path before he knew what had happened. He scrambled to rise, but his whip injury from yesterday burned like fire. His fingers returned from his pant leg damp with blood. The wound must have opened afresh from his exertions.

Hank forced himself to his feet. A wave of dizziness passed over him as he staggered forward. He clenched his teeth and tried to run, but after a few shaky steps he collapsed, heaving for breath. He forced himself up on his hands and his left knee. Heavy footsteps pounded toward him.

Hank moved his right knee frantically, trying to stand.

A large boot landed on his back and pushed him flat to the ground, knocking the wind out of him. The next moment, Schala was lifting him by the thrick and dragging him off the road.

Hank clawed at the ground, fighting to stay where he lay. He swung his arms and dug his fingernails into the dirt. He clutched at everything he could reach but succeeded only in tearing up his hands.

Schala dropped Hank into a small dip in the ground, hidden behind a gnarl of bushes.

Hank tried to sit up, but the taskmaster was on him in an instant. Schala slammed his knee into Hank's chest, pinning him to the ground. His iron-like fingers jerked Hank's head back by his hair. His hot breath gagged Hank.

"Where in the name of all evil do you think you're going?" Schala shook him.

Hank gasped for breath.

"Answer me!" Schala stabbed his knife into the dirt

beside Hank's cheek.

Hank squeezed his eyes shut. A tear slid down his face. He shook his head from side to side but said nothing.

"Do you not fear me?" Schala asked with savage fury. "Then fear this!"

Hank opened his eyes and stared in horror. Leaning back, Schala rolled up his long sleeve. Tattooed in fiery red on his attacker's bicep was a monstrous, hideous dragon.

Hank took a deep breath. No words came. Only fear. Deep, gut-wrenching fear for his life.

Schala released the pressure from his knee, and Hank gulped in a deep draught of air for his burning lungs. With all his strength, he cried out, "Teacher! Teacher! Help! Oh, Teacher, please help me!"

Schala, clearly taken by surprise, grasped Hank by the shoulders and began shaking him. He yanked his long knife from the dirt and raised it high in the air.

Hank squeezed his eyes shut and prepared for the fatal blow.

"Stop!"

Footsteps approached and stood behind him. After a long pause, Hank dared to open his eyes.

Schala was shaking like a leaf, and his face had turned chalky white. He clenched his hands and screeched in obvious defiance, "Leave us alone! What do we have to do with you? Have you come to destroy us?" His eyes narrowed into fiery slits. "I know who you are, son of the king!" He looked as if he were trying to spit.

"Be silent." The answering voice was quiet, but also as strong as the mountains. "And leave this one alone forever."

Schala gave a final thrust at Hank with his knee and ran away into the woods.

Hank lay silent with his eyes closed, too overcome with exhaustion to move. He was aware of a faint breeze tugging at his hair and the dull throbbing in his leg. A strong hand gently touched his shoulder.

Hank opened his eyes and reached out shaking fingers to clasp the hand in response. "Teacher, thank you." He fought to hold back the lump that suddenly appeared in his throat. "I knew you would help me."

Teacher's hand gave Hank's hand a firm squeeze in return and let go. Then a pair of strong arms lifted him.

Hank looked into Teacher's eyes. A set of familiar, deep-brown eyes gazed back. A smile tugged at the corners of Teacher's mouth. A neatly trimmed beard covered his face, but not enough to hide the sunken cheeks.

"You don't have to carry me."

"I'm stronger than you know." Teacher stood to his feet with Hank still in his arms. He began to pick his way back toward the King's Road.

"Teacher, I'm so sorry for leaving you and leaving school … and everything else I did. I even ate wedding berries. I'm so sorry. Would you—" A sob cut off the rest of his sentence. He felt terribly childish for crying, but he couldn't help himself.

"Yes. I forgive you." Teacher's words were gentle. He smiled at Hank and squeezed him even tighter.

Hank closed his eyes and rested in the warm embrace as they made their way up the King's Road toward the school. "How did you know where I was?"

"I was looking for you."

Hank's eyebrows knit together, but his eyes remained shut. "But why?"

"I knew you would be coming. Your father has been looking for you too. He came to me earlier today and was surprised that you were not in school."

Hank's eyes flew open and he tried to sit up.

"Lie still. He will meet us at the school in a little while. It's almost the time we agreed on."

Hank settled back and rested in silence as they entered the schoolyard and began ascending the stairs. "Teacher?"

"Yes, Hank?"

"Was it true what Schala said about you? I mean, about being the son of the king?"

Teacher stood still and looked into Hank's eyes. "Do you not know already?"

Hank looked away. He thought he knew, but he wasn't sure.

"Then you must judge for yourself by how well I heal." Teacher shifted Hank's weight. "Your hands are cut to pieces, and your leg needs attention. Let's go inside and take a look at them."

ADAM III

Chapter 11

"How precious also are thy thoughts unto me, O God."
Psalm 139:17

It was a wretched month for Adam. Things went from bad to worse after Hank left.

Schala should been pleased with the work everyone had accomplished in the fields. The funja plants reached as high as Adam's waist, and the men predicted a rich harvest this year. His heart swelled with pride at all his hard work.

But Schala continued to shower him with daily rebukes. Adam's ears rang from the constant tongue lashings. His legs ached from Schala's whip. The sudden stings and lasting burns became routine.

Even worse than the physical pain, though, was the sting of his conscience. Adam had developed a strong lust for wedding berries and obtained them from Schala whenever he could.

He always regretted it afterward, especially when Schala

smirked cruelly and mocked him for his weakness.

It didn't take long for Adam to become hooked on wedding berries.

"Now you must pay for them," Schala demanded one day. "I want your coin."

Adam's heart sank. His coin? *No!*

For two days he refused, but on the third day—in a moment of weakness—he gave in. He traded Hank's coin the next time he wanted berries, even though he knew the coin didn't belong to him.

When the coins were gone, Schala told Adam he now owed a "blesseen." Then it rose to several blesseens in exchange for a handful of berries. Adam wasn't sure what a blesseen was, but in a short time he found himself in debt for over sixty.

Every morning Adam promised himself, "I will not break the law today." He determined to return to school, but it was no use. He couldn't go back. What would the other students say? How would Teacher respond?

Worse, he was deathly afraid of Schala's threats. He couldn't even tell Grandfather. He didn't want to be caught and punished for eating wedding berries.

And strangely enough, he didn't want to lose his "freedom."

The one bright spot in Adam's life was Christy. She waited at the creek every evening to tell him exciting tidbits from school. Sometimes she brought something for him to eat. She always shared her notes, handwritten copies of almost every word Teacher had said that day.

Adam had a large pile of notes in his room. He hadn't

read any yet, but their presence helped ease his conscience.

He shuffled the pages and sighed. *I need to talk to Grandfather.*

Adam left his room and headed downstairs. He paced back and forth in the hallway then touched the swirls on the wooden door leading to the sunroom. Dinner waited inside, along with a conversation he determined not to avoid this time.

But he dreaded it.

Out in the streets, the army was preparing to march. Garda had fallen, as well as Doene. Sheera had been calling all month for reinforcements. The Arsabians were overrunning the Twelve Cities, and now the Eirenians would strike back.

Adam's mind was consumed with a different mission. He had to speak with Grandfather.

Taking a deep breath, he swung the door open. Darkness had fallen outside an hour ago. Light from the hanging lamp danced in the sunroom's glass walls, reflecting back Adam's pale face.

A single trencher of food sat in the middle of the table, where Adam, Grandfather, and occasionally Roberts ate their dinner. Tonight the trencher contained not only rice and silfun but also a small pile of mango slices, a rare treat.

Adam ran forward and shoved his cheeks full before it occurred to him that no place had been set for Grandfather. Where was he?

Panic welled up. *Did Grandfather leave with the army without telling me?*

Adam grabbed a handful of rice and jammed it into his

mouth as he ran back down the hall and out into the courtyard. Torches glowed in the street. He saw the silhouette of Rhenda, the cook, leaning with bent shoulders against the gate.

He joined her.

She glanced at Adam and then back at the crowd in the King's Road. Soldiers in homespun uniforms marched past with bows on their backs and swords at their sides. Jackson marched with the men, his dark eyes somber in the flicker of torchlight. A brand-new sword hung from his belt.

A pang of jealousy stabbed Adam.

There was no sign of Grandfather. Rhenda tugged the corner of her apron with her long fingers. Her husband marched as one of the soldiers.

Adam tried to think of something to encourage her. "Thanks for dinner. The mangoes taste great."

She nodded and continued staring into the crowd. "It's a treat. You didn't forget it was Supplies Day, did you?"

"How could I forget?" The fact had been burning in Adam's head all day. Images of the morning crowd in the plaza rushed through his mind afresh—the supplies wagon, the drivers, the bundles, the outstretched hands, and especially the shock of the driver calling out his name: "Adam Sonneman the Third!"

It was the first time Adam had received anything by name from the supplies wagon.

Not long afterward, he'd watched the wagon roll away down this very road, with one little lamb tied to the back, following.

He remembered Hank watching his lamb move away, his father's hand resting on his shoulder. Adam could still envision the tears standing softly in their eyes. He sighed. Was it the sacrifice or their relationship that had touched him more?

No, he would not be forgetting this Supplies Day.

He drew his hand out of his pocket and looked down into his palm. There it lay, the dark, hard seed. It was not the one he had received from Teacher a month ago. That one had rotted into dust. This one was new, sent directly from the king to Adam ... by name.

King Eliab knows my name. He clearly had something he wanted Adam to do.

Adam couldn't believe the king still wanted him, or that he wanted to give Adam another chance, especially knowing all that had taken place this past month.

Adam dropped the seed back into his pocket just as the last soldiers in the column marched past the governor's dwelling. He wondered if he would ever see them again. He faced Rhenda. "Where's Grandfather?"

She jerked her chin back toward the house. "He's in the study with Father Dementiras. To be honest, it makes me nervous. I don't know what they have to discuss so much. That man shows up here almost every Supplies Day."

"Thanks." Adam started back across the courtyard.

"They'll be a while," Rhenda warned. "Might as well eat your dinner first."

Rhenda's words brought Adam up short. She was probably right. "All right. Thanks."

To his surprise, Rhenda followed him back to the sunroom. She flopped down in the seat across from him as he started to eat and crossed her long arms on the table in front of her.

Adam hesitated with a mango slice halfway to his mouth. What was she doing here? He squirmed.

"Do you believe the prophecies?" she asked.

Adam turned toward the window and furrowed his brows. In the reflection, Rhenda's gaze followed him. "I guess so. Why do you ask?" He turned back and finished his mango slice.

"I don't know what to think."

She stared into the palms of her hands. Strands of greasy hair slid down her cheeks and partially covered her face, but she made no attempt to push them away. "My Camdin comes home every day with terrible ideas from school. 'Prophecies,' he says. They're starting to worry me to death. Do you know what he's talking about?"

"Do you mean about the Goiim?"

Christy had said something about the subject just this afternoon. *I wish I had paid better attention.*

"Exactly!" Rhenda's head snapped up. "He says they're going to destroy our crops and ruin our city. They could come at any time. King Eliab himself decreed it. He says we've forsaken the king, and our judgment has been prophesied from the beginning. He says it's our own fault."

"Who says? Camdin?"

"No. Teacher says. He's been taking the children to study the King's Stones twice a week, and Camdin says these things are all written down." She pushed back from the table and stood up. "It scares me, but what am I supposed to do? You've been in school longer than Camdin has. What do you think?"

Adam crammed a spoonful of silfun in his mouth and said nothing. He wanted to speak, but he didn't know what to say. The thought of losing the funja crop turned his stomach.

"My father always says the king loves us," Rhenda went on. "If so, why would he let these things happen? Why would he prophesy something so terrible? Why would he leave us like he has? *Why?*" She raised her hands in obvious exasperation. "I just don't know what to think anymore."

The cook moved toward the door. She stood still, looking at Adam. "Maybe if you hadn't quit school you would have some answers for me." She left, closing the door behind her.

"Wait!"

The door reopened, and Rhenda poked her head through.

"I'm going back," Adam said. "To school. That's why I wanted to talk to Grandfather. I'll try to find you some answers."

The door slammed shut.

Adam drew out his seed and studied it. *The king is thinking about me.*

Adam wanted answers too. And there was something he needed to do with his seed.

But that was a secret he didn't plan to tell Rhenda.

ADAM SONNEMAN I

Chapter 12

*"While they promise them liberty, they themselves are the
servants of corruption: for of whom a man is overcome, of
the same is he brought in bondage." 2 Peter 2:19*

Governor Adam Sonneman glowered at the elderly man
sitting across from him. "Your price is unreasonable. I
can never get that many blesseens by next Supplies Day."

Father Dementiras smiled and stroked his beard, gliding
his fingers through the soft, white hair that ran almost as far
as his belt. "Unreasonable? My dear friend, a bargain is a
bargain. You and I most definitely made one, did we not?"

His plump red cheeks broadened into a grin, and he
spread his hands wide, palms up. "You can't get help like
mine just anywhere. Would you rather go to that Tyrant? I
hope you still value your freedom." He turned and spat on
the floor at the mention of the Tyrant.

Adam Sonneman turned his face away and released a
long, slow breath. "All right. I'll have the money by then."

Father Dementiras rose to his feet and bowed. "As I knew

you would say, my dear friend. Until then, may you live in peace. My blessing be upon you." Receiving no answer in reply, he smiled and made his way out of the study.

Sonneman stayed in his seat, his gaze fixed on nothing in particular. His fingers drummed the table, and his forehead furrowed deeper and deeper. He seized an old inkwell and hurled it against the wall. "I hate it!"

He pounded again and again on the table. With a final kick of his boot, he put his head down on his arms and lay still.

How long the governor stayed that way, he did not know. He roused when a voice called his name. He was dimly aware that the voice had called him several times already, rising in volume. He lifted his head from his arms and sat up to his full height.

A loud knock sounded on the door. "Grandfather?"

He let out an impatient snort. "What is it?"

Silence.

He was about to call even louder, but the door opened a crack. His young grandson Adam poked his head through. His voice came much quieter than before. "I brought you some dinner. Would you like me to bring it in?"

Sonneman relaxed and settled back in his chair. "That's fine." He brushed aside papers to make room for the trencher Adam set before him.

The food was surprisingly warm for the late hour. In addition to a first portion of mangoes, he noticed a second, smaller portion. Perhaps the boy had given him his share.

He frowned. Acknowledging it would open an unwanted conversation. He waited for his grandson to leave.

The boy, however, sat down in the chair across from him. "Was that Father Dementiras?"

Sonneman grunted an affirmative. Scooping up a bite of rice with his fingers, he shoved it into his mouth.

"Why is he so fat?"

"He's not fat. He's normal. You think he's fat because the only people you know have sunken cheeks and shriveled frames from having too little to eat."

Adam reached up and felt the side of his face. "All right. Then why is he so normal?"

"He's a Pre-Aardian islander. What would you expect?" This conversation was taking too long. "Is that all?"

Adam scooted to the front of his chair. "There's something I wanted to tell you—I mean, ask you." He shifted in his seat. "Is there any way I could go back to school again?"

So, that was the reason for this visit. Perhaps it wouldn't be too difficult to deal with, after all. Sonneman shook his head. "Adam, I'm really surprised."

Adam shifted again and rubbed the hair on the back of his head. "What do you mean?"

"I thought you wanted to be free."

"I do. Well, I did. It's just that it isn't turning out the way I expected. I thought you would train me and let me do important things with you. Or fight. Besides, I don't have to go to school forever. Just for now. Could I start tomorrow?"

"Sure."

Adam sat back in surprise. "Really? I can go? Just like that?"

Sonneman chuckled inwardly. He was playing the boy

like a fish on a line. "Well, hang on a minute. There's one thing you need to do first. If you're not working for me, then you need to return my coin."

Adam's mouth fell open. "B-but I thought you said it was the symbol of my authority. You said I might be the next governor someday."

"Perhaps, perhaps. But listen, I gave you a year's wages. I expect a good year of work out of you."

Adam clutched the arms of the chair. "The coin is a whole year's wages? I won't be able to give it back. Isn't there anything else I can do?"

Sonneman slid a large slice of mango into his mouth. "Listen boy, a bargain's a bargain, and you and I most definitely made one. Do you think that teacher of yours will want you back? In his eyes you're a regular criminal."

Adam sat still and picked at the calluses on his hands.

Sonneman chomped off half a hot pepper and said nothing more. Perhaps now he could be rid of this interruption.

"If you want to train me to be a governor like you," Adam said in a small voice, "do you think I could participate in some military drills?"

"Whatever for?"

"Well, now that the army's gone, we don't have them to defend the city. And the prophecies say—"

"Prophecies! You believe those old things? Why, there's about as much substance to those as the ribs and wrinkles of old Roberts."

Adam ducked his head.

Sonneman leaned back. "I get inside information from

Father Dementiras. He assured me we can expect to drive the Arsabians into the sea. Mark it, boy. I know what's going on."

He pushed back his chair from the table. He had money problems to work on now. Then again, perhaps he could turn this visit from Adam into an opportunity.

"On the other hand, it doesn't hurt to be prepared. Hmm. Come here. I have something to show you." He moved to an ornate chest beneath the window. Wooden lilies were carved around the lid. Stooping and undoing a latch, he opened the chest and reached inside.

"Here. What do you think?" He lifted out a small, red-handled sword in a leather sheath and handed it to his grandson.

The scabbard was covered with dust, but when Adam drew out the blade, the metal glistened like new. "It's beautiful!" He slashed the sword from side to side and thrust it into the air.

"Careful! If you're going to fling it about, then take it outside."

Adam turned the blade over in his hands, his eyes lost in wonder.

A pang of guilt touched Sonneman, but he pushed it away. "Do you like it?"

"Very much." Adam sparred and made another thrust at an unseen adversary.

"Then accept it."

Adam's eyes grew large. "Of course! Thank you very much." He made another wide swing. "This is an amazing blade. It must have cost a lot."

"Yes, indeed. It will cost you ten blesseens."

Adam's sword hand went limp. "What is a blesseen?"

Sonneman snapped his fingers. "A coin. The coin I gave you that day in the woods is called a blesseen."

Adam gaped. "A blesseen is the coin? A whole year's wages? It would take me forever to earn that much money. I thought the sword was a gift."

Sonneman gave Adam an expression of pain. "A gift? My boy, I'm sorry, but these are hard times. You don't think I could afford to just give it to you, do you?"

"Then take it back." Adam sheathed the sword and held it out with both hands.

Sonneman threw his hands up. "Oh, no. I could never do that, not after you accepted it. You'll have to pay the amount."

Adam let the sword hang loosely in his hands. "Please, Grandfather. We're family. I thought you would take care of me. If the sword is already yours, then why do you want me to pay you for it?"

The governor chewed the side of his finger. He suddenly regretted his ploy. For the present, however, he felt constrained by necessity. "It isn't mine," he said softly.

"I'm in debt for it to Father Dementiras and simply transferring the debt to you."

The boy drew out the blade. "But it has the symbol of the king. Father Dementiras doesn't serve the king, does he?"

"Not anymore."

Adam shoved the sword back in and returned to his chair. He blew the dust from the sheath and picked at it with his finger.

Sonneman reseated himself and took the last bite of mango. "You better get up to bed."

"Yes, sir. Good night." Adam shuffled across the floor and was halfway out the door when he turned back. "Grandfather?"

"Yes?"

"I love you." He stood where he was, leaning against the door.

"Is that all?"

Adam turned away. "I thought you would say—oh never mind!" He put a hand over his face and slammed the door behind him.

Sonneman furrowed his brows and gnawed on the empty stem of his hot pepper. If only times weren't so hard, maybe things with his grandson would be different. At least for now, he was a few blesseens closer.

ADAM III

Chapter 13

"Without me ye can do nothing." John 15:5b

"Bother these thorns." Adam tore his sleeve free and leaned against Red Rock, catching his breath. He had run all the way from the fields, but there was still a long way to go before dark.

He squeezed the seed in his pocket. *Am I making the right choice?*

Adam had intended to start for the Mount of Humility this morning, but Grandfather had sent everyone to the fields, even though they were normally free at the end of the week. The approach of harvest demanded extra hours.

Huge rhododendrons crowded the hidden path, just as they had the day Adam followed Grandfather. What dangers did their branches conceal? Would the Keeda attack? The hair on the back of his neck rose remembering their previous attack.

But Adam had made up his mind.

He squeezed the seed one more time. Then drawing his sword, he started into the forest. At first, he cut the thorns that hung in his way, but he soon realized this only slowed his progress. The sun was sinking farther behind the mountains. He lowered his blade and moved forward, dodging between the clutching branches.

Sorrow washed over Adam afresh—as well as a mounting panic—when he came to the place where Micaiah had been killed. What was he thinking, returning to such a dangerous place, and this time alone? *Alone.* How he was coming to hate that word.

Maybe Christy was right.

"The king never meant for us to go alone," she'd said.

Thinking of Christy brought a smile to Adam's lips and lessened his panic. She'd surprised him that afternoon. She sat on the bank, dangling her feet in the water. He'd stumbled over her with his buckets and almost fallen in the creek.

"Christy!" he exclaimed when he caught his balance. "What are you doing here?"

She smiled. "Resting my feet, of course. It was a long, hard walk following all those trails up the mountain and down so many times. I'm used to walking, but that was a considerable trek."

Adam cocked his head. "I have no idea what you're talking about."

Christy lay back with her hands behind her head, staring into the bright-blue sky.

"Teacher and I went to the Mount of Humility this

morning. I wish you could have come with us."

Adam set down the buckets and crouched beside her. "You've seen the Mount of Humility?"

Christy kicked her foot in the water. "I didn't just *see* it. We climbed it. Can't you hear? We went there to plant my seed. Teacher helped me. I didn't plant it in the normal sense, though. When we came to the second ridge, there was a horrible, hissing sound. I'd heard the noise before, but it was too much for me this time. Teacher showed me where I could hide my seed, and he said he would take care of it from there. After that we came back."

She smiled as if she had just returned from a picnic. "And here we are."

Adam's bewilderment at Christy's story led to stammering questions. She was forced to repeat her story several times before he finally caught on.

"I'm planning to go myself," he finally told her.

Christy's eyes widened. "You should wait for Teacher."

I can do this on my own, Adam thought, shaking his head. "I already know the way."

That was when Christy said those words: "The king never meant for us to go alone."

Now, as Adam moved down the path and descended into the riverbed, her words were still running through his mind. *"The king never meant for us to go alone."*

He scowled and tossed a rock against the riverbed's hard, cracked surface. "I wish he hadn't left us alone." The words came out louder than he intended, startling him. It wasn't the right thing to say. Everything else was so quiet that he felt conspicuous, perhaps even watched.

I've survived this far! He tightened his grip on his sword and kept moving.

Dirt crunched beneath Adam's feet. Shriveled branches rattled above him. There was no sign of life. Too bad those colored birds didn't fly here now. He imagined the river full of water, with the white-stone path beside it. He tried to guess where fruit trees and flowers might have grown. What would it have been like to walk here with the king himself?

He paused. A cool wind stirred the dust and blew it into his face. He closed his eyes and rubbed his arms. *What was that?* Adam opened his eyes. His heart thudded. For a moment he thought he heard whispers. But he saw no one.

His heart returned to normal. It must have been the wind. He shivered. This walk was taking longer than he remembered. Had he missed something? He gripped the seed in his pocket and looked up.

The sun was balancing on the mountain tops, brightening the sky with a parting flame of color. Adam pondered. It was getting dark. Maybe he should give up his mission and try again later. Maybe he should wait for Teacher.

He shook his head. No, Teacher wouldn't want him. *In his eyes, I'm a regular criminal.*

He smiled grimly. "I know what Christy would say." He put his hands on his hips and leaned forward in mock imitation, speaking in a high-pitched voice. "You *are* a criminal, Adam. But you still need to run to Teacher."

His arms fell to his sides. "It's easy for you to say, Christy," he whispered. "*You're* not a criminal. You've probably never broken a law in your life, or even wanted to. Maybe if I had parents like yours, things would be different.

But it's not that easy for me."

Adam drew his hand from his pocket and opened it. The seed clung to his moist skin. The king had given him this seed. He ought to plant it.

If Christy could do it, then so can I.

With his mind made up, Adam began to run. A few minutes later, the giant tree emerged out of the gloom. What a relief!

Without pausing, he climbed the steps to the platform. He grabbed a torch and tucked it into his belt. With only a quick glance at the darkening mountain, he descended again. He was making progress.

Climbing the opposite riverbank proved much harder. He paced in front of the wall of earth, searching for footholds. At last he found a spot where a large root from a nearby tree curved over the edge. After a few failed attempts, he managed to jump high enough to grab the root and drag his body onto the bank.

Rocky ground ascended into the sky. Adam took off at a slow jog, being careful to avoid twisting his ankle. His breathing grew labored, and he slowed his pace to a walk. His thighs ached, but he forced himself on, falling into a rhythm. He was pleased to see the sky growing close much sooner than he expected. Ignoring the throbbing pain behind his forehead, he bounded ahead with a final burst of energy.

Adam stopped short. More ground appeared as he advanced. He had been mistaken. Who knew how long it would take to reach the top? He gritted his teeth and dropped back to his monotonous rhythm, accepting the pain and trying to distract his mind.

Darkness fell. Cool wind snapped around him. His mind grew numb. But at last he reached the top and looked over the edge. *No. It can't be!*

Ridge after ridge rose higher and higher into the sky. The ultimate peak lay far in the distance. In between, black canyons gaped open like monstrous mouths. They threatened to swallow the scraggly pines that clung to their lips.

Adam's heart sank. What was the use? The ground dropped away only a few yards in front of him. He kicked a stone and sent it flying over the edge. This was impossible. *Unreasonable!*

Adam sagged. He had taken the worst possible route. The only way around this deep chasm would be to backtrack through a narrow gap on his right. From there he could descend into the valley. He squinted in the last of the fading light but couldn't see—or even guess—where a path might climb the next ridge.

"The king never meant for us to go alone." Christy's words echoed in his head.

"Then where is he?" Adam sheathed his sword. He jabbed his hand into his pocket and pulled out a couple of flint rocks. Sitting down, he propped the torch with his knees. He poured his frustration into striking the rocks until a spark caught. The torch burst into flame.

Adam rose and started for the gap. He slipped several times on loose rocks. *Slow down*, he ordered his legs.

Large rock walls enclosed the pass on both sides. His torch created shining streaks around him. Trembling, Adam unsheathed his sword, lifted it high, and entered the gap.

Almost immediately, the gap took a sharp turn, and the

sky disappeared. A sense of vulnerability clutched his heart and squeezed. He waved the torch and turned in circles, trying to see everywhere. Fighting his fears, he walked on.

The gap zigzagged its way down. Step after cautious step, Adam descended deeper into the valley. When he rounded the next bend, he sucked in his breath in surprise. The path opened as he reached the back of the first ridge.

He raised his torch and saw a giant, fallen tree, larger than any tree Adam had ever seen back home. It lay across the chasm. He held the torch higher and tried to see to the other side. Yes, the tree stretched clear to the opposite ridge.

Hope soared. He might save a lot of time with this shortcut. Holding his torch high, Adam began picking his way toward the fallen tree. Jagged rocks stabbed through his shoes, but he kept on going, afraid to stay in one place too long.

Hisss!

Adam froze and crouched. Was that whispering? He dipped his torch behind a rock, trying to hide its blaze. His back and arms cramped, but still he waited. He strained his ears listening to the night. All was still. No further sounds.

Cautiously, he advanced and came to the fallen tree. He examined it on both sides. It appeared to be holding fast, so after testing his weight on the trunk, he sheathed his sword, gripped the torch even tighter, and climbed up.

Adam didn't plan to walk across this tree bridge, not knowing how far the chasm dropped. He crouched to his knees and scooted forward, using his free hand for support. Partway across, he lowered the torch and tried to see how far the chasm fell. No good. His light stopped short of the ground, and his imagination guessed it was a long way to the bottom. He clung tighter to the branches and the bark, hardly daring to move his knees or reach for another handhold.

A large branch jutted up in front of him, blocking the way. He lifted his torch. *How will I get around this massive—*

Adam caught his breath. Chills raced up his spine. Etched in the wood with red ink was the image of a great red dragon. Its eyes blazed with hatred, and its jaws gaped wide with flames. Beneath the dragon were several strange symbols with the words I SeeK and I DeVOUR.

Adam's whole body trembled. The hand holding the torch shook so much he almost lost his light source. He peered into the darkness below and then at the way he'd come. He took a deep breath, trying to muster his courage.

How hard can it be to plant a seed? I can do this.

Refusing to look at the dragon, Adam reached behind the branch, seeking a handhold.

Hisss!

Adam jerked his hand back as if he'd been stung by a hornet. Then his legs and hands were propelling him backward as fast as they could go. His eyes flew about wildly, expecting a serpent behind every branch. He reached the base of the trunk and stretched his feet toward the rocky ridge.

Not there yet.

He scooted a few more feet.

Hisss!

Abandoning all caution, Adam threw himself from the fallen tree and landed on the rocky ground with a cry of pain.

His torch flew from his hand. It rolled toward the edge of the ridge, ready to plunge into the darkness below.

Adam dove for the torch and snatched it up just before it plummeted into the chasm.

Panicking, he turned and fled back the way he'd come.

ADAM III

Chapter 14

"Your land ... is desolate, as overthrown by strangers."
Isaiah 1:7

By the time Adam reached the riverbed, his strength was nearly spent, as was his torch. He had run as quickly as possible, stumbling and scrambling, but still, much time had passed. He had nearly lost his way in the dark. More than once, he tripped and fell, rolling on rocks and tearing his breeches.

Now, as he lowered himself to a sitting position on the edge overlooking the riverbed, he doubted he had the strength to climb down. The torch sputtered and went out.

Adam drew a long, painful breath, tossed the useless light source away, and looked around. Faint starlight allowed him to make out his way. He started over the edge, holding onto roots and large rocks. His fingers slipped, and he dropped to the ground, landing on his feet.

Stinging pain shot through his ankles, and he collapsed.

He lay there in the dark holding his legs, afraid to rise but equally afraid to stay. He began to crawl along the ground, inching his way to the platform tree.

When he came to its base, he pulled himself to his feet. He cringed. Fresh stinging shot up his legs, but his ankles worked well enough to climb the steps. He pushed the pain aside and made his way up to the platform. If memory served him well, there should be another torch or two. He fingered his way across the rough boards, feeling for a torch.

Nothing! "Where are they?" he whispered into the stillness.

A large splinter slid under his fingernail. With a cry, he jerked his hand back and squeezed against the pain. "I hate this!" he shouted into the night.

He looked back in the direction of the Mount of Humility. It was too dark to make out any details, but he knew it was there. "If you're supposed to know everything and love us, then where are you now? I'm trying my best, and you don't even care!"

Adam gritted his teeth, pulled the seed out of his pocket, and hurled it with all his strength at the mountain. His foot brushed up against something that rolled. He strained to see. A torch! He quickly pulled out his flint rocks and lit it.

The smoke burned his eyes. He coughed and fanned the smoke away. Only the platform and the lower branches appeared within the circle of torchlight. Everything else had turned inky black. He felt conspicuous up here.

"I'm going home." With a parting glance, he left the tree.

The journey along the riverbed dragged. Adam stopped every few steps to raise his torch and check the bank. He dreaded missing his path in the dark. His heart leaped when he found it at last, and he climbed up into the rhododendron forest.

Shouting in the distance startled him. He paused. *Am I imagining?* No. There came the noise again, faint but too clear to be mistaken. The clamor must be coming from the city. What was happening?

The smell of smoke arrested Adam's attention. He glanced up. *Oh, no!* His torch had caught the branches above him on fire. He dropped the torch and beat at the burning twigs with his sleeve. No success. He stooped to search for something to smother the fire, but his torch had now kindled the dry leaves on the path.

Adam jammed the torch into the dirt, extinguishing the flames. Grabbing a handful of leaves, he rubbed them back and forth against the branches. The small flames dissolved into smoke, and Adam was left in the dark.

He pulled his torch out of the dirt and prepared to light it but thought better of the idea, considering the brush he would be going through. He tucked his unlit torch in his waistband and looked around. The moon had risen, shining its pale, silver light between the bushes. There was just enough light to see his way. He inched forward, feeling in front of him with his hands. The thorns were hard to navigate, but he made constant progress.

The shouting in the distance continued.

All at once, Adam ran into a bush. His heart raced. He turned in a circle, tracing his way. *When did I move off the path?*

Everything behind him was clear. He frowned, puzzled.

Adam returned to the bush blocking his path and searched for a way around it, but the path had disappeared. He pushed at the branches. To his surprise, they yielded to his touch. The bush rocked backward. Encouraged by his success, Adam pushed harder. The bush moved farther. He reached down, took hold of it near the base, and shoved it by degrees out of his way.

The path opened, and Adam took a few steps forward. Then he turned back and looked at the bush. A tingle ran up his spine. The bush had not been there before. *Someone must have moved it!*

Ignoring the risk of fire, he dropped to his knees and dug in his pocket for the flints. He propped the torch between his legs and worked to light it. His hands shook so much it took several times to succeed, but at last the spark caught, and he lifted the light.

Adam saw nothing unusual at first. The path looked the same as always. He recognized the place as the spot which had captivated Micaiah's attention all those weeks ago. He must have noticed something the rest had missed.

Then Adam saw them. He gasped and knelt for a closer look. There was no mistake. Embedded in the loose earth from the uprooted bush were footprints.

"They can't be mine," he whispered. These were barefoot prints, and he was wearing shoes. He held the torch closer to the ground. There were multiple prints, overlapping and blurring each other. His stomach turned over. He glanced around, searching the black shadows, afraid to find a pair of eyes looking back.

No one Adam knew went around in bare feet. He

imagined the Keeda traveling in the dark, hunting for victims. He drew his sword with his free hand and held it out in front of him. A sudden increase in the shouting from the village turned his thoughts toward home.

He extinguished the torch and stood trembling and gripping his sword until his eyes adjusted. Then he pushed and twisted and stumbled to the end of the trail. He clung to the giant red boulder, heaving in draughts of night air.

His nose wrinkled. He sniffed and caught the familiar scent of smoke. His eyes flew to his torch, tucked safely in his waistband, but it was not the source. A breeze wafted against his face, and the smell of burning filled his nostrils to the full. Far away, an orange glow and plumes of smoke rose from the direction of the city.

Adam tried to scramble up the boulder for a better look. The rock was too steep for his aching limbs. On the back side, away from the view of the city, he found a better place, with handholds. He climbed high enough to poke his head over the top. The view was no better from here than on the ground. Disgruntled, he prepared to descend. Then something caught his eye—the silhouette of a man standing on top of Lookout Hill.

The man waved his arm. Several more figures joined the first, and they began to run down the King's Road—straight toward Adam. He ducked his head below the top of the boulder, but the suspense terrified him.

He *had* to see what was happening!

He lifted his head just high enough to see. Hopefully, nobody could see him in the feeble light.

More figures appeared. Some were herding goats, while

others carried chickens or geese. The animals did not go willingly. They kicked and flapped and struggled against the men. One goat broke free and ran away, but no one bothered to chase it. The creature fled down the road toward Adam and turned off into some bushes not far away.

Adam watched in open-mouthed horror as the men made their way closer, carrying away the few animals his neighbors owned. *It's a good thing for them I'm not armed with a bow and arrows! I suppose it's a good thing for me too. I'd only get myself killed.*

He could see their faces now. They were drawn and thin like the city people, but with bushy beards and huge eyes. Their clothes were rough and filthy. What stood out most to Adam, though, was the whiteness of their skin. It wasn't a "normal" white, but pale and milky.

Keeda.

Adam stared at them in horror. They were coming closer.

The men stopped near the boulder and grouped together, muttering among themselves.

Adam held his breath. *Don't move. Don't breathe. Don't sneeze.*

One by one, the Keeda raiders squeezed between the boulder and the bushes and made their way into the forest. The goats fought back, bleating and digging their hooves into the ground. It was clear the animals did not want to go through the thorns. The Keeda cursed and shoved, finally managing to force their prey into the rhododendrons.

Adam waited, barely breathing, for several minutes after they were gone, hardly daring to move. He shuddered. *What if they'd returned when I was still on the path?* He pushed that thought out of his mind and slid down from the boulder. He was about to take off running, when the sound of bleating brought him up short.

The escaped goat stepped into the path and bleated at him.

Up close, Adam could see a peculiar white patch of hair with a blemish on the goat's left shoulder. He gasped. It was old Samuel, the favorite goat of the Carpenters, Christy's family.

Adam shot a glance back at the forest and then edged his way toward the goat. "Come here, old boy." He kept his voice low and calming.

Samuel made no effort to come, but neither did he run away. A bit of broken rope circled the goat's neck, and Adam stooped and took it. He tugged on the rope. "Let's go home, Samuel."

He started back toward the village with the goat at his heels. Adam smiled, feeling a faint sense of accomplishment. He had not only rescued one of the animals but also learned important information about the enemy's location.

Without warning, another white-skinned person ran over the hill, wielding a long-handled hammer. Seeing Adam, his eyes widened, and he swung the hammer, aiming for his head.

Caught off guard, Adam leaped backward, bumping into the goat. He dropped the rope and unsheathed his sword barely in time. The clash of metal sent his sword out of his hand and flying into the dust.

Adam dove for the weapon, rolling on the ground and scrambling back to his feet. He felt the whoosh of air when the next hammer stroke skimmed past his shoulder. The enemy twisted for a closer strike and caught his foot against a rock. He sprawled facedown on the path with a painful yelp.

Adam stepped on the handle of the hammer, pinning it to the ground. He raised his blade.

The attacker let go of his hammer and rolled over. Their eyes met. This was no bearded, grizzly warrior. The face was of a boy no older than Adam, eyes wide with terror, wordlessly pleading for mercy.

This was Adam's moment of victory and revenge. *I have the chance to defeat one of the Goiim.* Then ... why couldn't he bring himself to do it?

Adam lowered his sword and removed his foot from the hammer. He nodded toward the forest. The Keeda boy jumped to his feet. His wide eyes blinked with surprise. They stared at each other for a moment, speechless. Then turning, the boy snatched his hammer and disappeared into the bushes.

Adam sheathed his sword, furrowed his brows, and grabbed Samuel's rope. Leading the goat, he followed the path up Lookout Hill.

All the breath left Adam's body at the sight that awaited him. Fields burned in every direction. The flames lay low, simmering, but the heavy smoke testified to their former fury. Small, black shadows of people ran everywhere. The whole city must have emptied out to fight the fires. Grandfather's fields lay smoldering.

Adam's stomach clenched in a tight knot. All of his hard labor was vanishing into a pile of ashes. The rich harvest of funja was ruined. He'd believed his freedom had helped him to really accomplish something, but now everything was going up in smoke.

ADAM III

Chapter 15

"Thou hast hid thy face from us, and hast consumed us, because of our iniquities." Isaiah 64:7b

The shouting increased in volume as Adam descended the hill. Now, he could hear crying as well. Villagers ran past him carrying water or hurrying their loved ones to safety.

Samuel's rope jerked Adam's hand. He turned to find the goat with his feet planted near the path to Christy's house. "All right. But you better hurry."

He trotted with the goat up the path, passing multiple people running to the stream. As he approached the Carpenters' home, Christy's father ran toward him carrying a bucket. His blue eyes reflected both the glowing embers around them and the man's own inner turmoil.

"Hey!" Adam called out, trying to catch his attention. "I found your goat!"

Between the surrounding clamor and his own distractions,

it was clear the man did not notice Adam. "Your goat!" Adam yelled, tugging on the rope.

The man shot him a blank look and tried to pass, but Adam grabbed his sleeve. "Your goat!" He yelled even louder, trying to make himself heard.

Christy's father pulled away. "Just let him go."

The goat was tugging hard. Adam gave in and let him go. Samuel bolted for home.

Mr. Carpenter returned to Adam. He seized him by the shoulders and bent close to his face. "Can you bring us some water?" When Adam nodded, he thrust the bucket into his hands. "Hurry! We need it now. Don't wait!"

Adam ran for the creek. He dodged past other running villagers and headed straight for his favorite watering hole. With a long jump, he cleared the stream, landing on his feet on the other bank. Pain shot through his ankles and over his whole body. The surge of adrenaline that had carried him over the last hour seeped out of his body, leaving him exhausted and pain-wracked.

He waited while a wave of nausea washed over him. Then he knelt to fill his bucket. Something in Mr. Carpenter's eyes had warned Adam that his mission was critical. A moment's delay might be perilous.

He heard someone coming up behind him, so he raised his bucket and moved out of the way. Before he could take another step, a giant hand gripped Adam's shoulder, reeking with the smell of fish.

"By my beard and my belly," a familiar voice growled in his ear. "This world will end in a bad way when people go running off into the night." He drew a deep breath. "As if they didn't have masters and grandfathers to take orders from."

"Roberts!" Adam twisted around. "Let me go. I'll be right back. The Carpenters need me to—"

"Oh no!" The old man held him fast. "You're coming with me. I'm not going to lose you again. Bring the bucket. We can use it."

The grip on his shoulder told Adam that arguing was futile. Roberts dragged Adam through the fields toward the King's Road. The fires looked almost quenched at this point, but men still hurried by. Most bobbed their head to the chief servant.

Roberts gave them little notice, but trudged forward awkwardly, as always. He led Adam over burned-out rows and through muddy puddles.

Adam swatted at curls of smoke and rubbed his eyes to make them stop stinging. When he opened them, Doke was running toward them. "Roberts! Roberts!"

The chief servant stopped and frowned. "Fumes and furies. Can't you see I'm busy right now?"

Doke dipped his head in respect but then drew up close like an old friend and laid his hand on Roberts' arm. "Surely you can spare a minute. What I say concerns us all."

Roberts frowned and didn't reply.

"Can't you see what's taking place around us?"

"I've got eyes, haven't I?" Roberts tried to yank his arm away.

Doke held on tight. "We can all see the fires, but do you recognize their significance? The prophecies are being fulfilled before our very eyes. You were in the plaza when

King Eliab gave us his covenant. We heard what would happen if we rejected him. He predicted this."

Roberts' hand on Adam's shoulder trembled. He breathed heavily and scanned the fields. "I remember."

"Then we should repent. Turning back to the king is our only hope. If we don't, we can expect even worse judgments."

Roberts stared at the smoking rows that would have been harvested in a few days. He took a deep breath but remained silent.

"Roberts?"

The chief servant jerked his arm away. "What do you expect me to do?"

"Will you talk to the governor for me? Tell him what I said. No weapon can prevail against the king's purposes. Will you tell him this for me?"

"All right!" Roberts' grip on Adam's shoulder became a vice, and he marched away from Doke at a rapid rate.

Adam had to run to keep from being dragged along. When they arrived at the governor's dwelling, Grandfather was standing in the courtyard shouting instructions. His right hand clutched a sword. Servants crowded around him.

Roberts stood aside until the other servants had been dispatched. Before approaching, he whispered in Adam's ear. "Say nothing about the old man. It might fire the governor up even more."

"But you said you'd—"

The squeeze on Adam's shoulder cut off his words, and Roberts pushed him forward.

Grandfather scowled at his chief servant.

"Where in the island have you been this whole time?"

"I've been doing just as you asked, trying to find this-here young one. A time I've had of it too! Never got to finish my dinner, and what thanks do I get? Not a word."

"You should have left him." Grandfather turned to Adam. "Where have you been?"

Adam considered his wording. "I was on the King's Road. I saw where the Keeda entered the forest, and I think I know where they came from too." He explained about the uprooted bush near the place where Micaiah had been killed.

Grandfather scratched his chin. "Roberts, take a handful of men with you and check the place. You've been there before. Quickly now!"

The old man shot a parting glance toward the kitchen before leaving. Adam started to follow Roberts, but Grandfather gripped his shoulder. "Not you, boy. Come with me."

He pulled Adam to the side of the courtyard behind a giant stone planter, cracked and caked with dirt. Grandfather checked around before looking Adam full in the face. "Why were you in the forest?"

Adam ducked his head, but Grandfather grabbed him by the chin and forced his face up. "Were you trying to plant that seed? Answer me!"

"I thought I would, but I couldn't do it. It was horrible, Grandfather. I threw the seed away in the forest. I won't ever do it again. Honest. I'm sorry for being late to dinner. Please don't be angry."

Grandfather dropped Adam's chin and stared across the courtyard at a second planter. He was silent a long time.

"I've been getting too lax," he muttered. Then he turned his gaze on Adam. "Do you know how your parents were killed?"

Adam's eyes widened. It wasn't the answer he expected. "Sir?"

"I said, 'Do you know how your parents were killed?' Do you?"

"No sir, I don't. You told me they were lost in the forest." Adam licked his dry, cracked lips. "I … I always hoped they'd be found someday or —"

"We found them," Grandfather said. "They'd been killed, Adam. Killed by Goiim. They were trying to plant their seeds on that mountain." He pointed in the direction of the Mount of Humility.

Adam's heart squeezed in sudden grief. *Mother and Father are dead.* The hope he had clung to for years was snuffed out in an instant. A hard lump grew in his throat. His eyes stung. *My parents are gone forever!*

Grandfather's passionate voice jerked Adam back to attention.

"I told your father what would happen. We stood right there." Grandfather jabbed a finger at the second planter across the courtyard. "I told him to his face that he was throwing his life away. But he was too much under the influence of that teacher of yours."

Adam's numb mind focused on the cracks in the opposite planter, trying to picture his father.

Grandfather went on. "Your father said it didn't matter what happened to him, as long as he followed the king. Well? See where it got him? And now, you've come near to suffering the same fate. If you want to murder yourself, then go ahead and try to plant those seeds. But don't say I didn't warn you. Understand?"

Adam quivered at the somber tone in his grandfather's voice. "Yes, sir. I'm sorry, Grandfather. I'll never do it again. I don't even want to. Please don't be angry with me."

Grandfather studied him. "It isn't your fault so much. It's that teacher of yours." His lips twisted into an irritated sneer. "I'll settle with him once and for all. I've been patient for far too long."

Adam covered his face. The tears he had so valiantly held back rose to the surface.

"Oh, stop your blubbering."

Grandfather went on in a softer voice, "It's late, Adam. You've been out a long time. Get up to bed." He paused. "Yes, sir?"

"Yes, sir."

Without waiting for a reply that probably wouldn't come anyway, Adam ran to his room, fighting back his tears. He dressed for bed in a daze and then, overcome with exhaustion, he collapsed into bed.

SCHALA

Chapter 16

"For we wrestle not against flesh and blood, but against principalities, against powers, against the rulers of the darkness of this world, against spiritual wickedness in high places." Ephesians 6:12

Schala hesitated as he approached the meeting place. Moonlight glistened on his moist skin. Around him towered the jagged peaks of the Mount of Humility. He took a deep breath and clasped the rocky wall of the ridge he was climbing.

He hated to admit the fact even to himself, but he was afraid. Always in the past he had been eager to come to the officer meetings—eager to boast of new slaves or of his growing mastery of the old ones. He patted the bag of coins tucked into his vest, trying to reassure himself. There was certainly gain to boast of, two Sonneman boys in particular. But there was also a loss. He spat on the ground, cursing Immanuel.

Schala continued his climb. It was a greater offense to miss this meeting than to come with a reported failure. He could make out a few of the others just ahead. They were gathered in a large circle, where a natural clearing formed among the rocks. He approached the ring and seated himself on a fallen log as far from the center as he dared. Pushing his boots against the ground, he glanced around, careful to avoid eye contact.

The officers filling the ring—all of them fellow Dragonians—carried axes, clubs, or long knives. As the circle began to fill, the buzz of low conversation grew in intensity. "Hey, hey, everyone!" someone shouted in a harsh, croaking voice. "Here comes old Legion! Look at him now. Not so big and bad after all, is he?"

A nasty round of laughter rippled around the circle.

"Where's all your boasting now?" called another. "Can't hold onto your prisoner any longer? I know some other animals you can attack with your spare time!" This mockery was followed by an even greater roar of laughter.

Legion shook his fist at the group but said nothing.

Under normal circumstances, Schala would have laughed as loud as the rest. Legion was a wiry man, with shaggy red hair and a bushy beard. Physically strong, he always drew quite a following. Schala had been secretly pleased to learn that Immanuel had driven Legion away from the coastal region several weeks ago. The Dragonian had taken out his anger on a herd of pigs, driving them into the sea and frustrating their owners. Schala had laughed out loud at the time.

Now, though, he had to face up to his own loss. He pushed

his fist into his hand and squeezed against his knuckles until they turned white.

A shout drew Schala's attention back to the circle. Insults flew back and forth, followed by accusations and curses. Men began throwing dust at one another and hissing. The entire ring exploded into an uproar.

An enormous shadow passed over them. The uproar faded into an eerie silence. Schala dropped on his face alongside the others, trembling.

Their master had come.

The hair on the back of Schala's neck rose and refused to lie down. He felt the dragon's presence without having to see him. The sound of his heavy breathing filled the clearing. He heard the serpent tearing up the earth with his enormous claws. A deafening roar filled the air, followed by a wave of heat. Schala cracked his eyes open enough to see the dragon belch flames from his mouth, engulfing a small pine in the middle of the ring.

"Let's begin," the dragon hissed.

Schala rose. He drew the bag with coins from his vest and joined the others at the fire. One by one, the islanders threw their coins into the flames. Some offered only a few coins. Others threw in handfuls. Schala normally threw his coins one by one, with a bit of flourish to emphasize his successes. He always paused on the last coin and spit on the picture of the crown before flinging it into the fire.

This time, however, he tossed his coins with a single cast and moved on, hoping to avoid attention. Chills raced up his neck. He felt the dragon's gaze upon him, the fiery eyes burning. Never in all his years of servitude had Schala been able to meet that gaze. He fought to keep from scuttling back to his seat.

Schala's regional supreme commander, Dos Lenguas, bowed low before the dragon. When he rose, he stood at least a head taller than most of those gathered and wore a long black cloak and hood. "You see, Excellency, we have reaped much from the city this season."

The dragon snorted. Two plumes of smoke billowed from his nostrils. "Coins are nothing, you fools. We want debts. We want slaves. Where are your receipts of debt?"

Dos Lenguas trembled but maintained a crafty smile. "They are here, Excellency."

He drew from his cape a bundle of notices. Gall, the regional commander over the coast, and Kamosh, the supreme leader over the Goya nations, drew out similar bundles.

The dragon eyed the parchments. "Give me your reports." The beast whirled on Kamosh, his tail flinging the rocks behind him. "What of the Goiim?"

"They are almost completely under your dominion, my lord." Kamosh sneered at Dos Lenguas and added, "As *always.*"

Dos Lenguas returned the sneer but held his tongue. His rule over Mount Eirene was the coveted position among Dragonian leadership, in spite of the challenges it afforded.

The dragon turned to Gall. "I heard of your losses along the coast. Do you have anything to say for yourself?"

Gall shook his head and studied the dirt.

"Then you know what punishment awaits. I will deal with you later. Dos Lenguas, what of the city?"

"We have made wonderful gains, your Excellency, including two grandsons of the governor. We have had no losses, either." He smiled and bowed.

The dragon flashed a mouthful of teeth. "You are an excellent liar, Dos Lenguas. But you don't fool me. You lost one several weeks ago."

Schala stiffened. His fist pressed even harder against his palm.

Dos Lenguas shot a glance at Schala. "Your Excellency, it was only a boy, and he will easily be retaken. I did not think to mention him."

Legion leapt to his feet. "Liar! We all know that a prisoner released by Immanuel can *never* be retaken." He raked a fierce glare across the circle. "I defy you to tell me otherwise."

A horrifying hush fell over the Dragonians. No one spoke. Schala cowered.

The dragon's tail snapped like a whip. It caught Legion around the neck and lifted him off the ground. "And how would you know that?" He held the islander close to his face.

Legion turned as white as a Keeda. He clawed at the dragon's tail, fighting for air.

"Short of breath, are you?" The dragon roared. "Let me give you *breath*."

Rearing back his head, he belched a ball of flame, engulfing Legion in fire. Flicking his tail, the dragon flung him across the circle. The islander rolled on the ground, screaming and beating himself until the flames were quenched. Then he lay still, moaning.

The dragon dug at the dirt with his claws. "Let that be a lesson to you all. I'll have no more playing around. We can ill afford to lose our prisoners."

"Hear! Hear!" croaked a voice from the outskirts. "We are far stronger than the Eirenians. Let us storm Mount Eirene at once and destroy it. Why do we wait?"

The dragon's fiery eyes turned toward the speaker. "Fool! Do you forget so easily my orders? If we attack now, our Enemy would come with all his armies. No, we are too smart for that. Tell me this, since you are so ready to speak. Who is the Eirenians' greatest enemy?"

Schala watched with interest. The speaker was clearly afraid, but trying to make the most of the situation.

"The Eirenians believe their greatest enemies are the Arsabians—the ones they call the Goiim. But in truth, it is we who live among them who are their greatest enemies. We lurk in the shadows, deceiving them, preparing them for destruction. Someday they will recognize us, but then it will be too late. Is it not so, your Honor?" He bowed.

The great serpent's tongue flicked in and out of his mouth. "Sit down before I bite off your head." He glared at the group. "Who is the Eirenians' greatest enemy? Who can tell me?"

Schala spun his face away from the flaming eyes. There was silence except for the dragon's claws clicking on the rocky soil.

Kamosh tapped his mace in his left palm. "Surely you don't mean the Arsabians are more dangerous than we are?"

"No, never!"

"It can't be the king, can it?" called another voice.

"Dog! He is the Eirenians' greatest ally, if only they knew it. Curse him! Don't mention that name in my presence." The dragon spat on the ground.

In one accord, the islanders also spat.

"Listen to me, you fools!" the dragon hissed. "There is no one stronger than I. But there is an enemy more dangerous than any of us. It is the enemy the people fear the least and put their trust in the most—their own hearts. Do you hear me? *Their own hearts* are their greatest enemy."

No one moved.

"Their lust for what they think is *freedom* will be their undoing. They can be tricked into almost anything, as long as it makes them feel *free*. This longing is our greatest weapon. Our words—not our swords—will destroy them. Our words will turn them against the king."

Gall spat. "What good has that ever done us? They can't do anything to hurt *him*."

The dragon swished his tail. "Don't provoke me to punish you early, Gall. It's not what they can do against *him*, but what he will be forced to do against them that matters."

Schala listened with mounting interest.

"The Enemy's fate is bound up with these people he so much loves," the dragon continued. "He promised before the entire island that he would reign with them over the rest of us from Mount Eirene. He committed himself by an unbreakable covenant to the success of their foolish city. The entire island knows this."

He pressed closer to his listeners. His hot breath nearly seared Schala, but he dared not move an inch.

"Think what it would mean if the city fell. The king has

put all of his weight on this one branch. Its ruin would mean his utter humiliation. The whole island would see what a fool he's been, and they would follow me as you have done from the beginning. We will reign over the island, and I shall be like the Most High." The dragon raised his head and roared, "I will have triumphed over our Enemy at last!"

An officer from Ar Sabia spoke. "But how would the city fall? You told us not to attack it."

"If we play our parts right, the Enemy himself will destroy his city for us. Doesn't his covenant promise vengeance against all who rebel? That includes the Eirenians from time to time. None of them has planted his seed every month except one, curse him, and we'll come back to him. I tell you the entire city is condemned by the king's laws, and his anger continues to build. His own sense of justice demands that the Eirenians die."

The dragon's scales glowed with excitement. "The day is coming when he will be forced to destroy them. When he does, it will be his own undoing, as well." Two wisps of smoke curled up from the dragon's nostrils. He smiled. "There is one more matter to attend to. Tell me what you have found out about Immanuel."

Dos Lenguas stood forth. "If I may presume upon your Excellency to speak a few words—"

"Just say them and stop wasting my time."

"According to my spies' reports, Immanuel has been fasting for the last thirty-nine days. He is undoubtedly weaker at this moment than he has ever been in his life."

"Is that all?"

"No. He has resolved not to eat again until he plants this

month's seed on the ultimate peak of this mountain. We believe he will make that attempt tomorrow, on the fortieth day."

The dragon stared off into the distance, his eyes gleaming in thought. His mouth curved up in an evil smile. "We must prepare to make our move. I will take this assignment. Step back while I transform myself!"

Fire flashed from the middle of the clearing, and plumes of black smoke billowed outward.

Schala jumped backward. He covered his head with his hands, coughing and rubbing his eyes. When he was able to see, he looked toward the center of the circle. The dragon was no longer there.

In his place stood Father Dementiras.

"Ho, ho, ho!" The elderly man beamed and stroked his beard. "Go now, my children, to your places. Tomorrow is an important day."

For the first time in weeks, Schala smiled. Not only had he avoided punishment, but he would also be avenged.

Immanuel would soon be defeated.

ADAM III

Chapter 17

"The entrance of thy words giveth light; it giveth understanding unto the simple." Psalm 119:130

The sun was high in the sky when Adam woke the next morning. He bolted up and reached for his clothes. Then he remembered what had happened the night before and lay back again. It was the King's Day, anyway. Time to rest.

He stared at the rafters, and his brain became a storm of troubling thoughts. He wished he could return to sleep and stay there, but it was no use. He threw off his bed covers and went to the window.

In the courtyard below, Adam could see the planter where he and Grandfather had talked. Father had stood at the planter on the other side of the court many years ago in a similar conversation. "Father was willing to give his life for the king," Adam said softly. "But I'm afraid to die."

His gaze flitted back and forth across the courtyard. *How can I move from the one planter to the other?*

He looked out over the city. Wisps of smoke rose from the distant fields. The smell of burnt funja tugged at his nostrils. Hardly a soul was stirring. A quietness hung in the air.

A lone man with a large cape and hood plodded by on his way to the plaza. The cape's green color marked him as an outsider from Doene. Many Eirenians from other cities had fled to Mount Eirene and built camps around the outskirts of town. Adam watched the stranger until he disappeared.

"I know where I can get some answers." He threw on his clothes and darted down the stairs two at a time. His stomach convulsed, and a wave of nausea swept over him, reminding him that he had missed dinner last night. He scurried down the hall to the kitchen. Rhenda was there, ladling porridge by the fire with her back turned.

"I'm sorry I'm late." Adam took a seat.

Rhenda sniffed and put a hand to her face. She said something that started with "No," but the words were muffled.

"What did you say?"

The ladle clanged against the pot. "I said, you're the first one here." A sob filled her voice.

Adam moved from his seat toward the table near the fire, where the bowls of porridge rested. He lifted one and returned to his place. Maybe he could ease the tension. "I noticed one of the bowls has more. Is that for old Roberts?"

"It's for Camdin. I'm giving him my portion."

Adam dipped his spoon into the porridge. There was even less than normal. His stomach growled. "You need to eat too, Rhenda. You're just as hungry as the rest of us."

Rhenda turned to face Adam. Her eyes were red and puffy. White lines streaked her face, where tears had formed pathways through the dirt and grease. She shook her ladle at Adam, her hand trembling. "Do you really know what it's like to be hungry? Have you ever gone for days without eating a single bite?"

Adam stared blankly in response, not sure what to say. "I missed dinner."

Rhenda paid no attention. "Do you know what it's like to watch your mother grow weaker and weaker, until she can't get out of bed, and then die for lack of food and water? Do you?"

Adam shook his head.

"Well, I do. I've seen it before, Adam. When storms destroyed our crops, I lived to tell the story. But Mother never did." She pushed back a greasy strand of hair and fidgeted with her apron. "Maybe I won't either ... this time."

Adam stirred his quickly cooling porridge. It hadn't occurred to him last night what the loss of their crops would mean. He wondered if Rhenda would die, or if everyone would. Doke had said that if their city didn't repent, they could expect even worse things to come.

Rhenda studied her hands. "Why, Adam? Are we really that bad? I know I don't keep all the laws or plant my seeds, but I try to live a good life. I try to be good to my husband and Camdin. Why would he want us to suffer this much?"

"Who?"

"The king! Does he think we are worthy of death?" She looked around the room, wide-eyed, like a hunted animal. "If he or his son knew what it was like to be in our shoes—to be hungry all the time—maybe things would be different. Maybe he doesn't even care."

"I'm going to try to find some answers today." Adam hoped his voice sounded reassuring.

"You said that before!" Rhenda burst into tears.

Feeling helpless to comfort her, Adam spooned three bites of porridge into his mouth and slipped out of the room with bulging cheeks. He almost collided with a servant, who shot him a questioning glance. Adam rushed past and hurried through the courtyard to the King's Road. There he paused to catch his breath and swallow his porridge.

Far off to his right, a handful of men picked their way through the burned-out fields, perhaps trying to see what could be salvaged. He turned to the city center on his left. Above the rooftops, the King's Stones poked into the sky. He took a few steps toward the stones then stopped. He put a foot forward, and then pulled it back.

His breath came in short gasps. *Why am I so afraid to go there?*

Finding no answer, he forced first one foot, then the other, forward. An eerie stillness lay over the village. He glanced at the houses as he passed.

Soon the majestic stones lay open to view. He could almost make out the words, but not quite. He glanced around. Was anyone watching him?

He halted. *What am I so afraid of? Words?* Surely, words couldn't be scarier than facing the Goiim last night. A new thought stirred in Adam's mind. *Perhaps I'm afraid of answers because I don't think I'll like them.*

Perhaps I'll have to give up my freedom.

Adam pressed forward. He would not turn back, even though he wanted to. Something was drawing him on, in spite of his fears. A growing longing to know the truth entered his soul. He clenched his fists and continued.

The road cut through the giant plaza then headed downhill toward the coast. The plaza was large enough to hold the entire population of the city when they gathered for Supplies Day—with ample room to spare. Around the edge of the plaza rose thirty-nine massive stones. The stones faced inward and ran in order from Adam's left all the way around.

Near one of these stones on the opposite side of the plaza stood the stranger Adam had seen from his window this morning. He propped his boot up on a carved bench and pulled back his hood. His face was young and covered with a trimmed, black beard. A crooked nose poked out. He paid no attention to Adam. His focus was absorbed in the message of the stone before him.

Adam faced the first stone on his left. He raised his gaze to the top, where the writing began, and read,

In the beginning, King Eliab created Aard and its inhabitants.

The statement was simple enough, and nothing Adam didn't already know. But the effect of those words was like a lamp coming on in a dark room. It was like real life had suddenly come into focus, and he had never seen it before.

"King Eliab created me." There was something profound in that truth. It made everything else seem trite by comparison. "The king is good. I am here because of him.

He wants to do me good, as well as the rest of the city. Why else would he make this place for us?"

Adam closed his eyes and sighed. "Why did I never see this before? I guess I wasn't ready to listen."

Adam continued reading. The stone spoke of four great rivers that flowed from the mountains to the sea, running freely through the land of Aard. It spoke of abundant food, the flowers, the birds, and even the presence of King Eliab among the people. The words filled Adam with longing.

Anxious to learn more, Adam read about the preparations for the covenant. The king wanted to live in Mount Eirene and be joined to the people in a special bond. A list of promises followed—he would bless them if they were faithful to the covenant. He would provide for every need, protect them from every enemy, and make their joy abound in absolute peace.

Then came a list of curses if the people broke the law. A storm would ruin their food. Adam swallowed. *Is that what Rhenda described?* If the people continued to rebel, they could expect destruction by their enemies:

"And I will turn my back upon this city,
and not my face," says the king,
"And I will give up my city to be destroyed
because they refused to listen to my voice."

Adam's stomach twisted into a knot. Was this what was happening? He moved to another stone and read the account of the signing of the covenant and the triumphant feast. But then the writing spoke of a Pre-Aardian islander, an enemy of the king. He had tricked the Aardians, telling them the king was depriving them of their liberty.

Liberty, Adam thought. *That means freedom.* He winced, remembering his hasty words: *This Adam will be free.*

The writing then spoke of the governor dishonoring King Eliab and casting away the seed he had been given. His rebellion, along with the rest of the Aardians, plunged the land into guilt, fear, and shame. The king departed for the mountains. The land became cursed, covered with thorns, and the prophesied judgments began to unfold.

The morning slipped away, and Adam kept reading. The stranger left. Someone else entered the plaza, but Adam was too engrossed in his reading to give the new arrival more than a passing glance. He began to skim, taking in several stories about people who were loyal, and how the king blessed them and retained his honor in the city through them.

The sun soon shone high overhead. Adam's head throbbed. His belly growled with hunger, but he ignored the pain and kept reading. He couldn't stop. There was something about reading the words of King Eliab that made Adam feel as though the king himself was whispering in his ear. Adam's ambitions now seemed trivial in comparison to knowing and serving such a king. He turned to walk toward the next stone, but something caught his eye.

Between the first and the second great stones, lifted up on a pedestal of sorts, was a smaller stone, about half Adam's height. He had missed it before. What gripped his attention this time was his name, scrawled in large, black letters across the bottom: **ADAM SONNEMAN**.

His heart thudded. *What in the island?* He approached the

stone and gave a sigh of relief. His heart returned to normal. This was the stone of the covenant. The name at the bottom was Grandfather's signature, not his, signed so long ago on that happy day.

"If only we could go back and start over," Adam mused.

But how can we? The people had broken the covenant. The king was angry. He was punishing them, and perhaps soon they would all die.

Adam cringed. He too was a criminal. He had eaten wedding berries. He'd lied. He'd quit school. Worse, he was in debt to the king's enemies.

The memory of Rhenda's puffy eyes and frightened questions flooded Adam's memory. He was supposed to be finding answers. "How can I?" he whispered, reaching out and touching the stone. "This covenant was the promise of life. Now it is the promise of—"

Adam choked on a sob before he could stop it. He stomped his foot and rubbed a hand across his burning eyes. It seemed like all he ever did these days was cry, and he hated to cry.

A hand touched his shoulder. "The promise of what?" asked a gentle voice.

Adam spun around. A man was stooping, looking into his eyes. Trickles of water, sparkling in the sunlight, shone in the man's eyes and ran down into his brown goatee.

"The promise of what, Adam?" he asked again.

It was Teacher.

ADAM III

Chapter 18

"Rivers of waters run down mine eyes, because they keep not thy law." Psalm 119:136

N
ever mind," Adam said quietly. "I'm sorry I—" His eyes widened. "Teacher! You're crying too. Why?"

"Don't be alarmed, Adam. It is a good thing to shed tears at the right time."

"I don't like to cry. I'm tired of being sad. When could there ever be a right time to cry?"

Teacher brushed a tear from Adam's cheek. "When our city rebels against her king. When the king is ignored for years without end. When the precious covenant that was intended to bring life instead becomes the promise of death. These are things worthy of being wept over."

Adam bowed his head.

"But I can tell you this," Teacher went on. "The ones who weep now are blessed, for they shall be comforted. Their sorrow shall be turned into joy when Mount Eirene is restored."

Adam looked up into Teacher's eyes. "How can you be so sure?"

He smiled. "By faith."

"You mean, you just know it deep down in your heart?"

"No, Adam. I mean that I believe what my father has written."

Adam pondered. Teacher sometimes spoke of the king as the city's father. Adam also remembered Roberts saying something similar.

Teacher held out his hand. "Come with me, and I'll show you."

Adam took Teacher's hand as he used to when he was a small child. It felt safe to be with Teacher. Hand in hand, they crossed the plaza to the opposite side.

They passed by the King's Fountain, which stood in the center of the plaza. It was an enormous, white-marble structure with multiple tiers and a great spout at the top. Stairs along two sides led up to a platform that ran all the way around the fountain.

Adam dragged his finger through the dust in passing and sighed. The fountain had been gorgeous at one time, no doubt. Perfectly white and full of water. But now? It was dry, and had been dry ever since the king left.

"See what is written here." Teacher pointed near the bottom of one of the stones.

Rejoice with Mount Eirene,
And be glad with her all you that love her:
Rejoice for joy with her,

All you who mourn for her.

"In this place it tells you why," Teacher said.

"Behold, I will extend peace to her
like a river," says the king.
"As one whom his mother comforts,
so will I comfort you;
and you shall be comforted in Mount Eirene."

"Do you see now? That is a promise from my father."

Adam smiled for a second and then sighed. "But what about the covenant? Is it true that it is the promise of death?"

Teacher turned and looked at the fountain. When he spoke, his voice sounded far away. "Yes, Adam. It will mean death."

Despite the burning heat of the sun, an icy tingle crept up Adam's spine. He thought of Rhenda and her obvious fear of death. His own fear rose. He searched Teacher's face. "But why? Are we really so bad that we must die?"

Teacher nodded. He looked deep into Adam's eyes, speaking with a passion that caught Adam by surprise. "Yes, indeed. It is a grievous offense to rebel against the king. He is Lord, Adam. His word is true and right. He must enforce what he says, or else the city will ruin itself. Every crime is a matter of treason. And treason must be punished with death. There is no hope for deliverance until you see that."

Adam looked at the palms of his hands and traced the scars with the tip of his finger. He thought about his own crimes. He remembered all the promises he had made, and how he had never been able to keep them. *I tried so hard!*

"It isn't fair!" He balled his hands and squeezed until his knuckles ached. "It isn't right."

"What isn't right?"

Adam pushed against the ground with his foot. "It isn't right to make us follow these laws—ones we can't even keep—and then kill us for it. It's unreasonable. I can't do it."

After a long silence, Adam looked up. Sorrow filled Teacher's eyes, something too deep for Adam to understand. He knew, however, that his words had hurt Teacher. He wanted to say he was sorry, but he might never get another chance to say what he thought. "Isn't it unreasonable?"

Teacher gestured toward the great stones. "Which of these laws is unreasonable, Adam? Which is not good?"

Adam dug his foot even harder against the ground. "It isn't reasonable to make us plant seeds on the Mount of Humility. I tried my best, but I failed. I don't think anyone could ever do it." He rubbed his arm across his eyes and stood waiting.

"Did you read the king's instructions first?"

Adam's mouth tightened. He stared straight ahead and said nothing.

"My father never meant for anyone to go alone," Teacher said. "His help has always been available for those who ask. Is that unreasonable?"

Adam knew he was in the wrong. But he had come too far to turn back without having his say. "Then why isn't he here? Why did the king abandon us if he expects us to trust in him?"

"Did he truly abandon you?"

This conversation is so frustrating! "Didn't he?"

Teacher turned his gaze toward the bright sky. "Do you remember what I told you about the sun?" He shaded his eyes.

Adam's eyes followed Teacher's. "You mean when you said that night doesn't come because the sun goes away, but because our planet spins away from the sun?"

How could he forget? He had tried to explain it to Grandfather and Roberts at dinner one evening. Grandfather gave him a lecture, demonstrating with a dinner roll and the table how the sun moved across the sky. Roberts declared, "The world will end in a bad way when young people get such ideas," and stuffed his own roll in his mouth in one bite.

"Yes, Adam," Teacher replied. "I am glad you remember. It does not appear from this viewpoint that our planet is moving at all, does it? And yet it is. Every night, Aard turns away from the sun, not the sun from Aard. In the same way, the city has turned away from the king, not the other way around. It is not the king's fault the people remain in darkness. It is the city that has abandoned the king."

"Isn't the king angry, though?"

"Of course. His love is far too great for him not to be."

Adam paused in thought. "Are you ever angry, Teacher?"

"Yes, Adam. Do you think I could be passive? I and my father are one. Even now, my spirit burns within me."

"You don't *look* angry."

Teacher smiled. "You are thinking of the wrong kinds of anger. There is more than one kind, and there is a good kind. I promise you, Adam, that my father's anger is only the good kind."

Adam didn't understand, but he would consider it later. "What kind of things make you angry?"

Teacher looked at him for a long time. His face bore a mixture of love and sorrow, as well as something strong and penetrating. Adam turned his eyes downward and waited.

"I am angry whenever my father is dishonored. I am angry when my people hurt themselves, and even angrier when they hurt one another. I am angry when people turn others away from me and from my father."

Adam remembered the night he had accepted the coin. "Do you mean like Grandfather?"

Teacher raised an eyebrow. "Was it your grandfather who turned Liptor away?"

Adam winced. Teacher's unexpected words struck his conscience like a hand slap. *He's talking about me.* It had never occurred to Adam that anyone would care about Liptor, much less that Teacher would blame Adam for his cousin's departure. He clenched and unclenched his fists.

"Is there any hope left?" Adam whispered. "I'm a criminal and condemned to die. My whole family and city are guilty of forsaking the king. The king is angry, and so are you. That ... that *covenant!*" Adam pointed at the small stone across the plaza. "It is set in stone and condemns us to die."

He looked up with eyes full of desperation. "Is there any hope at all that we can be restored to the king?"

Teacher took him by the shoulders. "There is tremendous hope for you, and for this city. That is why I am here."

He showed Adam another stone. "See this prophecy?"

"Behold the days come," says the king,
"When I will make a new covenant
with the people of Mount Eirene,
Not the covenant which I made
With their fathers, the one they broke,
Even though I was
Exceedingly good to them.
But this is the covenant
I will make in those days:
I will put my laws into their hearts,
And write it within them.
I will be their king,
And they shall be my people."

A wave of comfort washed over Adam. "But what does it mean? Is it a second chance to start over? What if we break the covenant again?"

Teacher beamed. "It is a different—and better—kind of covenant, Adam. It will replace the first one. It is a promise of transformed lives, of a people who will be glad to please my father, when his laws are engraved in their hearts. It is a promise of eternal life. All those who are part of this covenant will live forever, and this gift can never be taken away."

It was a large bite to swallow. Adam's thoughts spun. "Can it be true?"

"It is a promise from my father, and it will come to pass. Look what else He promises."

*Their sins and iniquities will I
remember no more.*

"My father will forgive every crime. This is good news."

Adam shook his head. Surely there was something more to it than this. "When will these things come to pass? Will I still be alive?"

Teacher's eyes filled with pain, and he rubbed his wrists. "The first covenant must be fulfilled before that day. When it is finished, then the new covenant will be ready."

Adam sighed. "That means we still have to pay the punishment. We must die."

"It means death, yes. But trust me, Adam. My father has a wonderful plan. Come and see what he has prepared."

He led Adam farther around the circle, to where a second covenant stone cut exactly like the first one sat on a similar pedestal. Words of the new covenant were written there, along with other words, but there was a notable blank space at the bottom.

"What is the blank space for?" Adam asked.

"It is blank because it has not yet been signed. It is waiting for the second Adam."

Adam's eyes widened. "Surely you don't mean me?"

Teacher grinned. "No, but this city needs a new representative. When Adam, your grandfather, signed the original covenant, it was his promise on behalf of the whole city that the people would follow the king. But he broke that promise. Now, everyone he represents is bound to his fate."

Teacher scratched his small goatee. "When the second Adam comes and lives a perfect life, all whom he represents will enjoy the blessings of the eternal covenant."

"Who can live a perfect life?" Adam scoffed. "No one can do that, or even come close."

"Do you trust me, Adam?"

Adam considered, then nodded. "I suppose so. You're the teacher, after all. I'm just a boy."

"Good." Teacher held out his hand. "Then follow me."

Adam reached out his hand then paused. "Where are you going?"

Disappointment passed over Teacher's face. "To the Mount of Humility. Do you trust me?"

Adam looked at the mountain in the distance. His heart pounded violently inside him. He wiped his sweaty palms on his breeches. "I … " He swallowed. "I can't."

"You can if I am with you."

"My p-parents died trying to reach that mountain," Adam stammered. "They were loyal to the king, and see what it got them?"

"I know. I was with them in their final moments."

"You *were*?" Adam said in a hushed voice. "Is it true? Were they killed by Goiim?"

"It is true, but their labor was not in vain. Their reward is eternal because they trusted in me and my father."

"What good is a reward if they're dead?"

"They are not dead now. They live with my father until he restores Mount Eirene. Do you not know that the king has the power to give life? You think so much about the power he has to give death. It would be no power at all but for the power he has first to give life."

"Can I see them?"

"Not at this time." He held out his hand once more. "Do you trust me?"

Adam's gaze darted from the mountain to Teacher and back to the mountain. He stepped back. "I trust you," he said, trembling. "But you will have to go to the mountain alone."

Fighting to hold back tears, Adam turned and ran back through the plaza.

ADAM III

Chapter 19

"My little daughter lieth at the point of death."
Mark 5:23

The sun beat down without mercy on Adam's shoulders as he headed for the fields. He had just eaten lunch, but his stomach still knotted with hunger. It also twisted with uncertainty about what he would face. He studied the bucket in his hands—the Carpenters' bucket.

Maybe they wouldn't miss the bucket if he never brought it back. Perhaps Christy's father wouldn't remember giving it to Adam the night before. But the memory of his frantic eyes made Adam think the man would never forget.

Besides, doing something right eased Adam's conscience after rejecting Teacher.

Adam surveyed the field for at least ten minutes to be sure there was no sign of Schala. Then he hurried through the ruined funja, kicking at the blackened stubble he had watered so often. He crossed the stream and scrambled up the bank on the other side near Christy's house. Would Mr. Carpenter understand why Adam hadn't returned last night?

He scuffed the dirt. *Probably not. He'll no doubt be angry.*

More thoughts whirled. What had Teacher meant about different kinds of anger? Adam tried to distract his troubled brain by imagining the different kinds.

Grandfather certainly got angry. His anger was like a stormy sea, threatening for a while and then powerful in its damage when it struck. Roberts' anger was more like a boiling pot, not powerful but always bubbling over. Pots were for food, which somehow seemed appropriate for the old kettle-belly. Adam smiled.

Christy could be angry at times too. He imagined she was something like the stream. It was cool and refreshing, but if he threw rocks into it, he expected to get wet.

He smiled a little more. "I hope I can see Christy," he mused. "I wonder what she would say if I told her everything that's happened."

Then Adam tried to imagine the anger of the king. He thought about a river, the sea, rain, and fire, but nothing seemed to match. Perhaps the king's anger was the same as Teacher's. He frowned. That was difficult to picture as well. If there was a good kind of anger like Teacher said, Adam hoped it would be the kind Mr. Carpenter showed.

Coarse patches of green grass dotted the Carpenters' yard. No damage here. But wisps of smoke rose from the back, where they kept the animals. Adam hesitated, daring himself to approach. Old Samuel chewed on a floppy flanna plant, staring at him.

He scowled at the goat and marched up to the house.

He gave a timid knock at the door. When no one responded, he pounded. The noise of scurrying feet followed, and the door was thrown wide open.

Mrs. Carpenter stood there in her large, checkered dress. She stared at him, wide-eyed, as if she expected someone else. Her dark tresses were matted this morning, and wrinkles lined her delicate forehead.

Her face relaxed into a pain-creased smile. "It's good to see you, Adam. We were concerned about you when you didn't come back last night. Christy will be glad to know that you're fine."

She pulled up the corner of her apron and wiped her red eyes and nose.

Adam looked away. Was everyone crying this morning? "I brought back the bucket."

Mr. Carpenter appeared behind his wife. "You're a little late." His blue eyes stabbed accusation at Adam. He made no attempt to hide the hard edge in his voice. "I hope you're satisfied with whatever you thought was more important than keeping your word."

"I tried. I really did. But Roberts grabbed me. He wouldn't let me come back. I didn't know what to do."

Mr. Carpenter sighed and bowed his head. "I'm sorry, Adam. I was wrong to be angry with you. Will you forgive me?"

It felt strange to hear an adult admit being wrong. Adam bobbed his head, afraid to open his mouth.

Mrs. Carpenter smiled and reached for the bucket. "Thank you so much for trying. And thank you for returning our bucket."

Adam nodded again. He peeked around the Carpenters and into the house. Christy's little brothers stared back at him with wide eyes. "Is Christy here? I was hoping to see her for a minute."

The blood drained from Mrs. Carpenter's face. She touched her husband on the arm. The man stared blankly in front of him and licked his lips. "She was—" He stopped, swallowing hard. "She—" He closed his mouth tight and said no more.

Mrs. Carpenter took a deep breath. "Christy was badly burned in the fire last night. Unless the king intervenes, we … we don't think she'll make it."

Adam gasped. "Oh, no! I'm sorry. I didn't know." He longed to say something comforting, but nothing reassuring came out. He felt afraid to speak, and equally afraid to leave.

Mrs. Carpenter put the bucket back in his hands. "We could use a little more water if you would like to help."

Thankful to be of use, Adam took the bucket and ran back up the path. His mind felt numb. His footsteps thumped against the hard earth, and his breath came in short spurts.

Christy is dying! No wonder her father had been so urgent last night. Would bringing the water have made a difference? Perhaps she would die even now because Adam had failed her. No!

His hands shook as he filled the bucket and climbed the bank. A wave of shame passed over him, and he feared to go back to the house. He didn't want the Carpenters to see him.

If only I could have broken free last night and brought her the water!

Old Samuel still guarded the yard. Adam avoided making eye contact with the goat and rushed past. Water sloshed out at every step. He eased the bucket onto the porch and gave a loud rap on the door.

Without waiting for an answer, he turned and bolted for the road.

ASTERIK

Chapter 20

"And he was there in the wilderness ... tempted of Satan; ... and the angels ministered unto him." Mark 1:13

Can you see anything yet?"

Asterik peered around the rock, his fingers dropping from the velvet pouch encircling his neck to the polished hilt of his dagger. Nothing moved along the opposite ridge. He scanned the gnarled tree trunks and dark crevices that covered the rocky face. So far, the Dragonians had not shown themselves.

The stench of burnt flesh engulfed him, and he twisted back into hiding, his nostrils stinging. He shut his gray eyes against the dark sky and took a deep breath. "I hate this war."

He had spent the last month at home tending the king's gardens. But yesterday Eliab had sent their troop out, this time to the Mount of Humility.

The king had met with Asterik beforehand and given him

the pouch he now wore around his neck.

It was for the king's son.

Asterik touched the pouch and opened it slightly. The smell of fresh mint chased away the oppressive air that hovered over him. He slid his fingers in farther, feeling the soft touch of the different herbs. He counted them for the fifteenth time and got the same number as each time before.

"Did you see anything?" Asterik's companion Malakan was persistent.

"Nothing yet." Asterik dragged his palms across his smooth, dark hair and over his face. "But I know they're out there." He opened his eyes.

Malakan shifted his weight. His rough vest scraped against the rock they were both leaning on. "You can feel it too?" He rubbed massive fingers through his tangle of tight, blond curls.

Asterik nodded. "There must be hundreds of them."

"There are more with us than with them." Malakan rubbed his hand along the shaft of his bow and shifted positions.

"I'm glad you're the warrior and not me."

"Check again if you can see anything." Malakan's green eyes sparkled like emeralds. He drew out an arrow and held it to the string.

Asterik sighed. "It won't make any difference. We can't do a thing until Michael gives us the signal. See what he's doing."

Their rock stood halfway up the final ridge of the Mount of Humility. Asterik had positioned himself closer to the valley, while Malakan kept the ground closest to their commander. He grunted and slid over to his side to look. "He's still waiting. I suppose we'll—"

Asterik touched Malakan's arm, signing "quiet," and pointed to his ear. The rattle of rocks sliding down from the opposite ridge could clearly be heard. Spinning toward his side, Asterik took another look. Sure enough, a solitary figure had come over the ridge and was picking his way into the dark valley.

Malakan pushed up against Asterik and looked over his shoulder. "Who is that? There's hardly anything left of him. He must be starved."

With every step the man took, Asterik's fingers clenched and unclenched his pouch. He shuddered. "It is our Lord Immanuel."

Malakan drew in a sharp breath. "What do you suppose–"

A jovial voice cut into Malakan's words, and a white-haired man emerged on the opposite ridge. He was hunched over and extended his hand to Immanuel. "I am glad to see you. Please give me a hand." The words carried distinctly across the silent valley.

"I'd like to give *him* a hand," Malakan growled, gritting his teeth.

Asterik motioned him to silence. He hated Father Dementiras as much as Malakan did, but he wanted to hear the conversation.

Immanuel pressed forward, brushing past the old man. He kept his gaze fixed on the final peak.

Father Dementiras stretched out his arm like a cat and caught Immanuel by the sleeve. "I advise you to listen to me … if you really are who you claim to be."

Immanuel pulled his arm away and kept descending. The effort made him lose his balance. He slid through the loose rocks and fell backward, catching himself on his arm. He lay there, breathing heavily. Then he rose, with his face still turned toward the peak.

"He's fatigued." Asterik's fingers played with the herbs, counting them again.

Father Dementiras overtook his prey with ease and kept pace beside him. "Really, lad, you're going to hurt yourself this way. Look at you! You're nearly starved. None of the people in the city are as hungry as you are, no matter how much they complain. Stay a minute and eat something." He placed his hand on Immanuel's shoulder.

Immanuel neither looked at Father Dementiras nor acknowledged his presence. He shook loose from his grip and continued on into the valley.

Father Dementiras bounded after him. "Is this what your father wants? He's not the kind to make people hurt, is he? Besides, if anyone deserves to eat, it's you."

Immanuel did not answer.

"What is he trying to do?" asked Malakan.

"Immanuel is fasting," Asterik replied. "It must be part of the king's plan. That serpent is trying to prevent him."

"What happens if Immanuel gives in?"

Asterik swallowed. "He cannot give in, Malakan. It would be against the king. All would be lost."

Father Dementiras pursued Immanuel. "Look, no one is meant to come here alone. Where are all the people who should be here now planting *their* seeds?" He shook his head. "They're in their homes eating dinner. They don't deserve any love. Is it right for you to be out here hungry?"

Malakan's cheeks burned bright red. "Since when does *that* one know anything about what's right?"

"Or about love." Asterik leaned his head against his fist on the rock. His stomach convulsed. "Why do you let him do this to you, Immanuel?" he whispered. "Please, oh king, help him now. Please help him."

"Where did he get *that*?" Malakan pounded the rock.

Asterik's head snapped up. He peered around the rock. Father Dementiras held out an orange, a beautiful, bright spot of color in the lifeless valley.

"It isn't right!" Asterik reached for his dagger. His dry tongue, stuck against the roof of his mouth, longed for the fruit. *How much more must my master be suffering?*

Immanuel's eyes shone. He broke his silence and spoke in a tone that reverberated throughout the valley. "It is written, 'Man shall not live by food alone, but by every word of the king.'"

Malakan slapped Asterik on the back. "Ha, that's the way. Let him have it."

Asterik smiled and squeezed his dagger.

Father Dementiras' face turned red. He stood glowering when the king's son moved on. Then letting his face relax, he lifted his left hand and gave a signal. Sweet yet sickening music began to hum in the valley.

Asterik felt its hypnotic power at once. His body responded against his will, relaxing his mind and drawing him into the rhythmic vibrations. He slapped his face and began counting the herbs once more. *Keep focused, keep focused*, he ordered himself.

Father Dementiras burst into laughter. "Ho, ho," he shouted at Immanuel. "You have more endurance than I thought." He caught up and clapped him roundly on the shoulder. "You are a good man, lad, a very good man. Not another person in Mount Eirene would ever stand up for the king like you."

The steep path had forced Immanuel to a snail's pace. Yet he ignored his pursuer, putting one foot in front of the other. His face sometimes twitched with a depth of emotion Asterik could not understand. He recognized the clenched jaw, however, and silently cheered Immanuel on.

The music became stronger, throbbing with an eerie, whining buzz. Immanuel shook his head several times and looked up. His lips moved, but he made no sound.

"It is also written," Father Dementiras said, "that the king will send his servants to protect you, even from stumbling on a rock."

The old man's eyes scanned the ridge near the place where Asterik and Malakan hid. "If you are truly the king's son, then you need not torment yourself about descending this embankment. Call for your servants and then leap to the bottom of the valley. They will catch you in their arms and even carry you to the top of the mountain if you want. Will they not?"

Immanuel stood still, gazing from the valley below to the towering peak before him.

"Don't you trust the king's word?" Father Dementiras grinned. "Surely you wouldn't hesitate to put your complete confidence in what he has written."

The music swelled.

Asterik's heart raced. *How dare he say such things?* Immanuel always did what the king had written. A sudden vision filled his mind—the troop racing forward to catch their leader and carry him to the heights of the peak. *I'll lead the way!*

He took a step, but Malakan seized him by the shoulder and drew him back. His green eyes blazed. He shook his head.

Asterik grimaced and covered his ears. The music was affecting him.

Immanuel's voice rang out. "It is also written, 'You shall not put the lord your king to the test.'" He burst into rapid, jolting steps to the bottom of the valley. The momentum forced him against a dead tree, where he stood to rest. His sides heaved with exertion.

Fingering the herbs in his pouch, Asterik fixed his moist eyes on his master far below. *If only I could go to him!* His heart pounded with every painful step Immanuel took.

Father Dementiras remained standing where Immanuel had left him. He kept his gaze fixed on his prey. Fire danced in his eyes.

Malakan slid back into place to check with their commander. Asterik raised his eyebrows at him. In answer, Malakan imitated Michael's position, raising his hand above him and holding it there, ready to signal a charge at any moment.

The throbbing of the music deepened to a dull roar. The high, buzzing whine became a whistling scream. Asterik returned his hands to his ears.

Father Dementiras raised his hand a second time. The air

filled with hissing and howling, a horrible din that accented the thrum of music.

Malakan's eyes were riveted on his commander, his nerves clearly strained.

Asterik looked back into the valley. Immanuel had climbed almost halfway up the mountain. Sweat flowed down his lord's brow. Horrible cuts marred his arms and legs. Immanuel's breathing came slow and forced. His lips continued to move silently. But through the pain, his eyes gleamed with light, never wavering from the goal.

Not even for a moment.

An explosion from the opposite ridge filled the valley with smoke. Asterik recoiled behind his rock, coughing against the putrid, burning odor. He waved his hands and squinted to see through the smoke.

A hideous, fiery dragon soared across the valley. The wind from his wings fanned the smoke, creating miniature whirlwinds that tore past Asterik. Flames poured from the monster's gaping jaws. The beast swooped against the mountainside, heaved up massive boulders with his claws, and hurled them into the valley below.

Asterik turned to Malakan. His companion's arrow was drawn to his ear, but his eyes remained fixed on Michael. Still no signal.

The dragon circled and landed on the path, blocking Immanuel's way. The beast sat only one good arrow's flight away, but Malakan didn't fire. Asterik's fingers fumbled with his dagger. He looked toward his master for a signal.

Immanuel advanced.

The dragon lowered his head. A guttural noise vibrated

from his throat. "This is as far as you go."

Immanuel kept walking.

The dragon opened his wings and lifted off, moving back and coming down again. "The city is mine. It rejected the king's rule long ago. I alone can give you the authority you desire."

The path led straight toward the dragon. Immanuel's pace never slackened.

Smoke seeped through the dragon's scales. Fire flicked out of his mouth. The serpent dug his claws into the rocky cliff and leaned out. "If you go forward, you will find death. Even if you accomplish your little mission, the city will fall. Your own covenant demands the city's death. Would you be the prince of a dead city? Is that what you want?"

The king's son was coming closer, his eyes shining. The hideous music, the hissing, and the howling rose in crescendo.

"Worship me, Immanuel, and I will make you ruler over the entire city this very day."

Malakan made a choking noise. Asterik jumped to his side. "Is it time?"

But Michael stood as resolutely as ever, his muscular forearm raised above his head. His other hand clenched a great sword. His teeth were bared, his golden locks flapped against his sweat-soaked head, and tears poured down his face. He too was waiting for a signal.

Malakan's bow slid to the ground. A reddish glow appeared in the corners of his eyes. "Ruler of the entire city," he mumbled. "This very day." He glanced at Asterik then shook violently. He pounded his fist against the rock and gripped his bow once more.

"Worship me, Immanuel." The dragon reared back. Flames belched from his mouth.

For the first time, Immanuel shifted his gaze from the peak and locked eyes with his enemy, the serpent. The voice of the prince resounded throughout the valley. "Be gone, dragon! For it is written, 'You shall worship the lord your king, and him only you shall serve.'"

The dragon let out a tremendous roar and flung himself into the air, hurling rocks. Then turning his back, he flew away into the distance.

Immanuel remained where he stood. His sides heaved as he gulped air. Then he pressed toward the peak. He stumbled. A silence far worse than the horrible music covered the mountain. Everything seemed to hold its breath. Immanuel rose.

Asterik wiped his eyes against his sleeve and nearly squeezed the pouch of herbs into a pulp. When would Michael give the signal? Surely they could help now!

But Immanuel was already at the peak. As if on cue, the dark clouds covering the valley parted, and the last light of day broke through. The prince's feet plodded on the final steps. He rose above the rock and stood silhouetted against the sun.

Asterik watched his lord turn to look south toward Mount Eirene. Then he turned toward the mountains and his first home in the city of the king. With trembling hands, he reached into the folds of his thrick and drew out a seed. Lifting it high above his head, he waved the seed in a sign of triumph.

The sun dipped behind the mountains, leaving everything in twilight. Immanuel knelt and pulled at the rocks with his bare hands. He stopped and wiped his face. Pushing away the sweat, he plunged his hands into the dirt.

Shadowy forms rose on the opposite ridge. Immanuel pushed the seed into the hole he had dug and pulled the loose earth and rock over it. He rose, wobbling back and forth. With his last bit of strength, he lifted his empty hand before collapsing on the ground.

The hideous music exploded across the valley, followed by shouts of the inrushing enemy.

But Immanuel's empty hand had been the signal.

Michael shouted and led the charge. It was answered by Malakan and a hundred others. The dark figures on the other side of the valley turned and fled. Swords flashed. Glistening arrows filled the sky.

Asterik glanced at the islanders running past him, each one clothed in the gold and blue of the king. But he did not join them. His heart throbbed for one thing only—his lord.

He raced from rock to rock, leaping and running until he reached the peak. Dropping to his knees, he cradled Immanuel's head in his arm.

"My Lord," he whispered, choking on his words. He tried again. "Immanuel, drink this, please."

He pushed the water skin between his master's lips.

Immanuel drank, and his eyes blinked open. Then they closed. A faint wrinkle that resembled a painful smile passed over his face. He released the water skin and fought for breath before taking it in his teeth and drinking again.

Asterik's fingers flew in and out of the pouch. He

crushed up a handful of mint and held it under Immanuel's nose. Then he was pulling out each plant King Eliab had given him and mixing them under his experienced hands.

Immanuel pulled himself to a sitting position. "Thank you, Asterik. I knew you would come. I feel refreshed already."

"You won, Master. You won the victory." Asterik balled up two leaves between his fingers and slipped them into Immanuel's mouth. "Is this ... is this the end now?"

Immanuel chewed in silence, eyes closed. He furrowed his brow.

"I mean, will the war be over soon?" Asterik asked. "Will there be peace?"

Immanuel shook his head. "Not yet. Peace will come in my father's time."

Asterik looked away. "Can you promise me one thing?" When Immanuel didn't answer, Asterik continued. "Will you promise you will never make me stand by again while you suffer? I would rather die a thousand deaths."

Immanuel opened his eyes. "I cannot make you that promise." He took the islander's hand, infusing him with strength and comfort. "I can promise you this, though. When the war is over, we will rejoice together. There will never be suffering again. I promise."

Asterik gave a feeble smile. He had run to comfort his lord, but now his lord was comforting him instead.

Immanuel turned and looked back across the forest toward Mount Eirene. "For the present there will be war. Be strong, Asterik. Be strong."

ADAM III

Chapter 21

"Who shall ascend into the hill of the LORD? or who shall stand in his holy place? He that hath clean hands and a pure heart." Psalm 24:3-4

Adam urged his horse into a gallop. The distance was greater than he had anticipated, and not much time remained. He didn't want to imagine what would happen if he were late for dinner and Grandfather found out where he had been.

And if Roberts found out Adam had borrowed his spotted nag without asking? *I'll never hear the end of it.*

He rushed around a bend in the King's Road, and the towering golden gate came into view once more. This time Adam was sure it was close by, and not fooling him as it had earlier with its enormous height. He turned the mare into the shade of a nearby tree and tied her to a branch. He would go the rest of the distance on foot.

He inhaled deep breaths and eased them out again. His

hands felt sweaty, and he wiped them on his thrick. The letter was still there. He felt the folded papla leaf poking his side through the thrick's pocket. But what chance did he have to deliver it?

"I wish I had more time," he murmured.

Perhaps if Adam waited until the end of the week, when he wasn't required to work in the fields. He shook his head. *No!* What good would that do? Christy probably didn't have that long. Maybe it was too late even now.

The thought of Christy dying drove Adam out of his resting place and onto the last stretch of the King's Road. It led right up to the gate. The guards could no doubt see him, looking down from above, and he kept his feet to a steady, confident walk. What would they think about a boy coming to their city? Did anyone else ever visit?

His thoughts spun, trying to imagine what to say. How did one speak to Pre-Aardians? It was too late now to think of anything clever to say.

Adam stood before the solid golden gate, which rose as high as he could see. He didn't look at the guards that peered out from windows high above. Instead, he went straight to a small door built into the gate. Determined to make a good impression, he stood tall and thudded the golden knocker against the door.

An islander opened the door and stepped out. His muscular frame was trimmed in bright blue and gold with a large crown emblazoned on the front of his breastplate. Adam couldn't help gaping at the man's fullness of face and the glory of his appearance.

"May I help you with something?" The guard kept his

spear erect and non-threatening, but he raised an eyebrow and planted his feet.

Adam swallowed past the lump in his throat. He put his hand on his side and felt the letter's edges through his thrick. "I would like to speak to the king."

The guard's mouth twitched with a subtle smile, and he relaxed his spear. "I'm afraid that won't be possible, son. No one from beyond this gate is permitted to see his Excellency without a mediator."

"What do you mean?" Adam tried to hide the tremor in his voice.

The guard bent down. "The king is holy. He is set apart from all that defiles and will have no fellowship with those who rebel against him. The only way he will receive you is if someone completely loyal goes to him on your behalf."

"I don't have a mediator, and I doubt I could ever find one in Mount Eirene."

"Then there's no use trying to see King Eliab." The guard straightened, apparently to resume his post.

"But I have to," Adam pleaded. "It's a matter of life and death. My friend Christy will probably die. The king is the only one who has the power to heal her."

The smile disappeared from the guard's face. He looked out over the road toward Mount Eirene. "I'm sorry, son, but there isn't anything I can do. Orders are orders, and I'm not about to go against the king."

Adam squirmed. "Isn't there any way you can make an exception?"

"No!" The guard's jaw set like iron. "I can never make an exception to the king's rule. If I disobeyed even once, I would forever be guilty of breaking his law. I will never do that."

Then he sighed. "Perhaps something can be done for your situation, however. I'll see what my commander says. No promises." He disappeared through the open door.

Adam slid over to where he could peek inside. A display of brilliant colors dazzled him. Lush green grass danced in the breeze next to sparkling fountains of water. Flowers of every hue poked out of bushes, trees, and vines. The fragrance of their blossoms invigorated him.

He gasped. There were even peach trees!

Adam jumped out of the way and stumbled backward when several men appeared. They passed through the doorway, with the original guard following, and walked straight up to Adam.

He gulped. Had these men seen him peering beyond the gate? What would they say?

A short man with a white mustache looked Adam over. "This one wants to speak to the king?"

"That is what he said," answered the first guard.

"Is this so?" The man bored Adam with a dark, somber gaze.

Adam nodded.

"Do you have a mediator?"

Adam stiffened. "No, sir."

The man pulled on the corner of his mustache. "Do you realize that no one from your side has seen the king since the rebellion?"

I didn't know. But he didn't think saying "no" would help his cause. He stood there, eyes wide and jaw tight. *The rebellion.* He had never thought of Grandfather's decision in those terms.

The man raised an eyebrow. "Show me your hands."

Adam extended his palms with a sigh of relief. If they wanted to search him, he had nothing to hide.

The small man jumped back, his eyes wide. "I never—" He broke off.

The others exchanged uncomfortable glances.

Adam looked at his palms. Hideous scars crisscrossed humped-up callouses. Most noticeable, however, was the nasty maroon color his skin had become. He jerked his hands back and clenched them into balls at his sides. He'd become so accustomed to the changes that he had stopped thinking there was anything wrong.

The man with the mustache stepped forward. A scowl carved into his forehead above bushy eyebrows. He gripped Adam's shoulders. "Listen to me, son. The lands behind these walls are pure and good. We could never let them be defiled by someone who has sided with the enemy. You should fear for your life, coming to this city with hands like that."

Adam glanced behind him. Perhaps he should run. But then what? Would they pursue him? Worse, what if Christy died? The king was her only hope.

Reaching inside his thrick, he pulled out the letter. "Then can you please give this to the king?" He thrust the letter into the man's hands.

The islander held out the folded papla leaf by his fingertips and kept it at arm's length. He sucked in a breath through his nose and read the lettering, which was scrawled across the outside in Adam's most careful handwriting, "To his majesty, King Eliab."

The man turned the letter over in his hands. He tugged at the sealing string but left the letter folded. With a backward glance at Adam, he drew aside the other three men to talk.

In the stillness, Adam heard a sweet sound. A bird! It sang in a high-pitched trill that stirred his heart. Or was he imagining it? He strained to hear more. The sound came from inside the gates. *Oh, if only the bird would fly where I could see it!*

The men returned. "The king is exceedingly gracious," the mustached leader said, "and we do not always know what he will say. He may accept your letter or reject it, according to his pleasure. We will try to take it to him." He paused. "There is something we would like to ask in return, however."

Another, much-taller man stepped forward. "There are things we are eager to look into. Things we do not understand … about the prophecies."

"The prophecies?" Adam asked, confused.

The tall man nodded. With each word he spoke, he grew more excited. "The prophecies in the King's Stones tell of a servant who will be perfect, like none other in your city. He will judge the city and reign over it, restoring it to the king forever. We can't wait for this to happen, but there are some prophecies that confuse us."

Adam bit his lip. *What does any of this have to do with me?*

The man's forehead wrinkled. "The king also says the people will all be righteous, but … excuse me for saying so, not even one of your people has ever been truly righteous."

"At least not that we know of," the mustached man put in. "In fact, the city seems worse now than ever before."

"We want to know why the king promises that your people will reign with him forever," the tall man said. "Not even the most faithful of his Pre-Aardian servants have been given this promise. It doesn't make sense."

It didn't make sense to Adam, either. Nothing about this conversation made sense.

The leader with the mustache squinted. "What do the Stones mean when they say, 'He was wounded for our transgressions, and bruised for our iniquities'? Who is the king talking about? Who is wounded, and how can he bear people's sins for them?"

Sweat trickled down the back of Adam's neck. He could hardly catch a breath. This was his chance to impress these men, but he couldn't grasp what they were asking, let alone invent an answer.

"Why are you asking me?" he finally blurted. These people knew far more than he ever dreamed of knowing.

The tall man cocked his head. "Aren't you one of Immanuel's students? Doesn't he explain these things?"

Adam dug his fingernails into his palms, fighting to come up with something he could say. Yes, Teacher always talked like this. Adam had memorized piles of information, but he had never made an effort to understand it.

He was saved from having to answer when a trumpet blast sounded from behind the gate. A messenger rushed through the door and saluted the short man with the mustache. "Your honor, an order just came through to prepare the gate. An escort will be riding out within the hour."

The man gnawed the corner of his mustache. "Who are they bringing?"

"A little girl from the outskirts of Mount Eirene, your honor. She was burned in a fire two days ago and has died from her wounds just this afternoon."

ADAM III

Chapter 22

"All we like sheep have gone astray." Isaiah 53:6

A cool night breeze brushed Adam's face when he stepped outside. He closed his eyes, feeling the air tug at his sweaty hair. The courtyard of his home ordinarily looked barren, but tonight—in the light of a full moon—it looked ancient and ghostly.

Charging through the front gate, he pelted down the King's Road and then through the fields. Pale, broken stubs that had once been a promising harvest whispered to him their story of loss and death. Only the trickle of water in the creek broke the silence.

Adam sat beside the water and pushed his back against a firm spot in the bank. Bracing his arms against his knees, he bowed his head into them. Perhaps now the tears would release. They burned behind his eyelids, and it didn't matter if they poured out. No one would see.

But his tears refused to come.

His mind whirled from one thought to another. He'd ridden the brown mare hard every step from the gate, barely escaping friendly fire from a band of returning Eirenian soldiers. In spite of his raw emotions, Adam had forced himself to the dinner table on time.

"And what do I get from Grandfather?" he asked himself.

Concern? Appreciation for his work? No. Grandfather barked at him for slouching at the table, for not showing respect, and for coming to the table a sweaty mess.

It's not fair! No matter what Adam did, he could never please the man. He tried and tried. He worked hard in the fields, and for what? A coin? And where had his efforts gone? To dust ... and to debts. He'd lost everything.

Then there was his cousin. Grandfather appreciated Liptor, all right! He recruited him for the army, giving him full-time sword training. "He might as well make Liptor governor now."

No, it isn't right to think this way.

The bright moon shone peacefully, and the cool breeze promised comfort. But Adam felt empty. *Did Father and Mother love me?* They were gone, and he would never know.

And now, the one person who had ever been a friend to him—she was gone too.

"Christy." He raised his head and gazed at the opposite bank, where she'd always stood. Empty blackness replaced her. "Why?" he asked. "Why did she have to die?"

Surely, the king wasn't angry with her.

Who was he, this King Eliab? Did he care what happened in Adam's world? Did anything Adam do or say even make a difference? Or was King Eliab as impossible to please as Grandfather? If the Ruuwh were real, the king would have known about Adam's letter before he delivered it.

A lot of good that trip did, he thought. *A waste of time.*

Adam tried to imagine what King Eliab looked like, where he sat in his comfortable palace beyond the mountains. Yes, the king was angry. That much was clear. But Adam couldn't picture his anger or find a way to relate.

He slumped and pushed his face against his arms. *What does it matter? I'll never see Christy again.*

His tears finally spilled, a trickle at first, then flowing into a regular shower. He sobbed, letting his sorrow run down his face. He rested his head in his arms and relaxed into a state of partial sleep.

A scuffling sound jerked Adam to attention. Something cold touched the back of his neck. He leaped away, pitching himself forward into the stream.

Naaa, Naaa!

The Carpenters' goat stared down at him. Samuel tossed his head and bleated again. It sounded like a laugh.

"You ... you ... *goat!*" Adam sputtered, shaking his fist at the animal.

A peal of laughter floated down like the notes of a favorite melody. "Oh, Adam, I'm sorry for laughing, but you look so funny." Another round of giggles filled the air. "Your eyes are as big as mangoes."

Adam shot to his feet and whirled around to face the opposite bank. "*C-Christy?*" He gaped at her. Water dripped from his clothes. His shoes were completely drenched, but he didn't move. *Am I dreaming?*

Christy stood on the bank in her usual place, beaming down at him. Her eyes twinkled with merriment, and her long dress glowed in the moonlight. She jammed her hands on her hips and grinned. "Well? Are you going to stand in the creek all night?"

Adam scrambled out of the water and joined Christy on the bank. He shook his dripping clothes. His heart raced. Could it be true? Was his friend really alive? "Are you all right? I mean, are you a … a ghost? I thought you were dead. What are you doing here?"

Christy smiled. "I *was* dead, but now I'm not. Teacher healed me."

Adam began to shake, and it wasn't completely from his damp clothes. "That's … that's … *impossible*. You can't get healed if you're already dead."

"I was dead," Christy insisted. "I remember it. I was aching all over from the burns, and I saw Mother and Father crying by my bedside. I said goodbye to them. Then I was gone. Everyone knows I was dead. I'm telling you the truth, Adam."

Adam peered at Christy, trying to see if her skin had become translucent. She looked the same as always.

When Adam didn't say anything, Christy continued her story. "I had the most wonderful dream. Four islanders came to our house, dressed in blue and gold. Nobody could see them except me. The first one carried me out in his arms. We rode on beautiful white horses down the King's Road, all the way to the golden gate."

She twirled, and her dress spun around her ankles. "I saw you, Adam. You galloped past us on the King's Road back to the city, and you looked horrible. I think you knew I was dead. I tried to shout to you that everything was okay, but you couldn't hear me."

Adam's eyes widened. How did she know he'd been to the gate today? *Maybe she really—*

"The gate opened," Christy said, breaking into Adam's thoughts. "I could just see inside. I saw colors you never dreamed of! Birds and all sorts of fruits. Even fountains. I knew I was on the verge of what I've always longed for, that moment when I see the king."

Christy stared off into the distance, clearly wrapped up in a wonderful vision. She looked ready to break into a joyful shout. Then she caught herself and turned back to Adam. "A messenger came running toward us. The gate closed. And then"—tears glistened in her eyes—"I woke up. Teacher was leaning over me." She smiled. "It was like seeing the king, after all. He made me better. Look."

Christy held out her arms. "No more burns or scars or anything. I'm all better now. I almost wish I could have gone through the gate, but the king knows when I will go. I am glad to be here for now, for Mother's sake and Father's and for—" She broke off.

Adam thought he saw her blush, but he couldn't tell for sure in the moonlight. "Christy, I'm so happy to see you that I don't even care if you talk too much."

She scowled.

Adam laughed and took one of her warm hands in both of his cold, wet ones. "Welcome back!" He shook her hand.

Water droplets flew.

Samuel jumped across the stream and came up the bank,

pushing between them. *Naaa, naaa!*

Christy knelt and grasped the goat's long hair in her hands. "You're a rascal. Do you know what a lot of heartache you caused?" She rubbed her face against the animal's side and wrapped her arms around his neck.

"Why do you say that?" Adam ran his hand along one of the goat's horns.

Christy sighed. "We thought all the animals were safe when the Goiim came, but I found out Sammy had broken out of his pen. I went after him. I couldn't let him wander around with all the horrible things going on. I saw him in the distance and almost reached him, but then ..." Her voice trailed off in remembrance.

"The fires," Adam filled in.

She shuddered. "Yes. I got caught in the fires, and the Goiim took Sammy away. I thought I would never see him again. But you brought him back." Her smiled returned. "Now we're all together again."

Adam let out a disgusted breath. "You mean that dumb goat got himself in all that trouble because he didn't stay in his pen?"

Christy squeezed Samuel harder. "He's not a dumb goat. He breaks out of his pen sometimes, but that doesn't make me stop loving him. He's special."

Adam snorted. "Special indeed! He got you killed. If I'd known that, I might not have brought him back." He glared at the goat. "I'd love to see him sent away as a sacrifice. But he's got that white patch with the blemish on his shoulder, so he isn't even good enough for sacrificing."

Christy gasped. "That's a horrible thing to say! And to

think I came looking for you to thank you for saving him."

Christy held the goat at arm's length and peered at his shoulder. "You're right. He is blemished, but that's what makes him special. Because I'm blemished too."

Adam's eyebrows shot up. "You are?"

"Yes." Christy whispered. She clenched her palms and held them down in her lap.

"You mean you have a deformity or something? Is it from the fire?"

"Not a deformity." Christy shook her head. "Sins. I've broken the king's law sometimes. I've gotten out of my 'pen' too, when I wanted my own way and not the king's."

A cool night breeze started Adam shivering again. He should go home and change into dry clothes, but Christy's words kept him frozen in one place. "I didn't think *you* ever sinned." He wrinkled his forehead. "How is that supposed to make your goat special? I wouldn't want a reminder of my blemishes hanging around."

Christy looked into Adam's eyes, clearly searching for something. The moon's silver light reflected two beautiful brown pools. "He's special, Adam, because he reminds me of the king's mercy."

She ran her fingers through Samuel's hair. "It's something Hank's father once said. Whenever we send a sacrifice, Sammy is spared because he has a blemish. The goat with no blemishes dies instead. I, who committed a crime in the first place, am spared too. The unblemished goat dies, the one who never did anything wrong."

Adam chewed on his lip. Wisps of understanding floated in his head, but he couldn't quite grasp what Christy was saying. "That reminds you of the king's mercy?"

"Yes! Because *I* ought to be executed. Instead, King Eliab provides an animal to die in my place so I can live. Hank's father says the king will someday provide a perfect sacrifice—someone with no blemishes—who will die once for all in place of us blemished people. I don't understand it, not really. There's something about it in the King's Stones.

> *He was wounded for our transgressions;*
> *He was bruised for our iniquities."*

Adam stared into the sky. He had heard those words recently, but where? It came to him in a flash. *The men at the golden gate.* Too bad they didn't ask Christy what the king meant. She could have given them a better answer than he had. He hadn't been able to answer at all.

Adam couldn't think of a good response now, either. He opened his mouth to tell Christy how much he'd missed her, but she cut him off.

"Oh, look!"

A group of Eirenian soldiers was struggling toward them, carrying one of their fellows in a sheet. Their uniforms were filthy and tattered. One man wore a thick bandage around his head and over part of his face. Adam stepped off the path as they approached.

A lean soldier with a sleeve torn off nodded at Christy. "Is this the way to Charlotte Carpenter's?"

"Yes." She pointed. "That's our house with the lamp in the window. Mother will do all she can to help. Is the wound bad?" She nodded at the soldier in the sheet.

"If he lives, he might lose his leg."

Adam twisted his face so he wouldn't see the bloody leg and focused on the lean man. "How is the fighting? Are we gaining ground?"

"Not like we hoped. The Arsabians took Sheera before we arrived and have entrenched themselves."

The soldier with the bandaged face scratched where his skin was exposed. He nodded at his companion in the sheet. "This one's lucky if he lives. Too many have already died."

Adam's heart sank. War at a distance excited his imagination, but when it showed its ugly side at his back door it turned his stomach. The realization that Ar Sabia might defeat the Eirenians sank into his being like a rock dropped into the deep end of the stream.

Christy put her hand on the sheet. "There's still hope."

Adam thought about it. Of course. Christy had been rescued out of death itself. More than that, the king had showed he really did care. As the soldiers moved past Adam, a flood of ideas coursed through his mind, formulating into a plan.

Christy dropped in line behind the soldiers. Adam's heart leaped. He hated for her to leave.

"Christy, wait."

She stopped. "What?"

Adam wanted to tell her how he felt about her being with him again, but his mind couldn't come up with the right words. A voice from the house called her name. Mr. Carpenter stood framed in the light of the doorway.

"Coming!" she called. Then she turned back to Adam. "Father said I could come just for a short time to tell you the good news."

Chills crept up Adam's neck. "How"–he swallowed– "how did you know I'd be at the creek?"

Christy's eyes gave him a faraway look. She smiled. "I guess I was just hoping." Then she seemed to come to herself. "I have to go. Father and Mother will worry if I'm late." She took Samuel's rope and jogged toward the house. The goat kicked up a trail of dust.

Adam raced to catch up. "I wanted to tell you something else. I sent a letter to the king about you. The idea came to me because of the letter the class sent about me, when I stopped coming to school." He shrugged. "I didn't think the king had answered, but now I think maybe he did."

Christy pulled the goat to a stop and whirled on Adam. "I knew he would answer, since Teacher signed it." Her voice turned joyful. "I'm so glad to hear he answered it already. I've longed to hear you say that, and my parents will be glad too."

Adam felt himself blushing. "I'm talking about the letter *I* sent him. The one asking for you to get better."

Christy cocked her head.

"Now that I think about it, though," Adam admitted, "I guess he answered your letter as well. Because ... well, I do want to obey the king, as much as I can. He ... he *does* care."

Christy's face glowed in the moonlight. "I'm so glad." She turned and started walking again.

"One more thing, Christy."

She turned.

"I have a plan. A big plan. One that could save our city. I

need time to work out the details. Can you meet me here after school tomorrow?"

"There isn't any school tomorrow. Teacher let us out to help our families recover from the attack. He's spending a lot of time with the refugees that are pouring into town. I'll come if I can. Now I have to hurry." She started running.

"Tell Hank to come too," Adam called. "And anyone else you can think of."

She nodded and waved goodbye.

Adam watched Christy until she was out of sight. Then he leaped into the air and whooped for joy.

Splashing through the creek, he bounded for home.

HANK

Chapter 23

*"Lord, Lord, have we not ... in thy name done many
wonderful works?" Matthew 7:22*

Hank slid a heavy coil of rope from his shoulder and let
it flop on the ground beneath a tree. He tugged at his
thrick, freeing it from the sticky skin where a large band of
sweat had formed. Sitting on the coil, he propped his back
against the tree and looked through the foliage toward the
King's Road.

Two days remained before Supplies Day, the day Adam
said they would go through with their plan. For weeks they
had been rendezvousing here, hammering out the details. So
far, Schala hadn't discovered their meeting place.
Meanwhile, time passed and lives kept slipping away.

Can we succeed? Hank picked at an ink spot on his
breeches. A more serious thought came to him. *Can we
survive?*

If it were up to Hank, they would not go through with the

plan, certainly not in this fashion. But Adam said they had a chance. *"If we don't try, we'll probably die anyway,"* he'd told the group at their last meeting.

Hank shifted his weight and slid a knife and a piece of wood out of his pocket. Adam was probably right. Hank cut two notches with his blade, one for Mrs. Ridgewood, and the other for Mayleen's uncle.

He had always loved Mrs. Ridgewood. For years he had gone to her house with his two older sisters to collect field nuts. They always brought her a basketful, and she baked nut pastries for them.

No more. His sisters had cried themselves to sleep last night.

Hank had never thought much of Mayleen's uncle. He frowned all the time and kept to himself. But this morning he too had passed from hunger and disease, leaving his wife with three wide-eyed girls to feed by herself. He wished he had known the man better.

Hank counted eighty-two other notches. Some represented the dead brought back from the war, like Jackson three days ago. The rest indicated victims of hunger and disease. How would they survive the hungry months ahead? His own mother would have died of fatigue if it hadn't been for Teacher.

Hank closed his eyes, remembering that special moment. Teacher had smiled and taken Mother by the hand. "Rise," he commanded. Just like that, Mother rose, left her bed, and scurried around the room like she always did.

Teacher had such power in his words, power to transform lives in a second.

He sighed. *If only Teacher were here now.*

Hank pushed against his stomach, trying to relieve the hunger pains. A stick snapped behind him. Panic surged through his body, propelling him from the rope coil. He twisted backward and landed on the ground with a loud *thud*.

Adam stood several yards away, with Camdin close behind. The two boys slapped their knees and burst into laughter. "You have the best reactions ever," Adam said.

"It's not funny." Hank stood and brushed the dirt from his breeches. "Your grandfather's fields are a stone's throw across the road, and you-know-who is still going about with his whip. You should take things a little more seriously."

Adam leaned against a tree across from Hank. "I do take things seriously. That's why we're here. I wanted to check out that ditch behind us on my way here. Did you ask anyone else about joining?"

Hank lowered himself on the rope. "I tried. But Jacob didn't think it was a good idea." He held up the end of his rope. "I did bring this. Hope you're satisfied."

Adam handled the rope end and nodded. "It looks good and strong if we end up needing it. I hope we don't."

Camdin copied Adam's stance. "Why do you hope that?"

"From what I've seen so far," Adam explained, "we should be able to make it up the ridges and down again on foot. But the whole mount is mysterious, and I've only gone partway. It doesn't hurt to be prepared."

The bushes rustled, and footsteps crackled toward them. Camdin gripped Adam's sleeve, his eyes wide.

Hank smiled. Now who was jumpy? "It's just Christy."

She forced her way into the small clearing and stood

there, picking burrs out of her dress.

Adam grinned at her. "Do you think you could be a little louder next time?"

Christy scowled and threw a burr at Adam. "I'd like to see *you* waltzing through these thorns in a long dress." A clump of hair flopped in front of her face, and she slapped it away.

Adam leaned to the side and peered past her. "Where's Mayleen?"

"She isn't coming." Christy wiped the sweat from her face. "She doesn't like the idea any longer. I tried to tell her we have to obey the king and plant our seeds each month, but she won't do it. She said maybe another time."

Adam made a face. "It's a good thing *I* brought someone. Camdin has agreed to go. That makes four of us. It may be enough for the king to notice."

Christy rolled her eyes. "Of course he notices, Adam. His Ruuwh is infinite, and he cares about all of us. It doesn't matter how many there are."

"It might matter when we're trying to save the whole city," Adam argued. "Right now, ten of the Twelve Cities are in enemy hands. Their armies are encamped only a day's march to the east. It's not like we're asking the king for a favor. We want him to rescue us and make everything better, like it used to be. If he's been angry for so many years because we haven't planted our seeds, it doesn't seem likely he'd be satisfied with just one or two now."

"But the king is good," Christy said. "You never know what he might do. Even if he doesn't come now, obedience is the least he deserves from us."

Adam prodded a root with his shoe. "I hope you're right. If he doesn't answer, I don't know what else we can do. Perhaps nothing will satisfy his anger."

"We have to try," Camdin said. "My mother has been starving herself for weeks. I'm afraid for her."

Adam laid a gentle hand on his friend's arm. "We're all concerned for her." He turned to Christy. "Did you bring a weapon?"

Christy pulled a small knife out of her pocket. "I found this."

"You couldn't find anything bigger?"

"I don't see why we need it." She shrugged. "I never brought weapons when I went with Teacher."

"We both heard hissing," Adam reminded her. "I don't know what makes that noise, but I wouldn't want to face it empty-handed."

Camdin fidgeted. "I could bring a carving knife. Mother keeps a couple in the kitchen."

Hank looked into the forest, avoiding eye contact with Adam. Christy was right. Hank hadn't brought weapons when he'd gone with Teacher to the Mount of Humility the last two times. "Maybe we should wait for Teacher."

"We would if he were here," Christy said.

Adam sighed. "I've told you already, Hank. That's been done before, and what good did it accomplish? If we're going to impress the king, we should show him we can do it on our own. That this is our idea, and not just something we're required to do for school."

Adam reached into his thrick and drew out a folded papla leaf. "Here's the letter. We just need to sign it. Tomorrow, if all goes well, I'll deliver it to the golden gate. Then in two more days we'll ascend the mountain, around the same time King Eliab is perhaps reading our letter."

"What if he doesn't read it?" asked Camdin.

Adam's eyes glazed over. "I don't know. There wouldn't be much to hope for after that." He spread out the letter on a stump and fumbled in a bag until he drew out a quill and some ink. "Hank, what is the total count after today?"

Hank held up his piece of wood. "Eighty-four."

Adam wrote it down. "Hasn't the king let us suffer enough?"

He handed the quill to Christy. She looked over the letter and signed her name at the bottom. Camdin signed next without reading the words. Adam scrawled his name and handed the quill to Hank. "Your turn."

Hank took the quill and glanced at the letter. His heart raced. *What would Father do in a situation like this?* He wanted to ask, but Father might become suspicious, even if it was a good idea.

He studied Christy's signature. Surely, Christy wouldn't sign anything if it wasn't all right. Besides, asking the king was always a good thing, wasn't it?

He skimmed the contents of the letter.

Dear King Eliab,

Our suffering is becoming more than we can bear. At least eighty-four of us have died since the fire, and even your most loyal servants are starving with hunger. We know that you are able to help us, and we long for you to come and bless us like you used to. We beg of you to return for your servants' sakes. To prove

217

*our eagerness to do your will, we will be ascending the
Mount of Humility on our own, perhaps even as you
are reading this letter. Please consider our devotion
and accept our sacrifice.*

> *Your most dedicated servants,*
> *Christiana Carpenter*
> *Camdin Welder*
> *Adam Sonneman III*

The others had signed it. Hank held the pen out, letting
the ink drip on the ground.

Camdin jumped. "I heard a noise in the woods."

They held their breaths, listening. Adam shook his head,
but then Hank heard it too—footsteps crunching through the
forest, running toward the ditch. The four friends looked at
each other and then focused on Hank.

"Hurry," Adam ordered.

Hank put the quill to the papla leaf and scribbled his
name.

Adam took the letter and gently waved it to dry the ink.
"Be careful going home. Stay apart on Supplies Day, even
when we're getting our seeds. We'll meet here immediately
afterward."

Christy headed off toward the road. Camdin followed
close behind her.

Hank was about to join them when Adam took him by the
arm and pulled him close. "Make sure Christy gets home
safely. I'll watch out for Camdin. I don't know what those
footsteps meant, but it makes me uneasy."

Hank nodded. The hurrying footsteps made him more
than uneasy. They frightened him half to death.

ADAM III

Chapter 24

*"Go to now, ye that say, 'Today or tomorrow we will
go into such a city, and continue there a year, and buy
and sell, and get gain,' whereas ye know not what
shall be on the morrow." James 4:13-14*

Adam jerked a rock loose from the stubborn dirt and
glanced over his shoulder. A pair of fiery-looking eyes
met his, and he whirled back to his task. When would Schala
go away? He had hovered over Adam all day, watching his
every move.

At first, Adam had merely been annoyed. Now, though,
he was beginning to worry. Why was Schala so watchful?
Had he guessed what he and his friends planned to do?
Could it have been Schala's footsteps they'd heard in the
forest yesterday? *What if he finds the letter?*

Adam wasn't needed for carrying water now that the
funja was burnt, so Schala put him to work digging up rocks
from a new field. He guarded Adam all day, slapping the

whip against his palm but never speaking. The sun seemed to halt in the sky. Adam fixated on it, longing for the work day to end.

When at last the men set down their tools and Schala departed, Adam was worn to the bone and reluctant to carry out his plan. But he knew what would happen if he didn't. He saw the despair in the faces of the men. *Will any of us live to bring in next year's crops?*

Adam ran to the creek and splashed water on his burning face. He dried his hands on his breeches and then looked around, checking to make sure Schala had left completely. With his eyes still searching the fields, he reached into a space between two rocks and drew out the letter.

With a quick leap across the creek and a scramble up the bank, he was off. The road was familiar by now. He ran as fast as he dared until he reached Red Rock, and then he slackened his pace to a steady jog.

Sweat trickled down Adam's face. A breeze pushed his hair against his temple. The day was fading. He ran on, ignoring the cramp that throbbed in his side. His feet ached, but he willed himself on. Perhaps this would be a turning point. What if the king *did* come? What if the prophecies came true, and their homes were filled again with food, flowers, and laughter?

Just ahead, he spied a regiment of Eirenian soldiers guarding the road. Because of the advancing armies, makeshift patrols had been set up at different locations around Mount Eirene. Adam had studied this one the last couple weeks, familiarizing himself with its movements. Before anyone caught sight of him, he turned off the road and took a path to the west. It soon brought him to a small clearing in the woods, where the soldiers tied their horses.

A small brown mare whinnied a greeting. Adam had fed her nuts on previous visits to gain her trust. Lives depended on her cooperation now. He untied her, saddled her, and quietly led her through the woods until he was far away from the patrol.

The guards would no doubt be upset if they knew Adam was borrowing one of their mounts. If he did his job right, though, the mare would be returned before they discovered her absence. Besides, Adam's mission might save their lives.

An uncomfortable thought pinched his conscience. Would using the animal without permission please the king? He shook his head. "I'll think about that later," he told the mare.

When he'd crept along far enough, he guided the horse onto the road and climbed into the saddle. Now he would need to fly. "Giddup, let's go." He trotted the mare for a mile or two then nudged her into a full gallop.

On and on he rode. An hour and a half later, Adam reached the golden gate. He slid out of the saddle and dropped to the ground. He groaned. His legs wobbled, and his backside was saddle sore. He ran his fingers through his hair to push out the sweat and straightened to his full height.

This was his moment.

He knocked on the small door. The same guard appeared, stern at first, but he relaxed when he recognized Adam.

Adam didn't wait for greetings or a scolding. "Please give this letter to King Eliab." He held out the parchment.

The guard frowned, clearly hesitant to take the new letter. Then he sighed. "All right."

Adam let out a breath of relief. The petition had crossed the golden gate threshold and was on its way to the king. He smiled and climbed back into the saddle. He knew he should return home, but he lingered, marveling at the gate.

Fear had kept him from appreciating the gate the last time he'd come. Now, pure, solid gold as far as his eye could see reached up into the sky. It reflected the setting sun in shining rainbow colors. "If a mere gate is this glorious, what must the rest of the kingdom be like?" he whispered, awestruck.

Adam turned the horse toward home, but his mind retained the vision. What a powerful king he must be! And he was good. Adam knew this now. King Eliab had played a tremendous role in Christy's healing. Maybe he'd personally sent a message to Teacher.

Adam sighed with longing. What might the king do if he returned to Mount Eirene?

His mind envisioned the Arsabians fleeing before the king's advance when he reclaimed the Twelve Cities. He imagined the fountains spouting once more, and food. Yes, food for all! And the people would be healed.

Adam's imagination soared. *Surely the king will honor me, the one who was loyal and planted his seed, leading his friends to do the same.* Perhaps in time—his heart raced—King Eliab would even make him the next governor.

This idea so thrilled Adam that he continued to savor it, even after he'd returned the mare and left the patrol far behind. He rehearsed what the king might say to honor him. He practiced how he would respond. Ideas chased each other and whirled through his mind as he plodded up the road. He hardly noticed when the sky began to darken.

Twang!

An arrow zipped by Adam's ear, jerking him from his daydream. Bright moonlight poured over him. Realizing what a glaring target he must be, he dropped flat on the road that stretched over Lookout Hill. His heart pounded.

He scanned the foliage on both sides, but there was no sign of an attacker. Who had fired at him? He rolled off the road, curled up against a bush, and froze. The rocky soil jabbed his back and legs, and his position cramped him.

Adam ignored his discomfort and remained motionless. The sun had vanished behind the mountains. Perhaps he would be hard to hit in the dark. He could run fast.

He pushed his hands under him and slid forward. Then he froze, listening. When he heard no sound, he crept forward. His confidence grew as he neared the top of the hill. Perhaps he could slide into the rocks and gain a safe vantage point to look around.

Adam crawled along the side of the road until he was almost at the top. The bushes grew too thick here to continue. He would have to use the road. His throat turned dry. Perhaps his attacker was waiting!

He pivoted his head. Nothing behind. The danger was probably ahead of him, but so was home. He couldn't go back.

Adam held his breath and listened until his air ran out. *What should I do?*

He squirmed forward on his stomach, inching tightly against the rocks. At last, he reached the top of Lookout Hill.

The shadowy images of Mount Eirene and Grandfather's fields appeared in the distance. Home had never looked so good. "King Eliab," he whispered, "if your Ruuwh is as powerful as Teacher says, please help me now."

He scrambled to his feet, poised to make a run for it. His limbs were stiff, and he wobbled. Out of the corner of his eye he saw a shadow rise from behind the rocks. He was caught!

Adam shot away, but someone seized him in a flying tackle. Together, they crashed against the rocky ground, with Adam on the bottom. He yelled and flailed his arms and legs, but to no avail. He was pinned tight. A knee jammed his arm, and a rough hand jerked back his hair.

"Adam?" The hold on his arms relaxed. "What in the island do you think you're doing out here? I thought you were a Keeda."

Adam blinked several times, trying to make out the young man's face. He wore the uniform of one of Grandfather's soldiers.

"Answer me, Little Governor."

"Liptor!" Adam gasped his recognition. "Where did you get that uniform?"

Liptor released his grip and stood up, brushing himself off. "Yeah, it's me. Are you surprised? Didn't expect to see me looking so sharp, did you?"

Adam frowned and sat up. "If you call that *sharp.* Your clothes hang on you like an old sack on a fence post. Where did you get them?"

Liptor sneered. "For your information, this was Grandfather's old uniform from when he was my age. People had more to eat back then. At the rate I'm progressing, before long I'll be able to fit just fine too. Unlike you. Where's *your* uniform?"

Adam didn't answer. The moonlight glinting off a large brass button on Liptor's cap caught his attention. The image of a two-headed snake wrapped around a tree was set in a large, bronze circle. The snake held a fruit in one mouth and a bloody sword in the other. Beneath the tree was engraved the motto FREEDOM AND DOMINION, the Sonneman family symbol.

Sharp words sprang to Adam's tongue, but he bit them back. If he was going to impress the king, he must be on his best behavior. "Congratulations, I guess. Did Grandfather send you? Why were you hiding behind that rock?"

"No one sent me. I came on my own. I figured someone ought to keep a lookout for Keeda. The regular patrol is too far from the city." He picked up his bow and strung it with a new arrow. "You never answered my question. What are *you* doing here?"

Adam looked away. "I was keeping an eye out for the Keeda myself. Sometime, I can show you where I first saw them. How long do you plan to stay?"

Liptor shrugged.

"I better run before I'm late for dinner," Adam said. "You know how Grandfather is." Afraid to say anything more, he took off running down the hill. When he reached the bottom, he stopped and kicked the dust. Then he slammed a fist into his palm.

"I lied ... *again*," he accused himself. "Why did I do it? What will the king think?" He scowled. Why did Liptor have to be here tonight?

Another thought entered his tired mind. What had Teacher said about Liptor? That Adam was partly to blame for misleading him? Not that Liptor would follow Adam willingly. But maybe he had more influence with his cousin than he thought.

Why were they always fighting? They had plenty of enemies already without going against each other. What if they worked together instead?

Adam's hand combed through the hair on the back of his head. His mental wheels spun. He turned around and took a step back toward Lookout Hill. His stomach twisted. "Liptor won't listen. Why am I doing this?"

It was almost suppertime, and Adam was hungry. He would be late for sure if he didn't go now. But this was more important. He kept on walking, all the way to the top of the hill.

Liptor crouched behind a rock, gazing out toward the forest.

"Liptor."

His cousin spun around, clearly caught off guard. His hands flew behind his back. "What do you want now?" he snapped. "I thought you were going to be late."

Adam fought to control his breathing. "It doesn't matter if I'm late. I want to discuss something with you. Can we talk?"

Liptor stared without responding.

Adam moved a step closer. "First, I want to tell you I'm sorry for lying. I wasn't on the lookout for Keeda. I ... well, I'll tell you in a minute where I was. But I'm sorry."

"All right. Where were you?"

"Hang on." Adam bit his lip. "I also wanted to tell you I'm sorry for misleading you a while back. I mean, when you stopped going to school so you could work for Grandfather."

"Huh?" Liptor's brows furrowed. "You didn't lead me away from or into anything. I chose for myself, and it was a good choice. Is that all you came back to tell me?"

Adam shook his head. "No, there's more. We haven't always gotten along in the past, but maybe we need to now. I have a plan."

Liptor snorted. "You're always full of plans."

"Yes, but this time it's different. I've seen what the king can do. He has the power to heal. He could rescue our whole city. I believe he will, if we show him we're worthy of his rescue."

Liptor crossed his arms over his chest and grunted at Adam's words.

Adam took a deep breath. "Several of us are involved. Tomorrow afternoon, as soon as we get our seeds, we're going to ascend the Mount of Humility. It will be dangerous, but it's the only way. This evening I took a letter to—"

He broke off and squinted at Liptor's hands. "Are those wedding berries? I thought you never touched them."

Liptor uncrossed his arms and flung something into the bushes. "What if it is?" he growled. "It has nothing to do with you. Don't act all pious. I know what you've done."

Adam ground his teeth. "Never mind. I wanted to tell you that I took a letter to the king. Several of us signed it. We're asking him to return to Mount Eirene. If we climb the mountain, we think he'll listen." He took a deep breath. "I ...

I'm inviting you to join us. What do you say?"

Liptor's lips curved upward in a scornful smile. "*Really*, Adam? You're a couple years younger than me, but I thought Sonneman blood would at least do a little bit for you."

The hair rose on Adam's neck. "What do you mean?"

"I mean, you still believe in the king? I thought you had more sense than that." He shrugged. "But I guess I shouldn't assume anything."

"Of *course* I believe in the king. Who doesn't? I don't know what you're talking about."

Liptor shook his head. "You're out of touch. Go ahead, play your little game, but you aren't going to involve me."

Adam crossed his arms and frowned. "You make it sound like you don't even believe the king exists."

"Very good, cousin. There's hope for you, after all. You're beginning to understand."

"Understand what? You sound ridiculous! Everyone knows the king is there."

"Everyone? You mean the children who attend Teacher's school." He laughed. "They believe anything someone tells them." He leaned close to Adam's face. "You can't prove the king's there, can you?"

"Teacher wouldn't lie," Adam shot back. "He's the most honest person we know."

"That's just it," Liptor said. "You're assuming these things. You can't prove Teacher never lies. He's probably got an agenda and tries to make us follow him by scaring us with tales about a Judgment Day and 'Oh, the king is always watching you!' Well, I'm not going to fall for that one."

Adam sighed. "I saw the golden gate with my own eyes

just a little while ago. Actually, I've seen it twice. I've read the King's Stones. They stand in the plaza of Mount Eirene for anyone in the city to read them."

Liptor sat down on a rock and pulled off his cap. "Assumptions, cousin. All assumptions. Were you there when the stones were written? Did you see who built the golden gate? You don't know any of these things, not if you think about it."

"I *do* know." Adam kicked the dirt, sending small rocks into the bushes. "Just because I can't prove them doesn't mean I don't know them. If you want to carry on this way, then no one can prove anything to you. But the facts remain the facts. You can sit there and disbelieve them all night if you want."

"Do you think I enjoy questioning my beliefs?" Liptor asked. "I'd rather keep on assuming and be blissfully ignorant." He lowered his voice. "But I want to know what's really out there."

The tension in Adam drained out. "So do I. But don't you think it's better to trust someone who knows, rather than just doubting?"

Liptor glanced over his shoulder toward the forest. "More than you think." A slight smile crept back on his lips.

"Why? Did you—"

"Quiet!" Liptor raised his hand and peered through the shadows.

Adam followed his example, trying to guess what Liptor was looking for. Then he saw it. A small glow like a torch flickered up and then died away. Then it flickered again.

"What is that?" Adam whispered.

Liptor stood up and brushed off his uniform. "That's my signal." He put on his cap.

"Wait. Your signal for what?"

Liptor turned and sized Adam up. "All right, I'll tell you. Schala promised this morning to take me to meet his master, someone even more powerful than Grandfather. This will be a big step up for me."

"Are you crazy?" Adam's mouth dropped open. "You're a fool if you trust Schala. Don't you remember what he did to Hank?"

"I know what I'm doing."

Adam studied Liptor's face. His skin had grown pale, although his jaw was set. "It's not worth it, Liptor. You don't know what you're getting yourself into. Think this through—"

"I don't need any more plans of yours!" Without a backward glance, Liptor charged down the road.

Adam stood clenching and unclenching his fists as he watched him go. His face burned. Then he set his feet toward the city and began plodding. He didn't feel much like eating supper, but he didn't feel like missing it, either.

A torrent of arguments fired through his mind like burning arrows. *I must be right!*

Liptor didn't know. Adam counted off the reasons, point by point. But what good did it do? No one ever liked his plans.

Grandfather would certainly be angry when Adam arrived home late. It was better to skip dinner altogether. He didn't want any questions. He didn't want any scolding. He didn't want *anything*! Let old Roberts eat his food if he wanted. Adam was sick to his stomach.

He paused by the turnoff toward Christy's house. He should feel better walking that path. But his heart ached with every step. He splashed across the creek at his usual place and lay down on his back. He looked up at the full, bright moon.

"Why do so many things always go wrong?" he asked.

The king, Adam's plan, and his dreams of success spun around in his tired, aching head. Then he started a mental argument with Liptor. The roots under his back jabbed at him. Dirt stuck to the sweat on his neck. He rolled onto his elbow—

His breath caught. The moon shone its light on a splash of red peeking through the grass. His blood warmed, and a tingle slid down his spine. He flopped back down. It couldn't be wedding berries. Not here. Not now.

He swallowed. *I have to get away!*

Adam couldn't give in to any weakness now, not when he'd come so far. He scrambled to his knees. How could that splash of red be wedding berries? Did someone leave them here by accident? His heart pounded. He had to check and see if they were really wedding berries.

He made his way over to the pile and peered closer. Yes, these were definitely wedding berries. Trembling, he reached out his hand and picked one up. The sweet, familiar aroma enticed him.

Throw it away!

But he couldn't. He held the berry at arm's length and stared at it. The idea of tossing it away filled him with an aching misery.

The thought of the berry's stimulating taste overpowered him, and he popped the fruit into his mouth.

Just one. No one would ever know.

Adam made a face at the flat taste. All this mental struggling for nothing? He picked up three more berries and rolled them under his tongue. Juice slipped through his teeth, but he felt no sensation. He ate several more.

His heart slowed down, and his brain felt numb. There was no joy in this. Maybe, if he kept eating, he might feel better.

When Adam reached for another berry, he felt a piece of parchment poking out from under the pile. Pinching it with his fingertips, he tugged it out. The writing was so large that he could make out the scrawled letters, even in the shadowy darkness.

Adam, you can pay me later. Fifteen blesseens.

Schala's writing!

Adam let the parchment slip through his cold fingers. Fifteen years of work for a bunch of berries? His gaze swept the pile. He hadn't eaten all of them. He pushed the remaining berries together and slid the paper underneath. Maybe Schala hadn't counted them. He tried to recreate the pile. No use. Schala would know right away half the berries were gone.

Adam seized the parchment and wadded it into a ball, with the remaining berries inside. Then he flung the whole mess into the field. *How dare Schala tempt me here. Here!*

How dare the evil man tempt Adam in his special place and on a night like this. A worse thought stabbed Adam's thoughts. "How did Schala know I would be here?" He groaned. Would the man ever give him a moment's rest?

Guilt washed over Adam. What would the king think? Had he gained the attention of royalty with his letter, only to have it focus on his crimes? Adam jumped to his feet and began plodding toward home. He had to move. He had to get away from his misery.

But he could not get away from himself. Neither could he undo what he had done.

All too soon, Adam found himself in bed, his emotions spent, his mind numb. He pounded his sheet with his fist, but his act brought neither answers nor comfort. Maybe he would feel better in the morning.

Adam buried his head in his pillow. He had sold fifteen more years to Schala. How many did that make in all? Far more years than he would ever live. "I'll be a slave for life," he whimpered.

He had no way to ever redeem himself.

MALAKAN

Chapter 25

"And there appeared an angel unto him from heaven,
strengthening him." Luke 22:43

Malakan leaped up the stairs three at a time, his feet skimming the cool, white marble surfaces. His green eyes blazed with excitement. Where was Asterik?

The expansive marble porch was empty. How different it felt from this morning, when he had joined the throng pouring in through the twenty-four golden doors that led to the Great Hall. The swell of their harmonious praises still rang in his ears and stirred him to the depths.

The king of all glory has triumphed alone.
He wields full control from the seat of His throne.
Holy in Wisdom!
Holy in Power!
Holy His plan to unite all in One!

Malakan ran along the walls of a narrow pool, leaping back and forth over the sparkling water. Surely, this was the day he had longed for. Surely now, the king would take back his special land. The judgment of Mount Eirene had come.

"Where *is* Asterik?"

On impulse, he diverted his steps and mounted the steps to the Tower of Trumpets. The walls of solid, white gold were so clear that the light from the sky poured through, engulfing him in radiance. The colorful bands of ruby, emerald, or sapphire lining each stair guided him higher. He burst up the last flight and onto the circular landing. His heart throbbed, and every muscle strained for action.

"Hail, trumpeters of the Most High." He saluted the men positioned around the wall.

"Hail to you, servant of the Mighty Warrior." They pounded their fists across their chests. "Do you bring tidings, or have you come for our music?"

"Or for the grand sights below?" added one.

"Everything!" Malakan bounded past a trumpeter into the embrasure behind him. "This is the greatest of days, and I want to experience it all." Grasping the crenels on either side, he leaned out. Air rushed around him, flapping his blond curls against his face.

Taranim, the leader, smiled and lifted his trumpet. "Then you are in the right place and in good time, as usual. We are about to sound."

Malakan feasted on the view. Miles upon miles of garden arranged in intricate patterns were accented with golden gazebos, crystal fountains, and monuments of countless victories. By the king's design, millions of colorful flowers danced in patterns that mimicked the galaxies. Beyond the garden lay homes and fields beyond number, stretching into the shining skyline.

These were normal sights to Malakan, but today armies covered the fields, blanketing every inch of standing ground between the garden and the horizon. They came rank upon rank in perfect order, marching behind their banners.

Malakan recognized the different emblems and began counting off the provinces one after another. "Look!" He pointed. "Even the Sagheer peoples from the far northern reaches have come."

"Yes, and from here you can see the Tauweel banner of the eastern giants," answered a trumpeter.

Malakan closed his eyes. He could almost taste the coming triumph on the tip of his tongue. "King Eliab has spared nothing in assembling his hosts. Can any of you doubt that today is the day we have longed for?"

Taranim waved him down. "If you doubt, you will know for certain in a moment. Stand by me, where you can see the front of the Hall. We are about to sound."

The circle of trumpeters moved into position around the wall. Each man stood in front of an embrasure, his feet planted, his instrument lifted to his lips. Taranim stood in the center. At his signal, the trumpets blared in unison. These were followed by rounds of rapid battle paces, one trumpet after another. They held at the end, until all joined in a single sound. Then with a sudden break, they concluded with three sharp notes and lowered their trumpets.

"I've never heard that before," Malakan said. "It moves me. What does it mean?"

Taranim gestured toward the Hall. "It is the announcement of wrath against Mount Eirene. See for yourself."

An enormous white flag snapped in the wind, shooting out from the battlements above the Hall at the sound of the music. A silver cup overflowing with red wine covered its face.

"Long has the anger of our king lingered," said Taranim. "But now it overflows and will not be withheld any longer."

He signaled with his hand, and one of the trumpeters sounded a different series of notes. A black flag was unfurled beside the first, bearing the emblem of a glowing sword.

Taranim nodded. "He has told the people of Mount Eirene plainly:

> *"If you be willing and obedient,*
> *You shall eat the fruit of the land;*
> *But if you refuse and rebel,*
> *You shall be eaten with the sword."*

He fingered his trumpet. "They have provoked the king to his face all these years. Now, his face is set against them for destruction."

Another trumpeter sounded. This time a red flag unfurled, covered with tongues of flame. A tingle went down Malakan's spine. "Our lord is a devouring fire. He is righteous to judge thus with eternal punishment."

Taranim lifted his instrument. "He is exceedingly righteous. None is like him. Servants of the Most High, raise your trumpets!"

As one, the men joined again in song, a familiar battle theme this time. Their music resounded to every corner of the vast fields below. The miles of armies stamped their feet and shouted, shaking the ground with the thunder of their rhythmic pounding. Thousands of voices joined in the singing, lifting the chorus with a triumphant crescendo.

"In righteousness he judges and makes his war,
Holy, holy, holy, is the lord, the King Eliab!"

"Amen! Amen!" Malakan seized Taranim by the shoulders. "You've never played better, my friend. I would love to tarry, but I must share the good tidings with Asterik. Our division will be at the front of the charge, and we must prepare at once."

Taranim smiled. "May the Ruuwh of King Eliab go before you, and may your arrows find rest in the hearts of the king's enemies."

Malakan saluted, placing his left fist over his heart and stretching out his right hand, palm up. "May he bless your instruments as the trumpet of the lord at his appearing."

Whirling toward the stairs, he bounded back to the marble porch and then on toward the garden. He imagined Asterik was tucked away somewhere in the privacy of his own thoughts.

He found him, as he expected, in Beulah, Immanuel's special section of the garden. Asterik sat on a bench carved from diamond. His right hand fingered the bark of a small cherry tree, while his eyes remained fixed on the crystal-clear stream in front of him.

Malakan approached from behind and clapped him on the shoulder. "Now I know beyond doubt that today is the day of battle. This is the first time I've ever seen you with arrows." He gestured at the crude bundle on Asterik's lap.

Asterik sighed and kept his gaze on the flowing water. "I know they're pathetic compared to yours, and the bow's not much better. But I doubt it will matter."

Pathetic seemed a generous term for Asterik's weapons, but Malakan let it go. "Have you heard the news? Our division will be the first to ride. We must hurry to prepare."

Asterik looked up, his gray eyes somber. "I won't be going with the division."

Malakan stepped back. "What? Why, we wouldn't be the same without you. What are you talking about?"

Asterik turned back to the stream. "I've been given a special mission."

Malakan whooped. "All praise to His Majesty! I'm glad for you, Asterik. This is a rare gift, and a special opportunity."

His friend shook his head. "And yet, I tremble at it."

Malakan removed his bow. "Don't be afraid. You can take my weapon. It will never fail you. Besides, the Ruuwh of the king will protect you."

Asterik pushed the bow back toward Malakan. "I'm not afraid of any danger. I tremble rather for our Lord Immanuel."

"Don't speak in riddles." Malakan hiked the bow back on his shoulder. "How can you tremble for him? He holds complete control over everything."

"He still can feel pain and grief. Have you forgotten that

it's the middle of the night in Aard?"

Malakan sighed. "True, the glory has departed from them. They rejected King Eliab. Let them live in darkness. Better yet, we will retake the land this day and destroy the rebels. Then the land can be delivered."

"Is that what you think the king wants? To destroy them?" Asterik ripped a piece of bark off the tree and tossed it in the water. "Why then does Immanuel toil until he is a scarecrow while he lives among them? Is it to condemn them?"

"I don't see why not." Malakan rested his boot on the bench and bent forward. "The king has written in the stones he gave them:

> *Surely you will slay the wicked;*
> *Do not I hate them that hate you?*
> *I hate them with a perfect hatred;*
> *I count them my enemies."*

Asterik shook his head. "But he loves them, too. He will certainly save those who repent and convert to his side. He has also written:

> *Mount Eirene shall be*
> *redeemed with judgment,*
> *And her converts*
> *with righteousness.*

Besides, what about all his promises to bless the city and raise up Aardians to rule with him?"

Malakan shifted to the opposite foot. He hated arguing. But Asterik always got the last word. "We've covered this ground before. You can't deny that the king must punish lawbreakers. He wouldn't be a righteous judge otherwise. The writing states beyond question that the penalty for breaking the covenant is death."

Asterik opened his mouth, but Malakan raised his hand. "Let's not argue anymore. King Eliab will work it out perfectly, no matter what we think. All we have to do is follow orders." He held out his hand. "Come on. Let's walk while we're talking. You can tell me about this special mission."

Asterik clasped the extended hand and rose to his feet. The two friends walked beside the stream. Asterik took a breath as if he would speak, but then he sighed and said nothing.

Malakan glanced at him. A silky, green canta bird perched on Asterik's shoulder and trilled his song, but his friend appeared not to notice. His eyes were gazing into the heavens. It was a familiar expression, and Malakan knew not to say anything for the moment.

The bird flew away, and Asterik spoke. "My orders are to stand by him and comfort him."

"Comfort whom?"

"Immanuel. I must leave at the next trumpet to join him." Asterik closed his eyes. "I can only imagine what kind of agony he must be feeling. I wish I were there now."

"Why?" Malakan's hand flew to his sword hilt. "Do you think he's in danger?" His knuckles whitened from the force of his grip.

Asterik opened his eyes. "No, I think he is alone. It is the agony of anticipation that he feels."

Malakan frowned. "Why do you say that? What does he anticipate?"

"I do not know. It is something King Eliab said."

"What did he say?"

Asterik put his hand on Malakan's arm. Looking around, he pulled him close and whispered,

"He told me 'Today is the moment of decision for my son. It is the turning point on which everything hangs. Stand by him, Asterik, and comfort him.'"

Malakan searched Asterik's eyes. "We know Immanuel will make the right choice. It surely can't be as bad as our last mission on the Mount of Humility."

"I wish I could agree. I mean … I know he'll make the right choice. But there is something … " Asterik's words trailed away. He turned his head and took a deep breath. Then swallowing hard, he turned back. "When I left, King Eliab put his face in his hands, and—"

"He wept?"

Asterik nodded. "He cried so hard his shoulders shook. I didn't know what to do."

"What can it mean?"

"I don't know. Something has been predetermined between Eliab and Immanuel, but what it is I cannot guess."

A trumpet sounded from the tower. Asterik sprang into action, swinging his homely quiver over his shoulder. "That's my signal. I must hurry to Immanuel. Farewell, Malakan, and may the Ruuwh of the king go before us and bring us together once more."

Malakan reached out to give the customary salute, but Asterik was already gone, bounding away through the garden. "Farewell, my friend," Malakan whispered. "I expect we will know the answer to these puzzles when next we meet."

ADAM III

Chapter 26

*"If I regard iniquity in my heart, the Lord will not
hear me." Psalm 66:18*

C hristiana Carpenter."
The islander glanced up from his list and shaded his
eyes against the blazing sun before continuing to read the
names. On most Supplies Days, the plaza was crowded, but
today the crowd had swelled to twice its size. Waves of
refugees had poured into the city over the past several
weeks. Like the arms of a whirlwind, the people circled a
central eye, where the king's servants distributed the
monthly goods.

Christy pushed her way toward the king's supplies wagon
and took a large, dark seed from an islander. She half turned
in Adam's direction but then caught herself and looked at the
plaza's central fountain instead.

Good, Adam thought with relief. She remembered the
instructions for everyone to stay separated. He did wish she

had at least glanced his direction, though.

She left the plaza with her parents and little brothers.

So far, so good.

"Adam Sonneman."

Grandfather moved from Adam's side and shoved his way toward the wagon. Several servants followed. The governor received a larger portion of goods than most.

Adam fell into line behind the servants. He wiped his sweaty hands against his breeches and hoped Grandfather wouldn't pay him any attention. *I have to plant the seed. I just have to.* After failing again last night when he'd eaten the berries, this might be his only hope of escaping the king's anger. And it was a faint hope at that.

He stood near the wagon and waited his turn. He should be next. The man with the list looked down at him but called out a different name.

Wait. It's my turn! Adam glanced around. The islander continued as if nothing was amiss. Perhaps there had been a mistake.

Adam's heart raced. Was it an oversight? He had no idea, but now he would have to wait until the entire list had been called to find out.

Families filed by, collecting their gifts and their seeds from the king. Adam felt conspicuous, standing in front of the crowd. He wanted to duck out of view, but so many people had crowded behind him that he couldn't move without drawing unwanted attention.

Hank came up with his family when his name was called. He stood so close that Adam could touch him. When he took his seed, he glanced at Adam and raised his eyebrows.

Adam shook his head and motioned in the direction of their meeting place. Hank nodded and made his way out of the crowd and down the King's Road.

From the corner of his eye, Adam noticed Camdin forcing his way toward him. He groaned. What was Camdin doing? They were supposed to keep separate to avoid attention, and now he was coming while Adam stood right at the front. Camdin waved and kept coming.

Adam looked the other way. What now? Maybe if he ignored Camdin, the younger boy would remember and stick to the plan.

"Adam!"

Adam cringed. He pushed his way through the crowd over to Camdin. He grabbed his arm and yanked him along toward the back. "What are you doing?" he demanded in a low, harsh voice. "I told you we need to stay apart."

Camdin jerked his arm free. "I know, but you didn't tell me what to do."

"Yes, I did." Adam led Camdin farther away from the crowd. "I told you very clearly two days ago. We have to stay away from each other to avoid getting ourselves into trouble. Do you want someone to figure out our plan?"

"Not that," Camdin said. "You didn't tell me how I get my seed."

Adam slapped his forehead. "I forgot. You're not old enough to get a seed yet." This was another complication.

"I could ask for one," Camdin suggested eagerly. "They probably have extra."

Adam shook his head. "Let me think." He stared at the giant King's Stones that circled the plaza and tried to focus.

"I could ask Father and Mother for theirs," Camdin said. "Mother can't go to the mountain right now. Maybe if I plant her seed, the king will help her get better."

"You better not. They might tell you not to go. Why don't you come along and help us plant ours?"

Camdin didn't seem to be listening. "I see them. It won't take long. Let me try." He disappeared into the crowd.

A wave of helplessness washed over Adam. His grand plan appeared to be unraveling before they even set out for the mountain. Teacher's words came back to him. *"Did you read the king's instructions?"*

Adam turned in a circle, taking in the stones that towered overhead. Hardly a soul in the plaza gave them any notice. Yet, they declared the words of the king regarding his laws and his judgment against them all for ignoring him.

He remembered his own words to Teacher: *"It isn't right to make us follow these laws—ones we can't even keep—and then kill us for it. It isn't reasonable. I can't do it."*

But Adam had to do it or face the consequences forever. "Maybe I should have studied the Stones," he muttered. There wasn't time now. He would have to plant the seed. He must.

A jerk on the tail of his thrick snapped Adam out of his thoughts. He spun around.

"I got it. I got it. Look." Camdin held up a seed. "Father gave it to me. He doesn't care what I do with it, and I didn't tell him where we're going."

"All right, listen." Adam leaned down. "Go meet the others as we planned and explain that I'm coming late. I'll be there as quickly as I can. Right?"

"Right." Camdin sprinted off through the plaza.

Adam straightened and took a deep breath. How long would it take for the rest of the people to receive their supplies? Sometimes, he enjoyed watching and waiting until the end.

Not today.

The sun beat down on the back of his neck and shoulders. The islander had stopped calling names and was consulting with his fellow about a scrawny man demanding a larger share.

Can't they make him leave so they can move on?

He wondered what his friends were doing. Had they gone straight to the meeting place? How long would they wait? The thought of them lingering out there bothered him, especially after hearing those footsteps the other day.

"Hey, look what I found."

Camdin reappeared and thrust a coil of rough rope into Adam's arms. "Isn't this your grandfather's?"

The rope was thick and dyed a peculiar black color. There was no mistaking it. But that was beside the point. "Camdin, why haven't you left? I thought you were long gone by now."

"I was on my way, but I found this beside the road right outside the plaza. It's your grandfather's, right?"

Adam made a face. "Yes, it's Grandfather's. So what? It doesn't do us a lot of good. Get going."

Camdin turned away.

"Wait!" Adam stopped him. "I have an idea. Can you remember instructions?"

"Sure."

"Then listen. We've lost time this morning. Tell the others to go ahead and get started. Let's meet behind Red Rock." He described it and then straightened and swung the rope over his shoulder. "Can you remember?"

Camdin smiled. "Of course. You'll see." He dashed off.

The crowd had thinned while Adam and Camdin were talking. Adam waited, heart pounding, while person after person filed forward for their supplies. What would Christy and Hank think of this new change of plans?

The last family gathered their supplies and left. The king's men took their seats in the wagon. Adam knew he should approach them and ask for his seed while he had the chance. Fear held him back. He had talked to Pre-Aardian islanders before. What made him hesitate?

The first man clucked to the horses, but the other touched his arm. Reaching down, he took something in his hand and jumped over the side. He walked straight to Adam. "I'm sorry for the delay."

Adam suddenly recognized him as one of the men from the golden gate, the tall one who had been the first to ask him questions.

"I hesitated to give you these in front of the whole city." He thrust something into Adam's hands, ran back to his partner, and leaped onto the wagon seat. The driver urged the horses into a trot, and the wagon rolled out of the plaza and on its way toward the golden gate.

Adam opened his hands. A large seed rested on top of two folded papla leaves. He stuffed the seed in his pocket and studied the leaves. Excitement mounted. Had the king responded? What would he say?

No. Disappointment settled into his stomach like a stone. These were the two letters he had delivered. He turned them over. Neither had been opened. A blob of red wax stamped with the emblem of a crown sealed the documents closed. Across the front, large black letters scrawled the words **no MEDIATOR**.

What kind of answer was this? After all of Adam's work, the king had apparently turned him down. "Was I mistaken about King Eliab responding to my first letter?" he wondered. If that was the case, then what chance did anyone have of talking to the king?

He turned the letters over again in his hands. There was no mistake. It was a flat denial because he had no one to mediate for him. And who would?

He crammed the letters into his pocket. *Now what?* What good would it do to plant the seed? But his friends were waiting for him. He had told them he would plant his seed.

Adam ground his foot into the stone pavement. No mediator. No help. It was unreasonable!

"I *will* plant that seed. Let the king say what he will, but I'll prove I'm worthy if it kills me." If this was his only chance, then he would make it happen—no matter how many snakes and pitfalls stood in his way.

HANK

Chapter 27

"Be not afraid, but speak." Acts 18:9

Hank flopped his sack of grain against the planks of the storage wall and stood up, rubbing the soreness out of his arms. "We'll be able to eat a little longer, won't we?" he asked as his father lowered a heavier sack beside his.

"The king has been gracious, as always. Did you think he would let us starve? Look at what his son did for your mother." Father smiled, ruffling Hank's fiery red hair with his hand.

Hank left the shed and walked out into the yard. *I wish Teacher were here right now.* His stomach twisted. A gnawing feeling told him Adam's plan wasn't right. But how could he explain it to Adam? He had never been strong at arguing, and Adam would demand a good explanation.

Father rubbed his sleeve across his forehead and meandered back toward the house, whistling. The heavy scent of grain filled Hank's nostrils. He heard the door close behind Father and stooped to lift the bundle of rope he had left here two days ago.

What am I doing? Teacher never asked him to bring rope. Neither did he make plans in secrecy. Planting seeds honored the king, but surely not without Teacher. He would come and help them if they waited.

Hank threw the rope down and let it lie. He wiped his sweaty palms against his breeches. "We have to go with Teacher." Saying the words aloud told Hank he would have to speak up. Adam wouldn't like it, though.

Hank met Christy on the path coming from her house. She was straining to carry a large basket. He ran to help. "What is this?" He took one of the handles.

Christy sighed with relief and pushed the hair away from her face with her free hand. "Mostly waterskins." She panted. "I also included some bananas and a few other foods. It's too bad I didn't have time to make daidoush, but we only got the bananas today from the supplies wagon."

She let out a long breath. "It sure is hot. We'll be glad for the water."

Hank nodded. Perhaps he should ask Christy what she thought about going without Teacher. But she had made all these preparations. He swallowed.

"I wonder how long we'll be gone," Christy said. "It didn't take that long when I went with Teacher." She frowned. "Adam is making everything different."

This might be a good time to say what I think. Hank cleared his throat, but no words came out.

"Do you know what Sammy did this morning?"

Hank fumbled with the seed in his pocket. "No. What?"

He sighed inwardly. Never mind saying anything now. He would have to listen patiently while Christy prattled on about her dumb goat.

When they reached the King's Road, Hank saw Camdin flying toward them. A cloud of dust trailed behind him. He stopped and hopped from foot to foot.

"Change of plans," he announced, gulping air. "Adam's been held up. He wants us to meet him farther up the road. Are you ready?" He started moving past them. "Let's go."

Christy let go of the basket. Her side clunked to the ground. "Wait a minute." She put her hands on her hips. "That doesn't sound like a good idea to me. What do you mean *he's been held up?*"

Camdin ran back. "He had to wait for his seed, but he's coming soon. He told me where to go. Come on, I'll show you."

Hank was about to protest, but Christy frowned and said, "Well, all right then."

Camdin took off.

Christy lifted the basket handle and started after him.

Hank had little choice but to let Christy drag him along while he held up his end of the basket. They trudged down the road. Camdin bounded in circles around them, urging them to hurry. They passed the school and Teacher's house. Hank gave a longing look toward the door.

If only Teacher would open it.

"Why don't you take a turn with the basket?" Christy called to Camdin.

But he was out of range, standing at the top of Lookout Hill. Christy harrumphed. Hank took a deep breath. Maybe now was his chance to see what she thought. "Christy."

She didn't respond.

Hank shook his head and studied the dusty road. Perhaps he shouldn't say anything. She'd agreed with Adam, so this trip couldn't be as bad as he thought.

Clunk!

Christy's side of the basket hit the ground, jerking Hank out of his thoughts. His head snapped up. "Hey!"

"Look at Camdin." Christy pointed. "Just leave the basket." She took off running.

Camdin waved his arms back and forth, signaling them to join him. He gestured at something on the opposite side of the hill.

Hank heaved the basket to the side of the road and sprinted after Christy.

By the time Hank reached the top of Lookout Hill, he was panting. He threw himself down next to Camdin, who was flattened on his stomach. Christy lay on his other side.

"Down there," Camdin whispered, pointing. "What are they doing?"

At first, Hank saw nothing. Then far away, he made out the form of a wooden structure. It rose above a boulder-sized rock with red stains running down its sides. Several men, merely dots in size at this distance, crowded around it.

"It's a bleeder," Hank said. A shiver passed through him.

Father had showed Hank a diagram of a bleeder once. Worse than the gallows, the rugged instrument of execution did more than just kill. It tortured and tormented its victims. A rope suspended the body from the wooden beams. Then a giant spike was hammered through both wrists, prolonging the criminal's agony. The outcome was always death.

Hank shuddered and turned away. *I feel sick.* He put his hand in front of Camdin's eyes. "Don't look. Let's go back and wait somewhere else."

Camdin peeled Hank's fingers away from his eyes. "Adam said to meet at Red Rock. We have to follow the King's Road. It might go right past where those men are." He bit his lip. "Why are they doing that?"

Hank and Christy exchanged worried glances. The path Teacher took to the Mount of Humility started behind his house. Why would Adam want them to go so far out of the way? It seemed like a waste of time.

"Never mind." Christy said. "Adam is making the wrong decision if he wants us to meet there. I'm going to stick to the right path, the one Teacher showed us. Let's go back. I'm sure Adam would agree, especially if he saw all those men."

Without waiting for a reply, she turned and marched back down the hill.

Hank looked at Camdin and shrugged. "I'm going back too." He headed down the hill, smiling when he heard Camdin's footsteps close behind.

Hank and Camdin caught up to Christy near Teacher's house. She had grabbed the basket and dragged it along the way. Now, she sat on a stone beside the road, ankles crossed and waiting for them.

The small group waited for Adam in silence. From time to time, Hank glanced at the top of Lookout Hill. What were those men up to with the bleeder?

"There he is." Christy pointed.

Adam hurried toward them. A black rope hung from his shoulder, and his sword bounced against his leg.

I should talk to Adam alone, before he joins us, Hank thought. But how? Camdin might come along. That would be awkward. He pondered a few minutes more. By the time he decided to run back and meet him, it was too late.

Adam started talking before Hank could say a word. "What are you guys doing here?" His brows knit with frustration. "Camdin, I told you—"

"It isn't Camdin's fault." Christy stood up. "He told us you wanted to meet farther ahead, but that didn't make sense. It's better to meet you where the path starts."

"Besides," Hank put in, "men on the other side of the hill are building a bleeder. If we go that way, they might see us."

Adam glanced toward the top of the hill. "I'll have to take a look."

Christy sighed. "Just trust us, Adam. Why do you have to see for yourself?"

Adam shifted the rope to his other shoulder. "What do you want me to do, give up? Lives are at stake, including ours. We've got to get over there."

"That's ridiculous," Christy said. "What's the point of going over the hill? The path to the Mount of Humility starts right here, behind Teacher's house."

"It does?" Adam glanced at Hank. "Is that where you started from?"

Hank nodded.

"Well, let's do it then. We don't have time to debate." Adam seized a handle of the basket and gestured at Hank to take the other one. "But if you want to talk about something

256

ridiculous, then we can start with this basket. We're on a dangerous mission, Christy, not a picnic."

She puckered her face. "I suppose you think you can make it to the top and back without water."

Adam glowered but said nothing. The four friends pushed through the gate to Teacher's garden and picked their way toward the forest. Rows of turquoise orchids danced beside them. Hank remembered when he had passed this way with Teacher. They had stopped and enjoyed the flowers.

Not this time. Adam's tugging from the front end of the basket kept Hank jogging to keep up. He wished he had the courage to protest. He kept trying, but his words would not come.

Time passed. They sped through familiar places, giving them hardly a glance. Adam took the lead at all times. He kept the group out of breath, pushing them as if they were being pursued.

Hank rubbed his hand across his brow and shook off streams of sweat. Even under the trees the heat was oppressive. "Let's take a break." He tugged on the basket. "We can't keep up this pace without water, and my arms are sore." He lowered his side to the ground.

Adam winced as the weight shifted and pushed his palms against his legs as if he was in pain. "Let's go a little longer." He reached for the handle. "We would have made it farther if it wasn't for this basket. Here, Camdin, take Hank's spot. Let's keep moving."

Christy tossed her head. "Oh, stop it, Adam. Are you trying to make our lungs give out? We can't go up the ridges at this pace. Let's drink some water and catch our breath. If nothing else, it will make the basket lighter. I'll take a turn at carrying it. Set it down."

Adam kept a tight grip on the handle, but Camdin reached around and jerked out a waterskin. "Thanks, Christy." He flopped down on a rotten log.

Hank took some water as well.

Adam sighed and let go.

Christy handed Adam a banana. "We're making better progress than you think. The steps are not far." She distributed bananas to the others.

"Steps?" Adam peeled the banana and shoved his mouth full.

Hank took a swig of water. "The steps go down into an old riverbed and then come up again on the opposite side. It isn't much farther from there to the base of the mountain."

Adam nodded. "Of course." He pitched his banana peel to the side and reached for the basket handle.

Christy jumped up. "I said I'd take a hand at it. Camdin, take the other handle."

"Adam can take it," Camdin said. "I'm going to run ahead. I want to see the steps."

Adam lifted the basket then grimaced. He let go and pressed his palm against his thrick. "Let's switch sides."

Hank raised his eyebrows. "What's wrong?"

Adam shook his head, picked up the basket, and he and Christy set off.

Hank found it much easier going without lugging the basket. He made a point to keep an eye on Camdin and also on the path behind them, just in case.

When they reached the steps, Hank crouched at the top

and waited until everyone had descended. Then scanning the woods, he darted down the steps after them. He almost crashed into Christy, who had halted right at the bottom.

"Has anyone noticed how dark it's getting?" she asked, staring through the branches high above.

"It's always that way in the forest," Adam said. "Especially at the bottom of a riverbed. It will be lighter once we come up on the other side."

Camdin had perched on the opposite bank of the riverbed and was dangling his legs over the edge. "You'll be surprised. It's even darker from up here."

Hank followed the others' gazes. Was a storm coming? He had read about such things in books.

"All the more reason to hurry," said Adam.

Camdin retreated back down into the riverbed. "Maybe we should go home."

Just then, the group was plunged into shadow. Darkness surrounded them. Hank could see nothing. He heard Christy shriek, and Adam grumbled. Hank rubbed his eyes with his fists and looked again. The forms of his friends began to appear.

"Help!" Adam was doubled over, rolling on the ground and wrestling with an unknown assailant.

Hank started toward them but then stopped. He could hardly see where he was going.

"Let go!" Camdin shouted. "It's just me!"

Adam shot to his feet. "Camdin? Why did you grab me? I might have hurt you."

Camdin's voice trembled as he staggered to his feet. "I didn't try to grab you. The clouds scared me."

Hank dug into the basket. He could see more clearly now and pulled out a waterskin. "Get some water, Camdin. We'll be all right. It's not even as dark as a normal evening once your eyes adjust."

"All the same," said Christy, "I agree with Camdin. We should go back."

"We *can't*." Adam's voice was adamant. "We've come this far already. We promised the king we would plant our seeds today. Don't you know what's at stake?"

"I know one thing," said Christy. "It's too dark to see our way, and it's better if we go home."

"I have a plan." Adam drew his sword. "If you follow me up the riverbed, I know where we can get some torches."

Hank looked up the black riverbed. He knew it wasn't yet evening. What was his family doing? How were they responding to this strange darkness?

Christy crossed her arms. "My father always says to come home before dark. He doesn't even know where I am. Now, you want to go off the normal path and take us with you. It's bad enough that you don't listen to anybody. What's worse is that you keep changing the plan."

"Fine," Adam snapped. "I'll go by myself. The rest of you can go home if you're too scared to finish the job." He took a waterskin and turned his back on the others.

"It isn't fair to force us that way," shouted Christy. "We're not going to go back and just leave you." She grabbed a handle of the basket and began dragging it after Adam.

Hank took the other handle and helped carry it. Camdin scurried to keep up. Little by little they picked their way forward. They rounded a bend and came to a stony incline. The dry riverbed grew shallower and smoother.

Adam went a few more yards then stopped. He looked back.

Hank read the confusion in his friend's eyes. "What is it?"

Adam frowned. "This isn't familiar to me. Perhaps we are in a different riverbed than I first thought."

Christy set down the basket and brushed the dirt from her dress. "That settles it. Let's go back. Maybe we can try again another time."

"It must connect with the other riverbed at some point." Adam closed his eyes and rubbed his hand through his hair. "This just means we'll have to hurry even faster to regain lost ground."

"It *means* it's time to go home," Christy said, a firmness resounding in her tone. "There's no way we're going to plant our seeds and make it back at a decent hour. This isn't the kind of thing Teacher would want us to do."

Adam stared at the parched, dry riverbed. His sword hung limply in his hand.

What is he thinking? Hank wondered.

Adam slid his fingers into his pocket and pulled out a crumpled papla leaf. "I said we were worthy, and I'm going to prove it." He lifted his chin. "I'm *not* going back."

Christy stomped her foot. Dust rose. "You make me so angry, Adam Sonneman! You want us to follow your plan, but it's all about *you*. You never listen to anyone else. You won't follow the rules, and then you think *somehow* you're worthier of the king than the rest of us. Well, I've had it."

She dug inside her pocket. Sniffing back tears, she tore out her seed and hurled it as far as she could up the riverbed. "If you want to plant it, then go ahead. I'm going home. Come on Camdin. Hank, you can do what you want."

Without a backward glance, Christy marched past the basket and back down the riverbed. Camdin scurried after her. Adam stuffed the letter back in his pocket. Lifting his sword, he proceeded up the riverbed.

Hank stood frozen with indecision. His heart raced. His friends were moving in opposite directions. He needed to act. But whom should he follow? He hoisted the basket, banging off the dust against his legs. His legs shook.

He stumbled after Christy and Camdin. Christy was right. It was foolish to go on in the dark. His gut had warned him right from the start that their errand was useless apart from Teacher.

What will happen to Adam?

Hank kicked himself mentally. If only he had talked to Adam sooner. But would it have made a difference? Even now, if he hurried back, he might catch his friend. But what about Christy and Camdin? Perhaps it was too late. He would just have to accept his failure and move on. He ached inside.

No! Hank had put off the right decision long enough. This might be his last chance. After all Teacher had done for him, and all his father had taught him, he must not falter now.

"Oh, King, please help me," he whispered. "You know my weakness. I—"

His foot caught at a root, pitching him forward. The

basket flew out of his hands. He slammed against the dirt riverbank before hitting the ground.

Shuffling feet on rocky soil and a whispered "who is it?" reached his ears.

He staggered to his feet. "It's me, Hank," he called, working to keep his voice steady.

His shoulder stung, and his left foot couldn't bear his full weight.

Camdin and Christy reappeared in front of him. "What happened?" asked Camdin. "Are you all right?"

Hank nodded. "Listen, Christy. Can the two of you find your way back without me?"

She knit her eyebrows together. "I don't see why not. Why? What are you planning to do? You aren't going to continue this wild goose chase, are you? What would your father think?"

Hank held his tongue until Christy stopped for breath. "I need to talk to Adam. Leave the basket here. If all goes well, he can help me carry it back."

Christy eyed him with a long, hard look. Then she nodded. "Very well. Come on, Camdin." They disappeared into the shadows.

Hank swung around and limped a few steps. His foot didn't feel sprained or broken. It would probably regain its strength in a few moments. However, his aching foot did not concern him right now. He thought about his words "on our way back." Christy had believed him. But could he believe himself?

Would he and Adam return?

ADAM III

Chapter 28

"There is a way which seemeth right unto a man, but the end thereof are the ways of death." Proverbs 14:12

A fly buzzed under Adam's nose. Then another. He swatted them away. If only the stench would go with it. He squeezed his burning eyes shut, hoping for relief. Instead, a hot wave of decaying odors doubled him over.

"This isn't working." He sheathed his sword and thrust his face into his thrick, fighting to breathe.

Old feelings of fearfulness tickled his spine. Images of his last visit to the mountain came tumbling back. Why couldn't the others have stuck with him? *I hate being alone!* He had lost track of time as well. How far had he come?

Blinking his eyes open, Adam saw a crooked tree on the bank. A branch dangled over the edge and into the riverbed. His spirits rose. Perhaps he could climb up and get some fresh air. He inhaled until it hurt and held his breath. Hurrying to the tree, he grabbed the branch.

The bark stung his hands. He jerked them back, and his precious breath escaped from his lungs. He bent over. Maybe he could endure the smell after he got acclimated.

He caught the branch again. Fire shot through his palms, but he held on and reached for a higher position. The branch cracked and swung against the dirt wall. Adam let go, and the branch snapped back. His wrists hurt.

"I need a different plan." He gagged against the noxious odors. Clearly, some kind of animal had died nearby.

The next time Adam grabbed the branch, he maneuvered his body to where he could walk up the dirt. Hand over hand, he edged up the riverbank. Then with a final, awkward twist, he pushed off and landed on his knees in the forest.

The air did smell better up here. If he kept going through the woods, he might work his way around the source of the stench and descend to the riverbed later. But the rhododendrons were dense. It would be slow going.

A scraping noise from the riverbed below startled Adam. He dropped to his belly and peered over the edge. With relief he recognized Hank. His friend was limping his way across the rocky riverbed.

"Hank," Adam whispered. Then louder, "*Hank.*"

Hank whipped around, his wide eyes scanning every direction at once.

Adam rose and shook the tree. "I'm up here."

Hank hurried to the bank and squinted to see. "Is that you, Adam?" Then he gagged, coughed, and turned away. "What's that awful smell?"

Adam's relief was so great, he laughed out loud.

"Something dead, I think. Never mind that. I thought you

left with the others."

"I … I decided to come back."

"I'm glad you did. Say, the air's better up here. Perhaps we can get around the smell. Do you need a hand?"

Hank shook his head. He whispered something Adam couldn't hear.

"I'm sorry. I didn't hear you." Adam leaned over the edge.

Hank gulped for air and spoke louder. "We need to talk."

Adam frowned. "What about?" Maybe Hank wasn't going to climb up and join him, after all. Had Christy sent him back to talk Adam out of going?

Hank reached out and shook the branch Adam had climbed. "Well, let's talk about this branch. Do you see these few leaves that are still green?"

Adam nodded.

"How did they get that way?"

Adam squinted, uncertain where this was going.

"The branch gets its life from the trunk and eventually from the roots," Hank continued when Adam didn't reply. "If I snap it off, the branch will shrivel and die. It doesn't have any life of its own. It has no power to make these leaves green by itself."

"What are you getting at?" Adam demanded. "We have a mission to accomplish, and it's getting late. You can give me plant lessons while we travel."

"Don't you see, Adam? We–you and I–are the branches. We don't have any power on our own, least of all to conquer the Mount of Humility. We must rely on someone else, on Teacher. The king never meant for us to go to the mountain alone."

Adam's face burned at Hank's words. Somehow, it always came to the same old thing—run to Teacher. Christy said it too. Sure, it had worked for Hank. But what kind of merit would that earn Adam with the king? The others weren't guilty of Adam's long list of crimes. Would the king say, "Oh, everything's fine now"? That was too simplistic.

Even if the king did say it, what then would be the point of all Adam's efforts? He gripped the branch and leaned farther over the edge. "So, you're saying I've been wrong all this time."

Hank winced. "Well, perhaps. I mean … I was wrong not to speak up sooner. But the main thing is what you do now."

"You think I'm wrong to plant my seed?" Adam tried to keep the edge off his voice, but it was hard to hide his feelings.

Hank took a deep breath. "What is wrong is trying to go without Teacher. You've got to come to him. If you don't?" He shuddered. "Adam, I've seen the strength of evil. You know what would have happened to me."

Adam couldn't deny Hank's story. A sense of longing stirred him. But maybe it wasn't the same for everyone. Teacher had made it clear that Adam had angered him. Then Adam had turned his back on him again.

How can I come to him now? What could Teacher do to help him, even if he did come?

"Why Teacher?" he asked at last.

Hank gave him an incredulous look. "Because he's the whole trunk, and the roots, and *everything*. This is what he was trying to teach us a long time ago. Who else carries such authority in his voice? Or such wisdom? He had the power to raise Christy from the dead. He loves us, Adam. Who else would you turn to?"

Adam remained silent.

Hank coughed several times into his fist. He blinked watery eyes. "You know you can't do it by yourself, Adam. Let's go. Let's get away from this stench."

Adam shot to his feet. The bushes scratched his back. His face burned with anger. "That's what everyone says. But I can do it. I *will* do it. I'll go to the very peak, even if it takes me all year."

He turned and pushed into the rhododendrons, fighting blindly to force his way through. His words sounded insane, even to himself. He knew he was wrong and wished he could go back.

But he was too ashamed. He couldn't face Hank.

It isn't fair! There was no way he could plant his seed. Every part of his plan had collapsed, and yet his very life depended on success. It was impossible to please the king. *Impossible.* Perhaps Grandfather was right. It was better not to try, better to be free from unreasonable laws.

Adam grabbed his sword and began hacking at the branches. He could hardly walk. Thorn vines clung to his clothes and yanked at him. He jerked away from one branch and got scraped by another. A clear place up ahead beckoned him to press on. He dropped to his knees and tried to wriggle through a gap near the ground.

Thorns caught his breeches. He heard the tearing cloth as he fought to keep going. But he was rewarded with a sudden release and tumbled free onto empty ground. Shaking himself, he looked around and realized he had found a path.

What a relief. He could follow it back to the riverbed. Once there, he would have to decide which way to go, but this was progress enough for the moment. He sheathed his sword and began easing his way along the path.

A voice caught his attention. He stood still and listened. Had he imagined it?

"Adam, hurry!"

Hank! Why was he yelling? Didn't he know how dangerous this forest was? Anybody could be lurking about. He bolted under a branch and around a corner.

The ground ended abruptly. Adam skidded to a stop just in time, sending a shower of broken, white rocks over the edge and into the riverbed below. Backing up, he drew a deep breath. The rotting smell of burnt flesh knocked him back like a wave. He doubled over, fighting to control his stomach.

"Adam, Adam! Get down here. I think it might be a soldier."

Adam squinted through burning eyes and saw Hank waving his arms in the riverbed below him. A rag was tied around his face, but it couldn't disguise the sound of Hank gagging. Swarms of flies filled the air, buzzing around his friend and a dark mass lying near him. *What is it?*

Then he knew. The blackened uniform. The remote location. The smell. Hank's words, "*I think it's a soldier,*" pierced his soul.

Adam scrambled over the edge and down the dusty bank, leaping the last few feet in a single bound. Angry flies scattered like plumes of smoke. Gagging, he held his breath and rushed to the disfigured body. His stomach heaved.

Reaching out a tentative foot, Adam turned over what was left of the body. A charred arm flopped to the side, exposing the face.

Hank jumped backward, but Adam stood frozen at the sight. The body was burned and decayed beyond recognition, but the cap left Adam without any doubt. Shining through the singed cloth was a large brass button. Adam knew it right away. He snatched the cap and then recoiled from the corpse as from a viper.

Hank watched, eyes red and puffy. He looked like he might lose his breakfast any moment. "W-who d-do you th-think it is?" he stammered.

Adam didn't reply. He couldn't. Tears clogged his throat. He tore the button from the fabric and dropped the hat. Gagging against the smell, he pushed Hank back the way he'd come.

Slowly at first, the boys made their way down the riverbed. Then Adam broke into a run, and Hank stayed at his heels. Their steps pounded one right after another, echoing the pounding of Adam's heart.

After what seemed like hours of stumbling through the eerie darkness, Adam finally made out the stone steps to their right. "Come on!" He clambered up them two at a time.

Once at the top, Hank collapsed on the ground. His sides heaved. "I have to rest."

Adam flopped down beside him, dropping the coil of black rope that still hung from his shoulder. He tried swallowing the lump in his throat, but it wouldn't budge. He stared into the forest.

"Adam." Hank clutched his arm. "Why did you take that button from the man's cap? Did you recognize him?"

Adam closed his eyes and fought to control his churning stomach. He shook his head and struggled to his feet.

"Adam! What's the matter?"

Adam's eyes filled with tears. It's *Liptor*! He wanted to yell, but his words couldn't get past his tight throat. He shook his head. *I can't tell him.* He brushed off his clothes and grabbed the rope.

"I need to talk to Grandfather."

ADAM III

CHAPTER 29

"Choose you this day whom ye will serve." Joshua 24:15

The governor's courtyard was a chaos of shouting soldiers and servants. Torches flashed past Adam as he staggered toward the house, but he hardly noticed them. He seized the door and clung to it to keep himself from collapsing. The image of Liptor's scorched body flashed through his mind.

He shook himself, straightened, and entered the main hall. "Grandfather!"

No answer. Where could he be?

Adam shifted his feet toward the side hall that led to the study. A discarded uniform caught his foot, and he shouted before he could stop himself. The memory of the corpse in a burned uniform was still fresh. He stood for a moment, shivering.

A heavy door beyond the study rattled open, and two soldiers emerged with drawn swords. Adam wanted to scoot out of the way, but curiosity bound him to the spot. It was the first time he had seen that door swing open since he was a small child. Why were the soldiers coming up from the dungeon?

A loud, cantankerous voice blasted from behind the soldiers. "Bullwhips and bloodbaths! What's this world coming to? Get out of my way or I'll tear you down."

Adam dodged past the side hall and ran the other direction. The last person he wanted to meet this evening was old Roberts, especially in his foul mood. He hoped the soldiers hadn't noticed Adam standing in the hall. What if they thought he was spying where he shouldn't be?

Their footsteps marched closer. Without thinking, he plunged through the closest entryway, dashed down a short corridor, and swung open the door to the sunroom.

Adam froze, mouth agape. Grandfather's foot was propped on a chair as he stood leaning into an earnest conversation with Uncle Tari, Liptor's father. His uncle's strong, sleek face shone whiter than the ivory in the table. He jumped to his feet when Adam entered, knocking his chair to the floor.

In three steps, Grandfather crossed the room and seized him by the shoulder. "Where in the name of all evil have you been? Can't you see what has happened to the sky?"

Adam bobbed his head, too afraid to answer.

Grandfather jerked the black rope off Adam's shoulder and threw it on the table. "And where did you get my rope? Roberts has upset the whole city trying to find it for me. Do you think you own this place?" He shook Adam and shoved him against the wall.

Uncle Tari's eyes were egg-sized when they met Adam's. He ignored Grandfather's rebukes and spoke in soft tones to Adam. "Do you know where Liptor is?" He searched Adam's face. "We thought he might be with you. He's been missing since last night, and he never showed up for distribution this morning."

Adam swallowed the knot that had filled his throat since finding Liptor's body. If Uncle Tari knew his son better, he would know that Liptor and Adam did not spend time together.

"Yes," he answered. "I saw him. In the woods."

Uncle Tari jumped forward, but Grandfather stayed him with a firm elbow against his chest. "What do you mean? Was he all right?"

Adam pressed against the wall. Digging a hand into his pocket, he brought out the brass button and placed it in Uncle Tari's hand. "I don't know what happened, but he was burned when I found him."

A cry escaped Uncle Tari's lips, and he sank into his chair.

Grandfather's eyes narrowed to slits. He scratched at his stubbly beard. "Why were you in the forest?"

Adam turned away and stared at the sunroom windows. His face reflected back to him, pale and empty. He had given no thought to what he would say about his adventure. He fell into his old thought patterns as his mind raced to find a way out.

"I … I was keeping an eye out for the Keeda," he said at last, flicking a glance into Grandfather's eyes.

"Go on," Grandfather barked.

"I was following one of the riverbeds, like the one where we went a few months ago. Everything got strangely dark, but I kept going. I was hoping to join the other riverbed and get a torch. Then I found Liptor. He was lying on his face—"

He broke off and stared at the floor, waiting for an explosion from Grandfather. But no sound came. Adam's ears and face grew hot. Was this the calm before the storm? Would Grandfather believe him?

When Grandfather broke the silence, his words were not at all what Adam expected. He rubbed Uncle Tari's back with a muscular hand and reached out with the other. "Let me see the button, Tari."

He held it up to the light, eyeing the twisted serpent's heads with the fruit and the sword. With a slight nod and a grunt, he extended the button to Adam. "Here, keep this."

Adam turned the button over in his hands. What did Grandfather mean? Didn't he recognize the Sonneman family's symbol?

"It appears I have been mistaken about your merits." Grandfather scratched his rough whiskers. "Is this the first time you have gone out on this kind of mission?"

Adam's mind raced. Was Grandfather praising him for spying on the Keeda? He felt ashamed to take credit for a lie. But would Grandfather finally respect him? "Only a few times." He lifted his chin. "But I haven't seen anything else since the night of the fire."

"You're a good boy." Grandfather chewed on each word as he spoke. "I believe it is time we promote you. Since Liptor can no longer fulfill his duties, I will give you his position. What do you say?"

A torrent of emotions engulfed Adam. He ached for Uncle Tari, who sat motionless with his head in his hands. Shock numbed Adam at this sudden reversal in his fortunes. His veins coursed with power, as if a door had been flung open before him and he stood on the edge of a new world of conquest.

Most of all, his longing for Grandfather's acceptance seemed to have a chance of becoming a reality. After yearning for it all his life, had he finally gained it?

A sense of warning pounded a drumbeat in his chest, but he pushed away the voice of his conscience. *Yes, I lied. But why not?* Adam had tried to please the king, and where had it led him? Only to failure at every turn. He rubbed the brass button between his fingers. Now, at last, he had a chance to gain position.

A tingle of doubt ran down his spine. What would Hank say? He squeezed his button. *Hank can't understand how much this means to me.*

A commotion in the corridor interrupted Adam's scattered thoughts. Roberts thrust his shaggy head through the sunroom's open door, glowering. "The prisoner has been secured."

Grandfather slid his foot off the chair and tossed the black rope to Roberts. "What is that to me? Here's the rope. It made its way back. Now, get on with it."

Roberts huffed. "Can't a man eat his dinner in peace first?"

Grandfather pushed up against Roberts, his muscles tight. "The Keeda are pressuring us for a human sacrifice. This execution will get them off our backs and rid us of a traitor, as well. The men will meet you at Red Rock."

Uncle Tari shook his head, clearly dazed. "Red Rock? But what about the prophecy?"

"This isn't the time to worry about foolish things like that. Roberts, get going."

The head servant withdrew, muttering about his beard and his belly.

"One more thing," Grandfather shouted after him. "Find Schala and send him to me. I've got a new soldier for him to train."

The words sounded like a thunderclap in Adam's ears. Send for Schala? Was *this* the door of opportunity Grandfather was opening? Schala may have been Liptor's trainer. Would he be Adam's now? Worse, wasn't it Schala who'd promised Liptor he would meet his master? Was Schala—Adam gulped—Liptor's murderer?

He flung the button across the room as if it burned his hand. "No! I can't accept. I won't."

Grandfather jerked back, his eyes flashing.

Adam knew that look. Grandfather would seize him any second. Clutching a chair from the table, Adam shoved it between him and the governor. Then he ducked under his arm and out of the room. He raced down the corridor, crashing into Roberts in the main hall.

"Pins and pigs' feet!" the old man hollered after him. "Where are you going?"

Adam wasn't about to stop and answer. He slammed through the front door, flinging himself out into the courtyard. His feet slipped, and he stumbled forward to recover his balance. *Faster, faster!*

Footsteps sounded behind Adam. The courtyard was long—too long. Thankfully, it was empty. He dodged to the right and crouched behind a giant planter. His breath came in frightened gasps.

He heard Roberts yelling and the sound of two or more men running past his hiding place. A few moments later, the quiet crunch of slow steps on broken tiles reached Adam's ears. He cowered and tried to make himself small.

"What gets into young people at times like this?" muttered Roberts as he shuffled past. "And the governor, for that matter. I don't like any of this business. Makes me sick to my stomach."

He trudged across the courtyard, swinging the tip of the black rope between his bony fingers. Adam watched him disappear through the gate. Then he waited until he was sure the old man was gone. Quietly, Adam padded to the center of the courtyard. *If I can just get out to the road, I might get away.*

The outer gate squeaked open.

Adam stood petrified to the spot. It was too late to hide. Where could he turn?

But the figure peeking around the gate reflected Adam's panic. Enormous eyes met his and then softened with recognition.

"Hank!" Adam whispered.

The boy gulped for air and gestured at Adam to go back. Uncertain, Adam returned to the planter. Hank followed, and the two boys ducked behind the stone planter together.

"Hank, I'm sorry for what I said."

"Shhh." Hank clamped his hand over Adam's mouth. "Be

quiet," he whispered. "He might arrive any minute."

Adam pulled the hand away. "Who? Roberts?"

Hank shook his head, glancing toward the gate. "No. Schala."

Adam caught his breath. His heart raced, and he fought to control his breathing. How could Roberts have found Schala so quickly? It didn't make sense.

"Schala was headed toward your house when I saw him. He had that look in his eye, the same look he had when he chased me. If Roberts hadn't stopped him on the way, I don't think I could have made it before him."

The words had just left Hank's mouth when Schala entered the courtyard. His fiery eyes scanned his surroundings. Drawing a long knife out of his belt, he slid it into his boot, marched to the house, and let himself in.

Adam swiveled away. He shoved his back against the rocky planter and squeezed his fingernails into his closed fists. The stabbing pain shooting through his palms snapped his eyes open.

Hank clutched his arm. "Adam, you can't stay here."

Adam whirled. "You're right. Thank you." He swallowed. "Thank you so much for what you said."

Hank nodded. "I know what that look on Schala's face means."

"Not just what you said now," Adam said. "I mean, what you said to me in the forest. You were right, Hank. I see it now. I'm going to run to Teacher."

In spite of his terror, a sense of great peace coursed through Adam. He felt that a great burden had been lifted, as if he was truly beginning to be free.

When he stood to go, a strange thought struck him. *Why, I'm standing in the same spot where Father stood all those years ago, the night he argued with Grandfather about planting his seed.* Chills skittered up his neck.

Hank broke into Adam's musing with common sense. "Hurry, Adam. Let's get out of here before it's too late." He smiled, despite the serious words.

They darted through the gate and onto the King's Road. Adam was glad they didn't encounter Roberts as they ran past the fields, although he couldn't guess where he had gone. "What next?" he asked Hank. "Where will I find Teacher?"

Hank didn't answer. He turned off at the path that led to his house and beckoned Adam to follow.

Adam hesitated. What would Hank's family think of him hanging around? Worse, he didn't want to see Christy. Her house was too close to Hank's.

"I want to go to Teacher's house," he told Hank.

His friend shot a backward glance toward the city. "He wasn't there this morning. Let's ask my father if he knows when Teacher is returning."

"I want to go straight to his house," Adam insisted. He looked around but saw no one on the dusty road. "It will be okay. Maybe I can find a clue if I look around carefully. I'll be back."

Adam took off running before Hank could argue. At that moment, he was glad to be alone. Once he made certain his friend was not following, he slowed to a walk.

"Now maybe I can clear my head," he said. "So much has happened in just one day."

His thoughts whirled. Was he right to reject Grandfather's offer? How many years had he dreamed of such an opportunity? Adam shook his head to clear it. *Yes!* He *had* made the right choice. Teacher loved him, just like Hank said. Grandfather had never shown love. "Why didn't I see it before?"

Images came to mind of Teacher's smile as he explained the laws of the universe or led the class in discussions about Mount Eirene's history. Adam remembered the tears in Teacher's eyes when he spoke to him in the city center. Adam couldn't forget the glow on his face when he explained the promised new covenant.

"If only I could talk to him now." Adam walked faster. How would he ever find the words to express how sorry he was? With Teacher, perhaps the words didn't matter. "If I can only find him!"

Teacher's house appeared through the gloom. Adam broke into a run, driven not by fear but by longing. He leaped over the fence into Teacher's yard. Halfway up the porch stairs something odd caught his attention. He stopped at the top of the steps and stared. A large notice was nailed to the door, with bold letters scrawled across its face.

His heart skipped a beat. Even without reading it, Adam knew this was not good news. He wanted to turn away, but his gaze remained fastened on the parchment. Trembling, he squinted to make out the writing:

THE OCCUPANT OF THIS HOUSE HAS BEEN CHARGED WITH INCITING THE PEOPLE AND IS IN CUSTODY OF THE GOVERNOR OF MOUNT EIRENE.

ANY PERSON CAUGHT ASSISTING THE PRISONER
WILL BE SUBJECT TO THE PENALTIES OF THE LAW.

The double-headed snake was stamped in wax below the writing. *Grandfather approved this!* Adam read the words again. Teacher a prisoner? Grandfather hated Immanuel, but what cause did he have to imprison him? "It can't be true!"

He ran to the window to peer inside.

Whack! The sound of splintering wood spun Adam around. He gasped. A hatchet lay buried in the door, right where Adam had been standing. Schala stood twenty paces away, glowering. Then he stooped and reached into the top of his boot.

Oh, no! Adam scrambled away and tumbled over the porch railing, landing on the ground in a heap. He ignored the stabbing pain that shot through his left leg and leaped up. *Behind the house*, he told his legs. *Run!*

He made it and was halfway around the other side when it occurred to him that Schala might head him off.

He froze. *Which way?* There was nowhere to hide. The darkness might help, but it wasn't enough. He listened for his pursuer, but he only heard a rumbling noise that filled the air with a dull booming. There was no time to guess what it was or where it came from.

His only thought was getting away from Schala.

A picture of Liptor's charred body flashed across his mind, and he gasped. *Run!*

Schala gave an answering shout and leaped at Adam from the side of the house.

Adam yelped and took off back the way he had come. He

expected to feel the knife blade any second. He paid no attention to the sharp pain in his leg but ran as if his life depended on it. *Go, go, go!*

He would have to run until his heart burst to get back to Hank's house. For now, though, if he could just make it through Teacher's gate. He charged past the right side of the house and saw Schala bearing down on him from the left. The rumbling noise thundered in his ears.

Adam flew through the gate with the enemy right on his heels. The road lay only a few paces away. Out of the corner of his eye, he saw a bright light and an enormous cloud rushing toward him along the highway. But there was no time to wait or think. He gathered his last bit of strength into one great leap and sailed across the road, past the onrushing noise. He crashed into the dirt and rolled over multiple times before he lay still.

Adam lay with his eyes closed, expecting the worst. Hundreds of shouting voices and neighs of horses burst through the thunder. He opened his eyes and saw white stallions rearing. The steady thundering broke into muffled roaring, and he realized the entire road for as far as he could see was engulfed in warriors wearing blue and gold, sitting astride their mounts.

Suddenly, they stopped.

A warrior urged his steed toward Adam. Before he could react, the warrior leaped out of the saddle, grabbed Adam, and hurled him onto the front of his horse. Swinging up behind him, he rejoined his troop.

A trumpet blasted. The horses leaped forward, and the army thundered on toward the city.

Adam glanced back to see what had become of Schala. A dark shadow scuttled away into the forest. *Schala!*

The green eyes of the warrior behind Adam gleamed with anger.

"Who are you?" asked Adam, trembling.

"I am Malakan, servant of the king."

"Thank you for rescuing me."

"I'm not rescuing you," Malakan answered. "Be glad I don't kill you at once, rebel." His muscles tensed into iron bands.

"The judgment of your city has come."

ADAM III

Chapter 30

"That every mouth may be stopped, and all the world may become guilty before God" Romans 3:19

Houses and fields flashed by as Adam fought to retain his balance on the horse. He had never moved so quickly in all his life. The combination of jolting bounces and thunderous hoofbeats dizzied him. Somewhere at the front of the line, a brilliant light illuminated the surrounding countryside.

Where is it coming from? What's happening? Adam's thoughts spun, but he dared not ask his captor any questions. He kept his mouth shut and his eyes open.

At the turnoff near Hank's and Christy's houses, the company halted. Riders displaying the king's colors fanned out in an enormous arch, spreading out to cover the entire countryside. Warriors in front of Adam shifted their horses, and for the first time he saw the king.

He could see only his back, but there was no doubt who

he was. The king was peerless in his physical perfection. The robe, the great sword, and the glowing crown marked him as the island's sovereign. But there was so much more. Power and authority emanated from him. Light sprang up all around him.

King Eliab lifted his hand and urged his horse forward. His troops followed him, sweeping across the territory that surrounded Mount Eirene. Sections of horsemen detached and rode off in different directions. Some plunged into the camps of Eirenian refugees. Malakan, however, moved steadily forward and remained in line with the king.

Adam squinted his eyes against the light. Behind him sounded the thundering from thousands of mounted soldiers. Were they still pouring over the hills? What had his captor meant by "the judgment of your city has come"? He shivered. *Has the king come to destroy us once and for all?*

They rode up the hill into Mount Eirene. People shouted and fled in every direction. The king turned and called to his army. His powerful voice filled the air. It rose above the pounding hoofbeats and the clamor of the city. "Gather them all. Let none be overlooked."

Royal soldiers swung to the ground. They entered homes, leading out wide-eyed citizens and marching them in line behind the king. A group of twenty soldiers charged into the governor's quarters, their swords raised.

King Eliab proceeded on toward the city center. When he entered the plaza, he rode directly into the middle. With majesty in his bearing, he dismounted his steed and ascended the stairs of the great fountain. Below him, still mounted on his horse, a muscular, dark-skinned soldier carried a heavy flagpole with a red banner tied around it.

Malakan turned his mount and circled the plaza. He checked his horse in line with several others and stood at attention, facing the king.

Adam tightened his grip on the saddle horn and trembled in the presence of the island's lord. Light continued to stream from King Eliab, expanding in radiant colors that covered the plaza, the buildings, and the whole sky. The giant stones glowed with brilliant whiteness.

Adam swiveled his head away in a daze, blinded by the intensity. He heard doors banging, wild shouts, and unbelieving gasps. When his eyes adjusted, the plaza had become a sea of chaotic citizens. No one resisted the king's forces.

A band of royal soldiers stood behind Grandfather, pinning his arms. Shock and terror spread across the man's features, an expression Adam had never seen before. No one spoke, but every person's wide eyes screamed the same silent message: *Woe! Woe to the city at the presence of the king!*

The people squeezed together as the king's vast army continued to file in. Soon, the city center was surrounded. Soldiers packed the rim of the plaza and beyond, clogging the streets. Archers streamed to the rooftops, notched their arrows, and pointed them at the crowd.

In the middle of the chaos, a band of Keeda clustered together. Adam shaded his eyes. *What are Keeda doing here?* Were they the ones demanding the human sacrifice from Grandfather?

A blast from a great trumpet sounded. The surging,

shoving crush of people grew still. A hush spread over the crowd.

The intense light softened to the brilliance of a summer day. Adam stopped squinting. The light was bright but different from sunlight. Why? The horse shifted, and Adam saw it.

There are no shadows! He glanced around. No shadows at all, not throughout the entire city. Everything was exposed in detail. Not even a grasshopper could have found a corner to hide in.

Then for the first time he got a clear look at the king's face.

Trembling gripped Adam to the core of his soul. His fear of Schala paled in comparison. It was a different kind of terror too. Adam was afraid of the evil Schala. Before King Eliab, however, Adam quaked at his own evil deeds.

Something strangely familiar radiated from the king, yet Adam never imagined such piercing eyes. They shone deeper than the sky, full of glory and wisdom. And Eliab's face was beautiful. Not like a flower in Teacher's garden, but breathtaking—like the golden gate.

Eliab held his head high and gazed into the people's faces.

Then the sound of trumpet blasts shattered the air. The king stepped forward on the ivory fountain's platform. Lifting his hands toward the sky, he spoke in a voice that resonated throughout the plaza.

"Hear, O heavens, and give ear, O earth, for the lord has spoken. I have nourished and brought up these people as children, and yet they have rebelled against me. The ox knows his owner, and the mule its master's feed trough, but Mount Eirene does not know me. My people do not consider."

Eliab lowered his hands and extended them toward the people. "Ah, sinful nation, a people weighed down with iniquity, children of evil-doers, descendants of corruption. You have forsaken your lord. You have provoked the Holy One of Mount Eirene to anger. You have gone away backward."

Ten thousand throats, the king's soldiers, shouted a unified answer in chorus:

"Our king is the Rock,
His work is perfect
For all His ways are judgment,
A king of truth and without iniquity,
Just and right is he."

Adam's limbs shook. The stone of the covenant, poking above the heads of the crowd, caught his eye. *If all the king's ways are judgment, then what hope do I have? I'm a criminal.* He shrank against Malakan's fierce grip. *I feel so exposed sitting up here!* He wanted to spring from the horse and hide in the crowd below.

"Why should I continue to strike you?" the king went on. "You will only revolt more and more. Your city is bruised and beaten into pulp, and yet you refuse to turn to me that I might heal you. Your country is desolate, and your fields are burned with fire, overthrown by strangers. And what good are your petitions? When you lift up your hands to plead with me, they are stained from the abundance of your crimes."

Adam glanced at his palms. The scars stood out, dark against the hideous red stains. People all over the plaza hung their heads and thrust their hands behind their backs.

"Where is your governor?" The king's voice thundered. "Where is Adam Sonneman?"

Soldiers dragged Grandfather through the crowd to the stairs of the King's Fountain. The great leader had been transformed into a trembling, pale shadow of his former self. He stumbled forward, knelt, and pressed his face against the dusty ivory stairs.

"Have we not met here before?" Eliab faced the prostrate governor. "Did I not give you a charge over this people, to lead them in following me? How then have I become a stranger to my own city?"

Grandfather raised his head a fraction but said nothing.

"Adam Sonneman, is that your signature on the stone of the covenant?" The king's finger pointed.

"Yes, your majesty."

"Then where are the seeds I entrusted to your people? Have you planted them, as you swore to me in this place?"

Grandfather shook. His answer was barely above a whisper. Adam leaned forward to hear him. "I ... my lord ... you have not been here for many years. How could I have known you would return and ask this of me?"

Eliab squeezed his eyes shut. "Though you have been unfaithful, yet I have remained faithful. I have not gone back on my word." Opening his eyes, he gestured with his hand. A troop of fifty leaped to hear their king's command. "Go," he ordered. "Search everywhere. We will know what has become of the seeds."

The troop dispersed into the city.

Spreading his hands wide, Eliab stepped forward. "How could you doubt that I would return? My words stand before you every day, as high as the sky in their glory."

Adam glanced at the King's Stones. Had the king prophesied his return? *Maybe I would have known what to do if I had only listened.* Tears pricked the inside of his eyelids.

"I have sent you messengers," the king said. "You slew them. Their blood cries out to me from the ground. Yea, even my beloved son has lived among you, and have you listened? No, you covered your ears and turned away your eyes to your own destruction."

King Eliab's son? Dizziness washed over Adam, and he clung to the saddle horn. *Teacher! How did I not see this before?*

The king signaled again. Soldiers raised their torches and set them ablaze. The fire was hard to see in the bright light, but smoke circled the stone of the covenant. The multitude writhed at the king's words and shrank back at the threatening torches.

None cowered more than the prostrate figure on the stairs. He gasped out broken, indistinguishable phrases that Adam could not make out.

"Do you accuse me of being unreasonable?" asked the king. "Are not *your* ways unreasonable? Consider how much I loved you from the beginning. When I created you, fed you, and built you this city, was that unreasonable? When we walked together in sweet fellowship and ate the fruits of the land, was I unreasonable then?"

Adam picked out Roberts in the midst of the crowd, standing near the fountain stairs. His face blushed deep red. He stared at his feet and rubbed bony fingers across his round belly.

The king took a deep breath. "When we met here and signed the covenant, was it not with joy? Did you not enter willingly into this relationship? No one in the island has received such promises as I offered you."

Clearly, the king did not expect an answer. "But you have forgotten me. You have ignored my words and cast aside my laws. You have broken your promises and dishonored me for days without end. My enemies have boasted against me because of your wickedness. Look!"

He pointed to the stones. "These stones testify against you, for they have witnessed for me day after day, and you did not hearken. You have broken my covenant, and you will pay what is written … until none remains."

The king turned his face away.

Hushed voices rose to a growing hum. Panicked whispers flew back and forth through the plaza. Women wrung their hands. Men shoved each other. The hum grew in intensity.

Then someone shouted, "It's Adam's fault!"

Adam jerked at the sound of his name. But no, the man was not shouting at him. He was shouting at Grandfather.

The crowd took up the chant. "It's Adam's fault. It's Adam's fault. It's Adam's fault."

A clap of thunder rent the air. "Silence!" The king lifted his hands. "Do you question my verdict? You are part of this covenant, every one of you. Adam's name stands for all who follow him. Can any of you say, 'I am clean. I have washed my hands in innocence'?"

As he spoke, the leader of the troop of fifty shoved his way through the crowd. He stepped past Grandfather and bowed to the king. "My Lord, we have searched the city. We found these behind every home. Are they not the remains of your seeds, which you have given?" He approached Eliab and poured black dust like ashes into his hands.

The king stared into his palms. Large tears filled his eyes. Lifting his fists, he let the dust go. A breeze caught the ashes and wafted them across the city.

Adam sneezed when the dark fragments blew into his face. He blinked his stinging, watery eyes.

The king signaled the rider standing beside him. "Let the city be burned. Let every citizen be hanged. The covenant must be fulfilled."

A red flag billowed into the wind, revealing the emblem of flames that covered its face. The crowd erupted into a pandemonium of screaming, wailing, and shouting. Soldiers raised spears and began unwinding ropes. Women fainted. Sobs and shrieks sounded from every corner. "Mercy, mercy!"

Adam heard his own voice cry out, "Mercy!" His conscience shouted back, *It's Adam's fault. It's Adam's fault. It's Adam's fault.*

And for the first time in his life, Adam was not blaming Grandfather.

ADAM III

Chapter 31

*"Therefore doth my Father love me, because I lay
down my life." John 10:17*

A royal soldier carrying a torch passed beside Adam, and
the smoke choked him. His mind snapped back to that
long-ago night in the tree, when he and Grandfather had
spoken by smoky torchlight.

"Unreasonable." That's how Grandfather had described
King Eliab.

Since then, Adam had often repeated that word, even to
Teacher's face. But now, before Eliab's glory, he could say
it no longer. "I cannot accuse the king of any injustice," he
whispered.

The king had remained steadfast. The fault lay not with
Eliab's laws but with the people, who refused to keep them.
And not just any people, Adam admitted silently. *With me
personally. Yes, with Adam Sonneman the Third.* He buried
his face in his stained hands and choked back his guilt.

The horse shifted beneath Adam, and Malakan steadied him as they turned. Strong fingers held him in place like a vice. *As if I could even think of escaping.* Giving the horse a nudge, the islander began to pick his way back toward the road.

A loud cry brought horse and rider to a sudden stop, and he swiveled. Adam craned his neck to see what had happened. *Grandfather!*

Grandfather had clambered up the stairs and now flung himself at Eliab's feet. His wailing rose in volume, and the people hushed to hear his words. At the king's bidding, Grandfather rose to his knees.

"Lord, lord, how could you condemn us for such a thing?" he pleaded. "You have seen that none here can plant their seeds in that mountain. My own flesh and blood have died trying. Will you kill us for not achieving what cannot be done? My lord, climbing the mountain is impossible."

The king raised himself to his full height. His nostrils flared, clearly checking his wrath.

Adam's heart wrenched. Now that he saw with his own eyes the king's anger, he began to understand. This anger was not a storm like Grandfather's, nor a boiling pot like that of old Roberts. Nor was it comparable to Christy's spouts of flashing frustration.

No, behind the king's moist eyes lay a mighty river, an endless source of peace and love. For decades this river had been dammed, rejected by the objects of that love. Now, that river had swelled into an ocean and begun to boil. The fury of rejected love would be held back no longer.

The dam was breaking, and everything before it would be

carried away by the destructive wave.

Adam hugged himself to keep from shaking. *This anger is overwhelming!*

"Impossible?" King Eliab roared. "Do you echo to me the lies my enemy has fed you? The serpent's hiss has ensnared your heart, but I have provided all that was necessary for success. Had you but read my words and come to me, you might have borne fruit."

He raised his hands toward the sky. "Let all the island hear and know forever. My command has been obeyed in every part by one Aardian. From your midst has come forth one who planted his seed in the highest pinnacle of the Mount of Humility. He did not come with strength, but in utter weakness. He did not go surrounded by helpers, but with only my Ruuwh. You have mocked me by your attempts when your stomachs were full, but he went after forty days of hunger."

Eliab looked in triumph across the multitude and even into the faces of his soldiers. "My servant trusted in my strength and found it sufficient to the utmost degree. He has glorified me, and he shall be glorified in my glory. Let him come forth!"

Adam searched the faces of the people. He picked out Christy's father and mother and saw them clinging to each other. Doke hung his head. Hank's father was weeping. Roberts was gasping for air and wringing his beard with his hands.

Then an islander on the outskirts called, "My Lord the King, he is here!"

The crowd parted, and a solitary figure staggered forward.

His hands were tied in front of him. From the side of his head a trickle of blood ran down into his beard.

Adam's breath caught. *Teacher!* He groaned and turned away. He had found Teacher, but it was too late. He couldn't bear to see him in such a hideous condition. Malakan squeezed his shoulder with trembling fingers. Adam winced. *That hurt!*

King Eliab beamed until the sky turned two shades brighter. He held out his arms. With tears streaming down his face, he thundered for all the island to hear, "This is my beloved son, in whom I am well pleased!"

Something leaped inside Adam's heart at the sight of such love and acceptance. How he had longed for such a look of approval all his life. How he yearned for a father's love. But Grandfather scorned him. *And I rebelled against the One who would have loved me.*

Adam sighed until he thought his heart would break. If only he could believe that the king's acceptance could be turned toward him.

Eliab signaled with his hand. "Release my son and let him come to me."

Two islanders leaped to Immanuel's side and sliced through his bonds. Offering him their shoulders they guided him toward the fountain.

Immanuel stopped and gestured toward one of the King's Stones near him. Swallowing hard, he spoke through parched lips. His voice echoed the king's tones:

> *"Lo, I come as it is written of me*
> *To do your will, O my king.*

Your law is within my heart."

Adam knew the words. How many times had Teacher quoted them in class? But what a powerful significance they had now.

Eliab beamed even more. "I have also written:

Rulers shall see you and rise,
Princes also shall worship
Because of the lord that is faithful
And the Holy One of Mount Eirene
And he shall choose you."

He paused. "I choose you, son. You will be honored before all."

Immanuel returned the smile, and Adam gasped. The likeness between father and son was unmistakable. He stared in wonder, captivated by his smile. Then Immanuel, still smiling, looked at Adam.

Adam jerked his eyes away, embarrassed.

An islander stepped forward. "My king, we found *this* around our Lord's shoulders." He held out a coil of black rope. "He was being taken to the bleeder for execution."

Lightning flashed. Thunder boomed. "I will withhold my wrath no longer." The king's voice filled the plaza. "You have added to all your evils this greatest of crimes. Would you murder my son? Let the family who owns this rope be hanged in their own bleeder at once, and let the city be torched!"

Screams and cries of anguish filled the city center. Torches flared, and smoke hung in the air. The archers surrounding the city center lifted their bows. Soldiers barked commands.

Panic surged through Adam. He tugged against Malakan's grip and tried to dive off the horse, but the vice-like fingers held him fast. *I'm going to die!* Adam could almost feel the black rope tightening around him, cutting off his circulation. At any moment, his bony wrists would be hammered together. His blood would cover him.

"Father!" Teacher's voice rose above the panicking crowd.

A hush fell. All eyes turned toward Immanuel. "Father, I pray you to grant me one request."

Adam's legs and arms shook as he tensed, listening.

The king locked eyes with his son. The two gazed at each other in silence, as if they knew each other's thoughts. From Adam's vantage point, he could see their faces mirroring one another—the same intense sorrow etched into both foreheads, the same unwavering resolve in the tightness of their jaws, the same faint spark of joy in their eyes.

Immanuel broke the silence. "Let your anger fall upon me. Let me be wounded for their transgressions. Let me be bruised for their iniquities. I offer up my own body as a sacrifice for their sins. Will you be pleased to accept my death in their place?"

All eyes turned toward the king. His eyes remained fixed upon his son. "Will you do this?" he asked softly.

Immanuel extended his pure hands toward his father. "What shall I say? 'Save me from this hour?' But this is the reason I have come to this hour. Father, glorify your name in me."

Adam felt the hand on his shoulder shaking uncontrollably. "Surely not this," murmured Malakan. "Can it be this that they have purposed? Please, let it be *anything* but this."

"I have glorified my name in you," King Eliab was saying. "And I will glorify it again. Let it be done as you have said."

He turned his face away.

Stillness fell over the plaza. The people stared at each other, clearly afraid to move or speak. The islanders stood motionless too. For once, they seemed to be doubting. Their faces reflected confusion. Malakan fought to control his breathing and mumbled under his breath.

When the silence became almost unbearable, the prostrate figure on the stairs lifted his head. He wobbled to his feet. "My king, if you seek a servant to execute this order, I place my men at your command."

The hiss of ten thousand swords being ripped from their scabbards sent the governor cowering back to his knees. Anger blazed in the eyes of every islander.

The king held them back. "Let him be."

Grandfather staggered once more to his feet. "Roberts, take the prisoner and your men to the bleeder. Do as the king commands."

The old man looked from the governor to the king, and then back to the governor. Shame covered his face. He stood motionless, his mouth gaping.

"*Move!*" Grandfather shouted. He descended the stairs and pushed his way through the crowd. Seizing the black rope from a soldier, he thrust it into Roberts' hands.

"Get it done, I say!"

The chief servant's expression remained cold as stone, but he took the rope and gestured to the men near him. They followed Roberts, along with the cluster of Keeda, until they surrounded Teacher.

One of the Keeda warriors ripped off Immanuel's thrick and bound his arms to his sides with the black rope.

"No," Adam whispered, but there was nothing he could do. He watched helplessly as they tightened the coils until the prince's circulation must certainly be cut off.

The Keeda seemed to enjoy their work. They laughed and mocked Immanuel, spitting in his face and striking him with their hands.

Teacher said nothing. He kept his eyes fixed on his father.

The crowd melted away as the Keeda pushed Immanuel toward the King's Road. Roberts hung his head and followed. Immanuel took a few laborious steps and stumbled. His bound arms could not check his fall. His face smacked into the pavement.

Adam winced. He wanted to cover his eyes, but he couldn't. His gaze was locked on Teacher's every agonized movement.

"Get up!" A Keeda kicked the crumpled form in the ribs.

Immanuel groaned and struggled to rise, but he could only wriggle. The crowd gaped at each other and sent furtive looks toward the king, but they made no move.

Another Keeda slid a whip from his belt. Multiple leather strips dangled from the glossy handle, each barbed with fragments of sharp rocks. "We told you to get up!" His muscles bulged as he flung back the whip. Then he struck.

"Get up!"

The lashes raked Immanuel's bare skin, tearing red furrows across his back and sides.

Adam gasped.

The king's soldiers cried out. Some sobbed. They trembled with emotion, their eyes huge, imploring the king with their gazes to speak the word that would allow them to attack.

But the king's face remained turned away.

The lashes whistled through the air. Roberts stood to one side, wringing his beard and watching. The first Keeda took out his whip and joined in, slicing Immanuel from the opposite direction. "Get up!" Blood flowed freely and puddled on the cobblestones at their feet.

Teacher could not rise. He twisted and writhed in vain.

Adam's hand ran down the side of his leg, feeling for the welts that Schala's whip had left. *I deserved the lashes*, he thought, *but Immanuel has done no wrong.*

"My king! My king!" The scream escaped Immanuel's lips, mixing with the snapping of the whips.

The king said nothing. He stood statue-like, facing the great stones around the plaza. Tears coursed down his cheeks.

One of the Keeda seized Immanuel's rope and jerked him to his feet. "Keep him upright," he ordered a nearby servant. The man hastened to obey. The group began marching the king's son out of the city to the King's Road. Roberts followed behind with the other servants.

At the edge of the plaza, Teacher struggled for breath. He turned back to face the fountain. "Father," he called, his voice full of heartrending pain. "Forgive them. They don't know what they are doing."

The king nodded slightly but otherwise remained motionless. A Keeda struck Immanuel's face and pulled back a blood-covered hand.

Immanuel turned once more and cried with a loud voice, "Father, I commit myself into your hands!"

Then the Keeda shoved him forward, along the streets, and through the gate. Then they were gone—on their way to the bleeder.

The earth began to quake. The horse under Adam whinnied and reared up.

Adam clung to the saddle horn for dear life, squeezing his eyes shut. When he opened them, the whole sky had turned black. The earth heaved. Roaring from loud, panicked voices and cracking rocks filled his ears.

Someone crashed into Adam's leg. He yelped and pulled it back just as the horse reared a second time. Malakan yelled and let go of him, trying to control his mount. The wind rushed past as Adam started to tumble toward the pavement. "Help!" His arm shot out, grasping for the saddle horn, the rider, for *anything* to catch his fall.

He missed … and plunged into the darkness.

Far above the city center, imperceptible to the Aardians beneath him, a great red dragon circled the plaza. Smoke eased out of his nostrils, and fire flicked between his teeth in a hideous grin.

"Foolish, foolish people," he hissed. "Who will save you now?"

ADAM III

Chapter 32

"In that he saith, 'A new covenant,' he hath made the first old." Hebrews 8:13

The wooden door gave a horrible squeal, cutting through the silence in the kitchen.

Adam jerked his head up from between his knees. *How long have I been asleep?* He pushed against the flour barrel on the floor beside him and scanned the shadowy figures at the tables. Lamplight danced across the servants' faces as they turned stony eyes toward the entrance.

The door creaked again, and a tall shadow with a heavy beard shuffled in. His head hung low, allowing gray hairs to trickle across his face. He moved one foot and then another, brushing them against the stone floor.

A noise snapped his head up, and his eyes opened wide. His nostrils flared at seeing the others gathered, sucking in a rattling wheeze. Clearly, he didn't expect this. He looked ready to flee.

Adam straightened. *It's Roberts. I wonder if—*

"Go ahead and sit down." Siraj, the butcher, indicated an empty chair. He crossed his arms. "We've been waiting for you."

Roberts glanced around the room, chest heaving. He scraped a chair away from the table and lowered himself into it. He picked up a spoon and rubbed it back and forth across the table, staring blankly.

The servants watched him in silence. Siraj nodded at Rhenda. The cook sat by the fire, barely moving. She reached weakly for the ladle.

"I'll do that, Rhenda," Adam offered, rising from his place on the floor. A wave of dizziness passed over him, but he shook his head clear and made his way to the fire. "You should be in bed," he whispered.

Rhenda sighed but made no other sound.

Adam took a bowl and filled it with a good-sized portion of silfun soup. *I should be in bed too*, he thought. But how could he, after everything that had happened? After his plunge off the islander's horse, he'd barely escaped the chaos in the city center. Thankfully, the rider hadn't come after him. The king's soldiers had departed.

Adam made his way home and gathered with Grandfather's servants in the kitchen, waiting. Now, Roberts had returned. *Maybe we can get some answers.*

Ears open to learn what he could, Adam set the bowl of soup before the chief servant. The knock of bowl against table broke the silence and seemed to pull Roberts out of his daze. He glanced at the food and then up at the finely carved rafters above.

Adam returned to his place by the flour barrel. No one else moved.

Roberts idly stirred his soup. Then he sighed and fingered his beard. "Well?" he said in a husky voice. "Can't a man eat in peace?"

"We want to know what happened," ventured Jaran, a young man standing in the corner.

Roberts ignored the remark. Instead, he went back to stirring his soup. With a final sigh, he shoved the bowl across the table and stood to his feet.

"Sit down." Siraj pounded the table and rose. "Tell us what you've done. Where is the king's son?"

Roberts eyed him. "I did what I had to do." He stepped toward the door.

Jaran moved from the corner to block the entrance. Others edged next to him, clearly hesitant to commit themselves to resistance but emboldened by the passions of the group. Under other circumstances, none dared to cross the chief servant.

Tonight they dared.

"Where is Immanuel?" asked Jaran.

Roberts growled and took a step closer to the exit. "Let me leave."

"Not 'til you answer us," said Siraj.

Roberts pushed against the group blocking the doorway. Jaran looked pale in the lamplight, but he held his ground.

"What did you do to him?" demanded Siraj. "What will happen to our city?"

The chief servant glared at the bristling faces like a bear caught in a circle of hounds. "I did what I had to do, what I was *ordered to do*. We nailed his wrists and hung him in the bleeder on Red Rock until he died. Then we buried him in the Mount of Humility."

Roberts grabbed Jaran and hurled him against a wall. "Now, get out of my way!" Barreling through the remaining servants, he stomped down the hall.

Adam's heart sank. Glazed-over images of the untouched bowl on the table and servants helping Jaran to a chair played in front of him. Standing on shaky legs, he meandered from the kitchen, down the hall, and out to the courtyard. He paced back and forth across the stone tiles, wondering.

"So, it's final." A hard lump settled in his stomach. "Teacher is … is … *dead*." He blinked back frightened tears. The king had not burned the city today. Not yet, but what hope was there for tomorrow? Was the king still angry? Had he forsaken them?

Adam flopped against the planter where he had talked with Hank. Was it only a few hours ago? He shuddered. So many horrible events had unfolded in such a short time. Resting his head against the smooth stone, he gazed into the sky. Bright stars twinkled, and he took hope from their light. His sense of time had unraveled. It was refreshing to see the stars and get his bearings. He sighed and closed his eyes …

When Adam opened his eyes, the sun was high in the sky. His head ached from leaning against the planter, and all his joints were stiff. How late was it? How long had he slept? He looked around. The courtyard was quiet. Too quiet. Where was everybody?

He thought back to his decision to run to Teacher last

evening. Or had it been late afternoon? Or—

Adam shook his head. Everything was jumbled together in a confusing mess. Whenever it was, he had left Grandfather to go to Teacher. Now, in the light of day, he wondered. Was it one of those flimsy decisions he was always making? Promising to do something and then changing his mind later?

"No," he said. "This is different." Something inside him had changed, and there was no going back. But where could he go? Teacher was *dead*.

The word left a bitter taste in Adam's mouth, especially when he remembered their times together in class. He thought about Teacher's excitement in the city center that day, when he showed Adam the promises in the King's Stones. He could see those deep, loving eyes in his mind's eye. "Have they closed forever?"

Suddenly, Adam pushed away from the planter and leaped to his feet. He pounded along the pavement with new determination. Swinging out the gate, he turned to the left and broke into a run toward the city center.

There was only one thing to do. King Eliab had said so. He needed to read and understand the king's words in the Stones. It was what Teacher would tell him to do if he weren't—

Adam broke off. The thought was too painful to finish.

The plaza was empty. The sun cast shadows from the buildings and reflected off discarded items from the day before. Tools and personal possessions lay strewn across the brick tiles, silent evidence of their owners' swift flight away from the place of judgment.

Adam turned from the litter to the first stone and began reading.

In the beginning, King Eliab created
Aard and its inhabitants.

The words had captivated him last time, but this time they overflowed with new meaning. King Eliab was right to be angry. This was the country he had made, *his* city and *his* people, only to be rejected.

He kept reading, searching, and skimming as he moved from stone to stone. There was so much to take in, and he yearned to grasp it all. Understanding and spiritual light beckoned him. He had only a small teacup, however, with which to take in an ocean of truth. His eyes fell on another passage:

Lo, I come as it is written of me
To do your will, O my king.
Your law is within my heart.

Teacher had spoken those words yesterday. "As it is written of me." How could Teacher say that? He must have known these words were speaking about him from the beginning. Were there prophecies here about his sacrifice? Was that what he meant, "To do your will"? Was everything yesterday part of the king's purpose from the beginning?

Adam's heart picked up speed. He remembered the islanders asking him at the gate what the stones meant, "He was wounded for our transgressions." Teacher had used those very words. Adam wanted to find them. He scanned the stones, searching.

Then his gaze came to a halt. There stood the stone of the covenant, lifted high on its pedestal. Goosebumps rose on Adam's arms. Fresh words had been scrawled across the stone. What could they mean? He stood too far away to read them. Did he dare go closer?

He couldn't stop himself. He was walking, wondering, trembling, getting closer. Now, he could make out the lettering. The words were scarlet and edged with gold tinting. The letters ran from one corner of the stone to the opposite corner and read:

It Is Finished.

"What does it mean?" Adam wondered. "*What* is finished?" His heart raced. Did these words free the city from judgment and death? Was their punishment paid in full for the broken covenant? *That seems too good to be true.*

Another thought troubled Adam. Did it mean that the relationship between the king and Mount Eirene was over? Finished? Was the king finished with Mount Eirene and his covenant with them? What about all the good promises?

Adam racked his brain. "If only I could ask Teacher."

He paused. *No, wait.* Teacher had told him already. Wasn't that what he had been so excited about? The new covenant!

Adam's feet flew across the plaza. He stumbled, caught himself, and ran faster. He saw the matching covenant stone before he reached it. It was the stone of the new covenant, just as Teacher had shown him.

"Behold the days come," says the king,
"When I will make a new covenant
with the people of Mount Eirene,
Not the covenant which I made
With their fathers, the one they broke
Even though
I was exceedingly good to them.
But this is the covenant
I will make in those days:
I will put my laws into their hearts,
And write it within them.
I will be their king,
And they shall be my people.
And their sins and iniquities
I will remember no more."

Just below the stone, in the blank space at the bottom, was a fresh signature written in bold, flowing letters:

Immanuel

Adam gasped. "Immanuel is the second Adam!" Teacher had known all along, even when he had spoken to Adam only a month ago.

"Oh, if only I had trusted him then."

Sorrow rose and threatened to suffocate Adam. What could he do now? His mind overflowed with questions, doubts, and fears. How could he be part of the new covenant? There were probably answers all around him, written on the stones, but how could he find them? A treasure was buried beneath him, but he had no way of digging it out.

He read the King's Stone next to him. Then he turned to another ... and another. Sometimes, a dart like sunlight seemed to pierce his mind in understanding. More often, though, he lost his train of thought and became confused.

Before he knew it, the day was gone. The sun was quickly sinking, and the shadows made reading difficult.

Adam felt more uncertain now than ever. If only Teacher were here to help him. "Oh, Teacher, why did you have to die?" His throat tightened. Sighing in pain and sorrow, he headed home.

So intent was Adam on reading and learning that he had ignored his growling stomach all day. Now, it throbbed for attention. He shuffled back to the governor's dwelling. A bowl of rice soup waited for him in the kitchen, a good sign for Rhenda, at least. He hoped she was regaining her strength.

Slurping down cold lumps of rice, he wiped his mouth and went upstairs. Maybe a good night's rest would straighten out his thinking. Exhaustion sucked the strength out of his limbs, and he stumbled into his room. Throwing himself on the bed, he almost missed the scrap of papla leaf dangling above him.

Then a slight draft from the window fluttered it, and he opened his eyes.

Pinned to the bedpost by a knife was a small note, hastily scribbled in familiar writing. Adam jumped out of bed. His skin crawled.

Oh, no, no, no! He looked around the room in every direction, expecting to be pounced on. He bolted the door.

His precautions didn't slacken his terror. He couldn't shake the feeling of vulnerability.

Adam jerked the knife out of the wood and took the tattered leaf. There was no mistaking the handwriting. *Schala!* There was no mistaking his message, either.

I know why you were in the woods.

Your debts are due upon receipt of this note.

If you can't pay in coin, then you can pay like Liptor.

Adam trembled. What had he gotten himself into? If only he could go back and never give in to Schala's temptations. But it was too late. There weren't enough coins in the whole house to pay his debt ... and the alternative was death.

He put a hand on the bolt. Perhaps he should go to Grandfather. *Maybe Grandfather has resources I don't know about.* His fingers began unlatching the door.

No! He yanked his hand away. There was a better way, the way he had chosen, and he wouldn't go back. Adam walked to the open window. Cool air from the mountains tousled his hair and blew across his face. He focused on the place where he thought the golden gate stood.

"Oh, King Eliab," he whispered. "I am so sorry for all I've done. I haven't kept your laws. I've broken all my promises. You already know I failed to plant my seeds."

Adam swallowed. "I'm especially sorry for not coming to your son earlier. I'm sorry I didn't return his love, and yours. But I want you to know that I would come to him now, if only I could."

He held up the death note and let the breeze ruffle it. "Schala has promised to kill me. I can't do anything to pay him or to redeem myself from the debts. I have nowhere else to turn, but I put myself in your hands. Please help me."

Adam couldn't be sure, but he thought he saw a bright light shine out from the base of the mountains. When he blinked, it vanished. Still, a sense of peace came over him, draining the tension in his body, just like the peace he'd experienced when he told Hank he would run to Teacher.

He tore Schala's note into pieces and tossed it out the window. The scraps floated out over the courtyard and into the city.

Adam returned to his bed and pulled his blanket to the floor. Peace or no peace, it might be wise to sleep on the floor behind the bed—just in case. He left the door bolted and laid his drawn sword beside him. As he drifted off to sleep, he imagined the bright light that had filled the plaza and the beautiful, deep eyes of the king. He sighed.

Whatever happened now was in Eliab's hands.

SCHALA

Chapter 33

*"And having spoiled principalities and powers, he made
a shew of them openly, triumphing over them in it."*
Colossians 2:15

S chala ran the smooth stone against the hatchet blade one
last time and tested it with his thumb. Razor sharp.
Lifting himself off the stump where he sat, he watched the
sun sink behind the mountains.

Time to finish the job.

Checking for any late travelers in the shadows of the
King's Road, he glided out of the forest. No one stirred.
Crunching over loose rocks, his boots carried him closer to
his prey. He grinned at the night's prospect. His recent kill
had made him hungry for more.

He reached Mount Eirene without being accosted. He
approached the gate to the governor's dwelling boldly and
peered through the bars. A slight movement caught his
attention from a second-floor window. Adam's window. He

glanced up. Bits of torn papla leaf floated on the breeze. Schala grinned. He would not be disappointed this time.

Reaching into his vest, he drew out a bundle of debts. He thumbed through them, smiling even wider. They were all here and ready to be put to good use. He reached for the gate's metal latch.

A hand touched his back. Schala ripped out his hatchet and whirled. The hair on the back of his neck rose at the sight of the tall, hooded figure.

"Easy, killer," hissed a familiar voice. "I'm glad I found you when I did. The master has summoned us."

Schala jammed the hatchet back into his belt. He wished he could bury it in Dos Lenguas' face, but he knew his limits and his orders. "I've got business to attend to first," he snarled. "I'll be there when I'm good and ready."

A sinister chuckling came from the hood. "I'll pass your message on. I'm sure the dragon won't mind waiting."

Schala's face burned. He hated being mocked. "Let's go then." He flashed a parting, irritated glare at Adam's window.

His commander drew up beside him as they walked. "Don't take it so hard, Schala. The prospects are better than you think. Before morning, you can have the whole family and not just the boy. We're making our move tonight."

Schala's pulse quickened. "What do you mean?"

"Wait and see."

Several faces came to Schala's mind. *I would love to finish off the old man, Doke, and Roberts, as well.* His heart sped up in anticipation. *It wouldn't take much to slit the throat of that desperate woman who does the cooking.* He wished he could have the governor too. But alas! The master probably wanted the man for his own prey. He would make great sport of him. *Can it really be tonight?*

The two darted into the forest, rushing along familiar trails. Dos Lenguas took the lead. "You should clean up after yourself," he whispered over his shoulder.

Schala made a face. "I didn't have time. Had to get back to my slaves. Some were attempting the mountain."

"Did you really have to throw the body into the riverbed? I could hardly stand the smell when I came looking for you."

Schala smirked. "It worked. His cousin fled like a rabbit."

Dos Lenguas said nothing.

They continued in silence into the mountains, darting back and forth through rocky passages. Schala didn't mind the climb as much tonight. He wanted to find out for himself. What did his commander mean about making their move?

The dragon was pacing in the meeting place when they arrived. The monstrous form blocked the faint stars behind him. The glowing skin cast a red light on the faces of those already present. "Late. All of you, late."

The giant tail flicked into the sky, hurling a boulder over their heads. It crashed against the rocks, splintering with a tremendous *crack!* The ground shook. "Can't you see what is in front of your faces? When, since the first rebellion, have we had such an opportunity? Yet, you drag yourselves here like a pack of rats!" Fire spewed out of the dragon's mouth.

Schala lowered himself to the ground beside Dos Lenguas and kept still. He pinched his nostrils against the acrid stench of burnt sulfur. Only a few officers had arrived so far. They filed in one or two at a time, rugged, evil men.

Hours passed. The throng of Dragonians, brimming with dark strength and cruel weaponry, continued to amass. The dragon paced back and forth.

Night turned into the dark hours just before dawn. Still, they waited.

Schala cursed under his breath. *If Dos Lenguas had left me alone, I could have finished off Adam with time to spare.* He rubbed his stiff fingers against his dew-moistened vest and cursed again. *What am I doing now? Waiting around, and for what?*

When at last the dragon spoke, his mood had changed. A soft, slippery voice indicated his cunning, if not his pleasure. "This is our moment," he purred. "Long have we waited in the shadows, biding our time. But at last the Enemy has given us the victory. Did I not tell you that he would be forced to defeat himself?"

No one answered.

The dragon flashed a mouthful of teeth in a sinister, devilish smile. "Behold, the city's savior lies dead. Did he think that he could spare the city with his sacrifice?" He shot fire into a tree at the side of the mountain. The clearing lit up.

Schala's eyebrows rose when the eerie glow illuminated a fresh tomb, sealed by a massive boulder.

"Immanuel is dead and defeated." The dragon roared his laughter. "And the Eirenians themselves killed him. They have sold themselves fully to do our bidding. It is now time to make them pay. In a short while, the Arsabian armies will make their move, but we will get there before them."

The circle burst into raucous shouting. Schala fingered

his hatchet. A smile crept across his hardened features. *Now comes the best part.*

"Enough," said the dragon. The crowd grew silent. "We have no need to burn coins this evening. Let us gather debts instead. Who among the citizens of Mount Eirene is not named in our records? And not one of them can pay … except in blood. Bring out the debts!"

Schala lagged behind, watching his comrades go before him. He wanted to be last, when he handed over the governor's grandson at the climax. His fingers itched to use his hatchet. It wouldn't be long before he could kill as many Eirenians as he wished.

The pile of parchments rose higher. Dos Lenguas handed over a large stack, and then Schala stepped forward. His hand held up the final debts.

"Stand down in the name of King Eliab!"

All eyes turned to the islander, who stood in front of the tomb, shining with a bright light. His feet were planted in defiance, and he brandished a short sword. A powerful bow hung from his shoulder.

"It's that fool, Malakan." Dos Lenguas strung his bow. "His grief has gotten the best of him."

Schala had no trouble recognizing the king's soldier. Decades had done little to change Malakan's complexion.

"If you'll excuse me," Malakan said as if he were addressing a class of school boys. "I have been sent here by His Majesty on an important mission."

Twang! Dos Lenguas' arrow shot forward. A volley of other arrows followed.

Malakan danced neatly out of the way. A silly grin spread

across his broad face. He thrust his shoulder against the tombstone twice his size and heaved it out of the way, revealing a black hole in the mountain's face.

Fury raged inside Schala. How dare Malakan mock them in their own stronghold? He roared in defiance, clawing his vest for a knife. The others echoed his rage.

Just then, not ten feet away, the dragon rose to his full height. The great, leathery wings fanned the wind, flinging the Dragonians into chaos. The dragon's neck towered over them like an oak tree, blotting out the sky.

The air left Schala's lungs in a *whoosh*. His skin burned from the heat of his master.

"Return the rock to its place." The dragon spoke in tones so deep that the earth quaked. His head swayed back and forth, moving closer to Malakan.

The king's faithful servant gave the dragon a cocky grin. "Sorry." He swung himself up to the top of the boulder and sat on it. "Orders are orders." He winked at the rebels below.

"You *fool*." The dragon swayed closer. "Your master lies behind you, dead."

"Not he!" Malakan leaped to his feet and danced on the rock in merriment. "I've a message of good news for all Aardians."

Throwing back his head and cupping his hands, he shouted until the mountain rang with his voice. "He is not here, for he is risen!"

No sooner had the words left his lips than the morning sun burst over the top of the mountains, breaking into the circle with brilliant light. The earth beneath Schala heaved, throwing him across the clearing. He rolled behind a log and lay there panting. When he peeked past the log, his throat went dry. *No! It can't be!*

Immanuel stood in the middle of the clearing. No longer thin, stooping, and weary, he rose above them in the very fullness of power. His garments blazed brighter than the sun in whiteness, and a golden crown was planted firmly on his brow. He raised a sword that could fell an army.

The great dragon was nowhere to be seen. Instead, a wriggling snake thrashed its body against the ground, its head squeezed against the rock by Immanuel's heel. The dragon's followers cowered on the ground before him.

"You are all usurpers and traitors," said Immanuel. "You have no right to collect debts from my father's subjects. You have no right to destroy my people."

He lifted his hand, and an army of the king's men appeared. Everywhere Schala turned, enemy soldiers surrounded him. Their clothes reflected the glory of their leader, and their faces radiated joy. At Immanuel's signal, two soldiers picked up the pile of debts and bound them in a cloth sack, which showed the king's emblem.

Schala saw his own handful of parchments. They had gone unnoticed in all the commotion and lay only a short distance from the log. Wriggling on his stomach like a serpent, he eased himself within an arm's length. If only he could grasp the one closest to him. *It's all I need to finish off Adam Sonneman the Third.*

His hand shot out like a whip and seized the debts. A smile cracked his face. *I have them!*

Then a piercing pain shot through his wrist. He screamed. A crooked, homemade arrow was embedded in his arm. His hand opened against his will. Next, the weight of an enormous boot smashed into his back, driving out his breath and pinning him to the ground. He tasted dirt.

"Sorry, Schala, but you won't be needing those any longer."

An enemy leaned over and snatched the papers from his open palm. Schala's eyes watered with pain and fury. He had always hated Asterik, and he despised him now. The smell of herbs surrounding the gardener made him want to vomit. How could this have happened?

Immanuel's voice rang out a second time. "It is not now the time when I shall hand out your judgment. But know this! You are a defeated enemy forever. Be gone!"

Asterik lifted his boot, and Schala darted away. Covering his ears and howling in pain, he scrambled away into the mountain with the rest of the Dragonians. When he was out of sight of Immanuel and his soldiers, Schala ripped the arrow from his wrist and threw it aside. Blood gushed.

He kept running, scrabbling at the ground in wild terror. His head pounded. Rocks tore at his feet and his hands. More blood flowed, but he didn't care. His only thought was to run as far away as he could and to be left alone.

Schala stumbled and fell, rolling into a crevice. He lay there a moment, fighting to breathe. From a distance, he heard a sound, a sound he hated more than any other. He pounded the ground with his fists. He burned with shame. His pride could never endure the slightest mocking.

But all his fury could not quench the peals of mirth that wafted throughout the mountains.

ADAM III

Chapter 34

"Come and see." John 1:46

Adam woke with a start. He grabbed his sword and leaped to his feet. What was that noise? Had it been his imagination?

No. The sound of shoes scuffing the floorboards came again from right outside his door. Schala! His hands shook in terror. *Where can I hide?* Should he call for help or remain silent?

Bang, bang, bang.

Adam wiped his sleeve across his face and squinted against the morning sun. *There's no way I'm going to open that door.* Where was the best place to defend himself? From the top of the bed? No, it was too unstable.

Bang, bang, bang!

Adam jumped, startled. He eased a chair to the side of the door. Heart racing, he scrambled up, planted his feet, and readied his sword. If Schala burst through the door, Adam might have a chance to catch him by surprise.

The enemy did not burst through the door. Adam unlocked the bolt and drew back the latch. Then he scrambled back up on his chair. *Might as well get it over with!*

More banging, but the door did not open. The latch was obviously stuck.

Adam reached out his foot and gave the latch a shove.

Whoosh! The door flew open, catching his foot and sending him flying. He leaned back to balance himself, but it was no use. He swung his sword wildly in a last attempt to save his life. Then crash! The chair and his body came tumbling down and smashed against the floor. He yelped in pain, with his sword arm pinned under him.

This is the end. He squeezed his eyes shut and waited for the knife to pierce him.

"Adam?"

Adam's eyes flew open. A pair of large brown eyes stared quizzically at him from the doorway. "C-christy?" he stammered.

"Are you all right?"

Adam shook his head. No, he was not all right. *Have I gone crazy?* Why in the island was Christy pounding on his bedroom door? He suddenly felt like a complete fool, waving a sword and wrestling with a chair. His clothes were disheveled from sleeping on the floor.

"Camdin said I might find you here." Christy stood in the doorway. "I'm sorry I caught you off guard, but you'll never believe the good news. I had to come and tell you. You won't believe it, but it's true, Adam. He wants to see you."

Adam untangled himself from the chair and rose. His thoughts were just as disheveled as his appearance. He set the chair in its place and sheathed his sword. Warmth crept into his face.

"I understand if you don't want to talk to me," Christy said. "I was wrong to throw away my seed and yell at you. It wasn't right what I said, and I shouldn't have said it. I want to be friends still. Will you forgive me?"

"Of course." Adam ran his fingers through his tousled hair. "Let's go down to breakfast." It sounded like a dumb thing to say, but it was the first thing that came to mind.

They went downstairs together. "I'm sorry too," Adam said. "*Really* sorry this time. To you, and to the king as well." He stopped at the foot of the stairs and looked to see what her reaction would be.

"Oh, Adam!" She clapped her hands. "I'm so glad. He will be too. Now, don't just stand there. You need to go quickly."

Go where? Adam hurried for the kitchen. Perhaps Christy was hungry. Maybe Rhenda would give her some porridge. If not, then Adam would give her half of his.

The kitchen was empty. He must have slept later than he thought. *No, wait.* Today was the King's Day. Everyone was probably sleeping in. He snatched up a bowl of porridge for himself and went hunting for an empty bowl for Christy.

"What are you doing, Adam? Didn't you hear me?" She drummed impatient fingers against the table. "I said to hurry."

She must be *really* hungry. "Sure. Okay." Adam grabbed an extra spoon and sat down on a bench by Christy's table.

"Here." He pushed his bowl toward her. "You can have as much as you want."

Christy sighed, flopping down on the bench across from him. "Thank you, but I've eaten already."

Adam started shoveling porridge into his mouth. Why couldn't she make up her mind? Maybe she could help him figure out what the Stones meant. "I went to the plaza yesterday," he said, his mouth half full of porridge.
"I saw—" He stopped to swallow.

"You've seen it too then!" Christy's eyes lit up. "Isn't it amazing? So cool and sweet, though not like it will be. The taste has been on my lips all morning. Can you imagine what it will be like someday?"

Adam stopped with a spoonful halfway to his mouth. "What are you talking about?"

Christy slapped the table. "Just what you said! The water trickling out of the fountain. I saw it this morning. I couldn't believe it, but it's real."

She shook her head in amazement. "The fountain's been dry for so many years, but now a trickle has returned. It made a tiny stream through the dust, ran down on the ground, and made a puddle. I climbed to the top where it was clean and took a drink. Didn't you say you saw it?"

"I said—" Adam's mouth was too full. He tried to swallow before he finished.

"Oh, Adam! Hurry and finish eating." Christy stood up. "Don't you want to see him?"

Adam struggled to stand and wipe his mouth at the same time. "See who?"

"Teacher!" Christy stomped her foot. "Can't you hear

what I've been telling you? He wants to see you."

Adam's heart sank. He slumped back onto the bench. "You must not have heard. Roberts told us the news. They killed Teacher and buried him in the mountains. I wanted to go to him like you said. I really did. But now it's too late."

"Adam!" shouted Christy. "He's *not* dead. He's alive. He's at his house right now. I saw him this morning."

Adam's heart squeezed. "Christy, I'm not in the mood for this. I don't know what you're talking about, but you did *not* see Teacher. Dead people don't come back to life and go back to their houses."

Christy stared at him. "Dead people don't come back to life?" She spread out her arms "Look at me!"

Adam opened his mouth to argue then snapped it shut. *She's right.* A trickle of hope coursed through his veins, making him shiver. The trickle turned to a flood of excitement. He caught her right hand in both of his and began shaking it up and down.

"Can it be true?" He was laughing and crying at the same time. Her hand felt so soft, so warm, and so alive. Perhaps Teacher—

Christy's face flushed red, and she yanked her hand away. She looked like she was trying to hide a smile, but why the sudden change? Had he done something wrong?

Adam looked down at his hands. The twisted, dark scars with their hideous red stain mocked him.

He looked at Christy's hands, so pure and smooth. He crumbled inside. No wonder she pulled away.

"Go to him," said Christy. "Hank told me that you wanted to go."

He looked into her deep-brown, pleading eyes. "Yes. I'll go."

Christy hurried Adam out of the kitchen. "Hurry."

Adam headed for Teacher's house. He started out at a fast walk, but the initial flood of enthusiasm soon faded. "What will Teacher think of me?" he muttered. "Will he draw back too?"

He shoved his stained, sweaty hands into his pockets. His fingers felt the seed. *Another reminder of my failure.* In the other pocket he felt a lump. He pulled it out. Sweat had melted the papla leaves together into a crinkly mess, but he recognized the king's seal and the printed words. *No Mediator.*

Adam shuddered. Is this what awaited him? Another rejection?

IMMANUEL

Chapter 35

*"Blessed be the God and Father of our Lord Jesus
Christ, who hath blessed us with all spiritual blessings
in heavenly places in Christ." Ephesians 1:3*

My Lord." Michael, the captain of the royal armies,
knelt on one knee and bowed his head. Dirt crunched
as thousands of loyal soldiers knelt behind him, flooding the
King's Road and the yard. "We await your command."

Immanuel smiled at his servants. How good it felt to be
restored to his former glory! Brightness pulsed through his
body and covered the land with light. The helmets and
swords of his men reflected the brightness. "Rise. For now, I
will send you to my father."

He stood in front of his house, watching the army march
across the hill and reveling in their songs of praise. The
harmony of so many islanders, united in their devotion to his
name, flooded Immanuel's heart with love. He could almost
taste the distant day, when the entire island would be united

in love as these soldiers were now. Who but Father and the Ruuwh could understand such joy?

With the music still echoing in his heart, Immanuel crossed the threshold into his home. The aroma of freshly cut flowers mixed with a pine scent from the fireplace. He breathed deeply, taking it all in.

Asterik rose from the flame he was tending. "Do you like it? I touched it up a bit to create the pleasant smell. The day is warm enough, though, that I hardly feel the need for a fire."

Immanuel rested a hand on his shoulder. "It's perfect, Asterik. The fire has a purpose other than for heat today. I'm glad you stayed so I could thank you again for the other night, when you stood by me in the garden. Your comfort meant a great deal to me."

Asterik bobbed his head, a flush of red tinting his cheeks with delight at the praise. He slipped across the wooden floor to a table at the opposite end of the room. Strings of herbs from the garden lay strewn across the tabletop in various patterns. Asterik seated himself and began organizing the herbs with lively fingers.

Immanuel stood by the fire and watched him. Then his gaze wandered to the window behind Asterik's back. Through it he saw the grass where he had knelt three days ago, wrestling in the night with his decision. The agony of that final surrender, when he had yielded everything to do Father's will, touched him even now. He rubbed the two hideous scars in his wrists, witnesses to his cruel execution.

"You know," said Asterik, his fingers flying through the plants, "I keep thinking of what you said this morning. The words 'defeated enemy forever' stir up this unspeakable joy inside me. I hardly know how to control my energy." A laugh escaped him.

He brought Immanuel a leaf that held a sweet-smelling paste. "I do wish, though, that you would have crushed the serpent for good."

"I know." Immanuel accepted the leaf. "But it's not the time. My father has a wise purpose in permitting him to remain free for a season."

Astcrik's brows knit together, but he returned to the table without a word.

Immanuel tasted the paste on the leaf. Honey-like. He closed his eyes and sniffed the pine scent in the air. The fire warmed the backs of his legs. He sensed Father's favor, as well as the presence of his Ruuwh around him.

"Father," he whispered, so quietly that even Asterik could not hear. "Thank you for choosing me. You have indeed glorified yourself in me, and I am glorified in you. I remember your promise to make me a covenant for the people, and for salvation unto the ends of Aard. Now, I ask that you give me these people for my inheritance, just as you said to me."

He felt the answer even as he spoke. Father had heard, and one of his students was coming to see him. Immanuel shivered with excitement. He would have endured all the suffering a thousand times over, if necessary, to experience the joy that now filled him.

"Asterik, hide yourself for a moment. You can listen, but do not be seen."

Asterik stood, looked around, and scrambled behind the

bed in the corner.

Immanuel chuckled and diminished the brightness of his glory. He ran to the front window and peeked outside. A boy trudged up the road, his head ducked. His clothes hung limply on his slender form. He looked down into his hands, shook his head, and paused, looking back. Then clenching his fists, he turned again to Immanuel's house.

Before the boy could take another step, Immanuel flung open the door. "Adam!" He leaped down the stairs in a single bound and charged across the yard. His heart throbbed with anticipation as he crashed through the gate and ran the remaining distance.

Adam stood rooted to the ground, eyes wide. Then he was folded in the arms of the king's son. Immanuel squeezed him tight, rubbing Adam's matted hair against his cheek.

"Teacher." Adam raised his head. "I've been so wrong. I've broken the law and made you suffer." He tried to pull away.

"I know." Immanuel drew him closer. "But now you have come to me. I am ready to restore you." *How I savor this moment!* He gave Adam a final squeeze and held him at arm's length so he could see his face. A tear brimmed over and ran down the boy's cheek.

Immanuel touched the tear and wiped it away. Then beaming, he reached into the folds of his robe and drew out a rolled-up parchment.

Tugging a golden thread free, he spread out the roll and placed it in Adam's hands. "See for yourself."

Immanuel followed the boy's eyes as they moved from the sapphire border, to the king's seal, and then to the words.

This scroll signifies the complete pardon of Adam Sonneman III. All crimes to his charge have been forgiven. The punishment he deserved has been paid in full. He is henceforth a free man and in perfect standing with his Majesty, King Eliab, not only at this time, but also for as long as the king shall live. He is herein also granted the gift of eternal life to serve his majesty forever.

The scroll showed Immanuel's signature.

Adam touched his finger to the name and read the message a second, and then a third time. When he looked up, his face streamed with tears. "How can this be, Teacher?"

Immanuel embraced him. "It can be because it is my father's desire and promise. It can never be revoked. It's good forever." He led Adam toward the house. "Come inside, so you can sign it as your own."

They entered and sat down at a small desk beside the window. Immanuel extended a quill toward Adam. "Will you accept this pardon?"

Adam kept his hands hidden under the desk and bit his lip.

"Father," Immanuel whispered in his spirit, *"I ask that you heal him for my sake."* He touched Adam on the shoulder. "Let me see your hands."

Adam's face turned white. He looked out the door into the yard and toward the city.

Immanuel couldn't keep himself from trembling. *This is the moment!* "Adam, do you trust me?"

The boy nodded slowly and lifted his hands. "I'm so sorry, Teacher. It's all my fault for not listening to you. If you don't want me, I understand, and I'll–"

His sudden gasp filled the room.

Asterik poked his head out, but the boy did not notice the islander. He sprang out of his seat so fast that the stool crashed to the floor. His mouth hung open as he gazed from his right hand to his left, and then back again. Both palms glowed with pure, white light. Not a scratch or a spot remained.

Adam flung himself into Immanuel's arms. "Teacher!"

Immanuel rocked him back and forth. He closed his eyes and imagined the rejoicing now in Father's presence. The whole throne room was certainly cheering this very moment.

"Now, sign." He pushed the quill into Adam's hand.

The boy nodded and wrote his name beneath his teacher's.

Immanuel smiled. "Your name is also in my father's book of life. You belong to him forever."

Adam nodded and wiped his hands across his face. "Thank you. I want to serve him and you for the rest of my life. When school starts, you can count on me being there from now on." He looked out the door, and a shadow passed over his face.

"What troubles you, Adam?" Immanuel asked.

Adam turned to Immanuel and clutched his hand. "I'm in dreadful danger. Schala is trying to kill me. I"—he hung his head—"I ate wedding berries. I owe Schala more coins than I can ever pay in my life. What should I do? Do you still want me?"

Immanuel reached into his robe and drew out a pile of papers. He winked at Asterik, who ducked back behind the bed. "Are these your debts?" He placed the pile in Adam's hands.

The boy shook as he scanned the writing. "Yes. What shall I do?"

"Give them to me. Schala's authority over you is broken. You belong to my father now. Your life of slavery is finished."

"What will you do with them?" Adam laid the debts in Immanuel's hand.

"Watch." Immanuel crossed to the fire, stoked it, and with a flourish tossed the pile into the flames. Within seconds, the parchments blackened and disappeared in a flurry of sparks.

"Oh, my," Adam whispered.

"Do you remember the new covenant? 'Your sins and iniquities will I remember no more.' Father has made me the true governor of Mount Eirene. It is my privilege to set you free from your former taskmaster."

Adam stared into the flames. When he spoke, his voice was filled with awe. "Then ... I have been redeemed."

"Yes. I have redeemed you. For the first time ever, you are truly free."

He led Adam out onto the porch. "There is one thing more." He reached into his robe for the third time and handed Adam a folded letter. It was sealed in wax with the king's emblem. "It is from Father. Open it."

Immanuel studied Adam's face with delight. He already knew the contents.

Adam fumbled with the crisp paper, breaking the seal and opening the letter.

Dear Adam,

I have loved you from the time you were born, and even before. Your parents are dear to me, and you are also. I have been observing your life and have been very involved, much more than you can imagine.

Your attempts to impress me while rejecting my words and my son were a deep disappointment. I have been angry at your repeated acts of rebellion. But my anger has given way to mercy, which shall last forever. I have made atonement for you through the sacrifice of Immanuel. That's why I sent him.

I cannot tell you what joy it gives me that you have trusted me and come to my son. He is the mediator that I provided for you, and now you are welcome to write to me any time you desire. I look forward to hearing from you.

There are many things I could say, but I will not tell you everything at this time. For now, I want you to know that I have accepted you not only as my servant but also as my son. I am adopting you into my family, so you have become an heir of my kingdom with Immanuel.

I love you, Adam. It is my honor and delight to call you Son.

Your father,
His Majesty, Eliab

Adam lifted his face to Immanuel. His eyes reflected desire and yet uncertainty.

Immanuel met his eyes with the same admiring look his father had given him in the plaza, the one he knew Adam had always longed for. "You are the king's beloved son, in whom he is now well pleased."

Adam shook his head. "B-but why?" he stammered. "I didn't do anything good, nothing worthy of this ... this ... everything! How can he be pleased in me?"

"You came to *me*, Adam. That makes all the difference. Didn't Christy tell you it would?"

The two looked at each other for a second and then burst into laughter. Immanuel let the tears roll down his face as he shook with joy. He reached into his robe one more time. In the depths of his pocket he felt the ring, white gold with a sapphire swirl. He lifted it out and held it to the light, allowing the sun to shine through.

"This ring is for you," Immanuel said. "It is a sign of your adoption."

The boy's jaw dropped, and he stretched out his hand in wonder. Then his forehead wrinkled, and he pulled his hand back. Fear danced in his eyes.

"What is it, Adam?"

Adam tried to speak and then faltered. Swallowing hard, he looked in Immanuel's face with searching eyes. "How much does all of this cost?"

Immanuel held back the lump in his throat. He bit his lip, checking his anger at the man who caused such confusion in this young boy's life. How evil that people could so abuse one another!

He pulled Adam tight against his chest and ran his hand through his hair. "It costs you nothing, Adam. Nothing."

Adam shook himself free and searched Immanuel's face. "Can it be true? Is this free?"

"I did not say *free*." Immanuel rubbed his thumb gingerly across his scarred wrist. "But it has been paid for already. Here. It is a gift." He took Adam's hand and slid the ring into place. "I will see you in school. You have a lot to learn."

Adam stood, speechless. He stared at the ring, his hands, and the letter. Then throwing himself into Immanuel's arms, he hugged him, allowing his tears to flow freely. "Thank you, Teacher. Thank you."

"Thank Father as well. He loves you and will be glad to hear from you."

Adam hesitated. Then standing straight and looking around him with questioning eyes, he said, "Thank you … Father." A look of wonder and joy spread across his features. "I have a Father!" He leaped into the air. "A Father who loves me!"

He turned back to Teacher. "I'll be there tomorrow for school." Then he was bounding off down the King's Road, leaping along the way.

Immanuel looked from his student toward the distant mountains. "Thank you, Father."

He entered the house to find Asterik sitting on the bed, shaking his head. "It's amazing. He has no idea what that cost you."

"No." Immanuel seated himself at the desk. "He doesn't."

Neither did Asterik. Only the Father and the Ruuwh could understand the agony he had felt being cut off from them. But that was past, and it was worth it to the utmost degree.

"In a minute I will send you to Father," he said over his shoulder. "But let me write this letter first. I want to send it with you. It is for Adam Sonneman the Second, the boy's father. Can you take it to him?"

"Of course."

Immanuel took a piece of parchment and dipped the quill into the inkwell. With a satisfied grin he began to write:

Dear Adam,

I will see you soon. But I have good news, news that you have waited for a long time, and I am too excited myself to keep back the tidings. The promise that I made to you here in Aard I have now fully kept. This past week, as you already know, I paid for your redemption. But I have done more, which you requested, namely that I have also saved your household. Today is the day young Adam came to me. May the blessing of my father abound to you until we meet again soon.

Immanuel

He folded the letter and handed it to his servant.

Asterik tucked the letter into his vest. "Is the king's anger quenched forever then? Will you burn all the debts?"

"Not all," Immanuel replied sadly. "Those who never come to me will remain enslaved. They will have nothing to shield them from Father's anger when it falls. What more can he offer them than his son?"

Asterik nodded and smiled. "Malakan will be glad to know. It wouldn't be right otherwise." Then he was gone.

Immanuel watched Asterik from the window as he disappeared over the hill. Soon, the Arsabian armies would pour over that same stretch of ground. There was so much to do in the meantime. But his work here was coming to a close, at least for a time. He was needed at the throne room. Now, the Ruuwh and the new handful of followers would carry on his work.

Immanuel knelt beside the chair and closed his eyes. "How I praise you for giving me Adam," he whispered. "I ask that you keep him from evil and transform him through the truth. I am coming to you soon, and he will need your power for the approaching war. Thank you."

He gripped the sides of the chair. "I praise you for all whom you will give me. I ask—"

Immanuel paused. He heard Father's Ruuwh answering his petition before he even said it. Yes, someone else was coming. Even at that moment.

With a smile he rushed to the window.

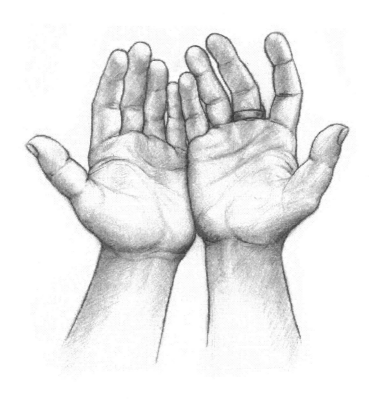

"And in that day thou shalt say,
O LORD, I will praise thee:
though thou wast angry with me,
thine anger is turned away, and thou comfortedst me."
Isaiah 12:1

AngeroftheKing.com

Why does the story emphasize anger?
What do the seeds represent?
Who are the Goiim?
How can I "run to Teacher"?
Is there a sequel coming? Or more?

Find the answers to these questions and many more at

AngeroftheKing.com

Are you *sure* you really understand this allegory?

ABOUT THE AUTHOR

J.B. Shepherd grew up in a Christian home, school, and church in South Carolina. He had the facts from day one. But only after he ran to Christ did he come to true life. He wrote *Anger of the King* out of his passion to help others make that same run to Christ and then to marvel at it.

He lives with his wife and two children in South Carolina when they're not traveling across the country in their blue Volvo wagon. The family plans to move to the Middle East in the near future for J.B. to pursue a teaching career.

To find the full version of J.B.'s story, check out the biography section of AngeroftheKing.com.

—

Made in the USA
Columbia, SC
23 June 2019